THE PIONEER BREWPUB WAS HOPPING. CROWDED WITH FISHERMEN, LOGGERS AND AN assemblage of locals, Frankie's table was one reserved for a small group of ladies who met every first Monday of each month.

The Margarita Monday Sisterhood.

"Kristin, he's way too young for you," Claire interjected loudly from across the table. "Besides, most of the younger lovers I've taken weren't worth breaking a sweat over. They can go and go forever but their technique needs refinement."

Kristen's pale eyes glittered in the smoky bar. The more alcohol she consumed, the more pronounced her Irish accent became. She ignored Claire. "Frankie, you don't know what you've been missing all these years. Now I understand why his nickname is The Swordsman. He really knows how to put the *fun* in dys*fun*ctional."

A few seconds passed before Kristin's meaning sunk in. Claire chuckled and even Frankie had to admit it was humorous. Fortunately or not, Damon's polyamorous reputation was legendary. Her junior crewman was incredibly popular with the ladies. She rubbed her itching eyes and threw a twenty on the table.

"You know what I heard from one of his old roommates?" Kristen twitched with mischief.

"No more, please," Frankie begged. "I can't take it."

"He said that Damon masturbates before a hot date so he can last longer in bed. How's that for dedication?"

Claire muffled a belch, reached over and patted Frankie's forearm reassuringly. "Drink up," she bellowed, pouring the dregs from the pitcher into her empty glass. "With any luck, you won't remember most of this by morning."

Frankie slumped in her chair.

"Don't bet on it."

The Bet.

This had all started with a stupid bet.

Guarding the Coast
Copyright © 2007 Samantha Gail
ISBN: 978-1-55487-250-3
Cover art and design by Martine Jardin

Published by eXtasy Books
Look for us online at:
www.extasybooks.com

Printed in the United States of America

Guarding the Coast

By

Samantha Gail

To Noelle Bachand… my good friend and muse.

I would also like to acknowledge the following people who were so very generous with their time and stories.

Captain Douglas J. Bucklew
Lieutenant Greg Pierce
Petty Officer Stacey Pardini
Petty Officer 1st Class Daniel Pye
Allen Rowley, Fire Control Technician, 2nd Class
Murry Taylor, Smokejumper/Author
Michael Coggins, Divemaster
JoDee Strong, Poetess
Jennifer Urrutia, RN

Chapter 1

MARGARITA MONDAY

"WHAT DO YOU MEAN HE HAS THE BIGGEST UNIT YOU'VE EVER SEEN?"

"What do you mean, what do I mean? What part of *all men are not created equal* didn't you understand?"

Frankie Moriarty stared at her girlfriend in horror.

"I can't believe you did him."

"What's not to believe?" Kristen yelled over the ruckus in the bar in order to be heard. Her bobbed auburn hair bounced while she spoke. "He had incredible stamina. I've done my share of younger men but he takes first prize for best sexual athlete. I came so hard I saw spots."

Frankie cursed under her breath.

Petty Officer Damon McGoldrick, free-ranging source of infinite trouble, had struck again. *Semper Paratis.* The Coast Guard motto was a fitting description of him. Damon was *Always Ready.* This time, however, his womanizing activity was a lot closer to home. Frankie slugged down the rest of her frozen margarita and motioned to the bartender for another.

The Pioneer Brewpub was hopping. Crowded with fishermen, loggers and an assemblage of locals, Frankie's table was one reserved for a small group of ladies who met every first Monday of each month.

The Margarita Monday Sisterhood.

"Kristin, he's way too young for you," Claire interjected loudly from across the table. "Besides, most of the younger lovers I've taken weren't worth breaking a sweat over. They can go and go forever but their technique needs refinement."

Kristen's pale eyes glittered in the smoky bar. The more alcohol she consumed, the more pronounced her Irish accent became. She ignored Claire. "Frankie, you don't know what you've been missing all these years. Now I understand why his nickname is The Swordsman. He really knows how

1

to put the *fun* in dys*fun*ctional."

A few seconds passed before Kristin's meaning sunk in. Claire chuckled and even Frankie had to admit it was humorous. Fortunately or not, Damon's polyamorous reputation was legendary. Her junior crewman was incredibly popular with the ladies. She rubbed her itching eyes and threw a twenty on the table.

"You know what I heard from one of his old roommates?" Kristen twitched with mischief.

"No more, please," Frankie begged. "I can't take it."

"He said that Damon masturbates before a hot date so he can last longer in bed. How's that for dedication?"

Claire muffled a belch, reached over and patted Frankie's forearm reassuringly. "Drink up," she bellowed, pouring the dregs from the pitcher into her empty glass. "With any luck, you won't remember most of this by morning."

Frankie slumped in her chair.

"Don't bet on it."

The Bet.

This had all started with a stupid bet.

She and Damon had been heatedly discussing his latest choice of playmates. She had used the letters HIV to make him see reason, get him to understand. Frankie was a gambler in most things but promiscuity was not safe for anyone nowadays, especially for someone with Damon's sexual appetite.

He was not easy to scare.

"Fine then," he had blurted. "How about fixing me up with one of the girls in the Sisterhood if you're so worried that I'll get some lethal disease?"

"I may be many things to you but *pimp* is not among them," she snapped. "Besides, by the time you score with any of my girlfriends, research scientists will have found a cure for AIDS."

Damon had whirled on her like a cyclone. "You like to travel, right?"

"You know I do."

"Then how about we make a little wager," he lured. "If you win, you'll be able to buy a plane ticket to anywhere you want to go."

Frankie had Prague on the brain.

Her European itinerary already chosen, she'd paid a small fortune for a three-pieced matched set of luggage and was ready, set to go. Before she could think rationally about the consequences of selling out her girlfriends,

Damon had twisted her words into a bet between the two of them. With the exception of herself, he would seduce the three unmarried, heterosexual women in the Margarita Monday Sisterhood within two months. There were two agreed-upon conditions: Frankie would not divulge the particulars to any of the women involved and Damon was to always use a condom.

They each had an entire paycheck hanging in the balance.

FORCING HER ATTENTION TO the present, Frankie let her head fall to the gouged cedar table and gave it a few solid knocks. A foot of thick, corkscrew curls the color of peach parfait tumbled out of the confines of her ponytail.

"I can't believe you did him," she repeated dolefully

Claire tapped Frankie on the hand to get her attention, pointing out the window to the parking lot. Three women were getting out of a red convertible, late arrivals to their group. "Maybe one of them can talk some sense into you."

"It's about time they got here," Kristin bellowed.

Frankie groaned. "Just shoot me and end my suffering." The Sisterhood, all nurses except herself, knew no boundaries when it came to acquiring juicy gossip.

Kristen puckered her ruby lips and offered up a toast.

"Here's to dipping your pen in the Coast Guard's inkwell."

"Dipping your pen!" Claire echoed.

Frankie made an ugly face and lifted her own glass to make a toast.

"Here's to lascivious girlfriends with no self control."

Half the heads in the pub turned their way.

"Hear, hear!" Their glasses clinked, sloshing liquid across the table.

CAPTAIN FRANCESCA MARIE MORIARTY was a helicopter pilot for the United States Coast Guard. And she was damned good at it. At five feet four, barely topping one hundred pounds, Frankie was the smallest package of piloting dynamite in the Coast Guard. "TB" a few of the old salts called her, short for "Tenacious Bitch."

Flying helos was the love of her life.

"Frankie?" Claire switched topics. "I don't understand it. You work with three of the best looking men in the state. Why aren't you having sex with any of them?"

3

"It's a tough job but somebody's got to do it," she answered. "Or is that, *not* do it?"

Claire opened her mouth to protest, Kristin interrupted.

"Haven't you seen her tattoo?"

"What tattoo?"

"The one on her right butt cheek," Kristin blurted with secret-divulging satisfaction.

Frankie threw her hands up in surrender.

"I can't say that I have," Claire confessed.

"Get her drunk enough tonight and she'll probably show you."

Habit dictated that at the end of every Margarita Monday, the Sisterhood made the brisk, quarter mile walk to the beach house that belonged to Frankie. Ensconced in their jammies and with all vestiges of party makeup removed, they spread their sleeping bags haphazardly across the living room floor and kicked the celebration up to the next level. The most sober nurse would start IV's on the rest of the women and prophylactic re-hydration would begin in the hopes of averting the dreaded hangover.

The other three women sat down at the table and began pouring drinks. Sophia, normally the shy one, asked, "What does Frankie's tattoo look like?"

"It's a black circle with the words 'pretty boys' in the center and a big red slash through it," Kristin eagerly answered.

"No pretty boys?"

"Frankie, you've got to tell us," Claire pleaded. "What's the problem having a little fun with the guys working for you? You're their commanding officer, right? Order them to perform."

"For the record," Frankie stated clearly, "Damon is like a brother to me. An evil one sent by Satan to endlessly torment and bedevil; yet a brother, nonetheless."

"What about Voice?"

"Married."

"Legs?"

Frankie wagged a finger. "Moriarty's rule number one. Never shag your co-workers."

Gage Adams let up on the clutch and eased his black Ford truck out of the parking lot of the hardware store. One more stop and he would be on his way home. Damned if he didn't hate coming into town on his days off. If that backed up sewer line had only waited a few more days! Tomorrow started a continuous stretch on duty until the following Tuesday morning.

One week on. Two weeks off.

He swerved to miss a jaywalking pedestrian. Mid-March, the springtime tourists had nearly doubled the population of the small town of New Harbor. Unconsciously rubbing the faint scar at his throat, he pulled into traffic along the Pacific coast highway.

He downshifted. The truck crept up an incline and Gage turned left under the massive concrete bridge. He could use a beer and some nubile female to stroke into until he forgot everything that was eating at him. It had been a long time since he sought such a welcome diversion.

"To hell with the sewer," he scowled.

Cruising along the bay front, he caught sight of his favorite bar, spun the truck around and pulled into the back alley behind a rusted old camper.

The night air nipped his face. An old man staggered past, huffing a brusque acknowledgment. Gage nodded, rammed his hands in his pockets and kept walking.

Jukebox music and heavy smoke blasted from open doors. A few heads turned to see the tall man with the build and swagger of a warrior. His icy green eyes assessed every occupant and found each exit.

Gage stepped inside.

"Ahoy there, Lieutenant," a raspy voice called to him from behind the bar. Edgar, the bar's owner motioned to an empty chair. "Pull up a seat."

Gage nodded. A pretty brunette made eye contact as he brushed by. Gage fixed her with a stare that was direct and steady. He *was* interested.

"How's business, Edgar?"

Gage kept his gaze riveted on the woman. Her push-up bra was filled to capacity.

"Life is good. No complaints here." Edgar shoved a frothy microbrew in front of him and flashed a crooked grin from behind heavy jowls.

"Glad to hear it," Gage answered.

"You missed them by a few minutes."

"Missed who?"

"Your captain and her crazy nurse friends." Edgar made a clucking sound like a hen. "Them gals have been coming here for years. Don't think I've ever seen them so drunk. They kept calling for one round after another. I tried to cut them off until they threatened to tie me up and do things to a part of my anatomy that ain't never seen sunshine and don't suspect ever will."

"Nothing is sacred when you get that wild bunch together," Gage agreed and took a hearty slug of his beer.

The brunette watched his mouth with open interest.

Invitation sent and accepted.

"Nurses." Edgar shook his head. "They all staggered off towards the beach about five minutes ago," he said with a twinge of conspiracy. "Might not be a bad idea for somebody to make sure they made it to Frankie's place safely."

Gage's dark eyebrows shot upward. "I suppose that somebody ought to be me."

"You're the local hero around this town," Edgar answered. "I'd do it myself but those gals scare me."

The hint of a smile creased Gage's mouth. He upended the pint of ale and set it down on the bar with a thud.

"HOLY SHIT!"

Frankie stopped dancing at the sound of Claire's exclamation. She twirled to the source and her mouth fell open in surprise. Lieutenant Commander Gage Adams was leaning against the doorway looking magnificent in a tight pair of jeans that hugged his lean hips. He was dessert for the eyes. Booted feet were crossed casually at the ankles and his black shirt delineated every muscle across a very broad chest.

It was a crying shame. Her co-pilot had the sexiest smile she had ever seen in her life—lazy, knowing and totally off limits.

What was he doing at her house?

"Legs!" Frankie stumbled over a casualty passed out in the middle of the floor.

Gage took a step inside and surveyed the carnage.

"Ith everything okaaay?" Frankie lisped.

Not many people knew her parents had provided expensive speech therapy lessons. The only time Frankie lapsed into lisping was when she was overly tired or intoxicated. Her glassy eyes crossed for a moment.

"Everything is fine," he reassured. "Edgar sent me to do a welfare check."

Her cottage beach house was warm and cozy. The white shutters were wide open and every light was on. The Gypsy Kings blared from surround-sound speakers. He had watched from the door while four half-naked women twirled in an awkward tango and was surprised that none of them lost their dinner.

6

"Did everybody make it here without a problem?" he asked.

The girls stared dumbly at him. Gage took a head count. Andie and Lauren were down, unconscious but still breathing amidst layers of sleeping bags. The other four women were still on their feet, barely.

"Ladies, ladies." He glanced at his watch and shook his head. "It's only ten o'clock at night. What time did you start drinking?"

"The usual," Kristen answered. She edged a little closer to him. Frankie reached out, grabbed her roughly by the back of her pink satin teddy and hauled her in like a fish. She let out a little yip of surprise.

"Which is?" Gage prompted.

"Cocktail hour," Frankie answered. "Wanna beer?"

"No thanks. I've got to get home."

"What's your rush?" Claire had crept up to join them, staring hungrily. Gorgeous and tanned, her long blonde hair set off sparkling eyes the color of moss. Frankie grabbed an elbow and pulled her in alongside Kristen.

"I've got a backed up sewer line that needs attention," he said.

Claire wrinkled her nose.

Gage grinned. "So, unless someone needs to be tucked into bed, I'll see you in the morning, Captain," he replied, staring at Claire a little too long.

"I need to be tucked in," Claire piped up.

Frankie gave her arm a yank and a "behave yourself" look.

"I'll see you at work," Frankie addressed him.

"On time?"

"You bet."

Sophia, watching quietly from a few feet away, feigned a cockeyed salute and promptly fell over sideways. Her face collided with a throw pillow on the sofa. She exhaled a small grunt and in a remarkable spurt of effort, crawled blindly onto the couch.

Chapter 2

TROUBLESOME TUESDAY

"**M**AYDAY! MAYDAY!"

Frankie heard the frantic call within the earphone of her helmet. The situation had gone from bad to worse. She gave a gentle forward nudge to the cyclic and changed the angle of the rotor blades to bite more air. She glanced at the airspeed indicator and coaxed a few extra knots of momentum. They would be on scene in less than a minute. The cutter from Station New Harbor was also en route. In the background, via her headset, came the calm response of her co-pilot to the mayday request.

No reply.

The distressed vessel's Emergency Position Indicating Radio Beacon began transmitting its location. Whether the activation was manual or by immersion in water was unknown. Gage tried the vessel again and then hailed the Coast Guard cutter.

Frankie's attention was concentrated elsewhere.

Helicopters.

They did not naturally want to fly. A delicate balance of forces and controls working in opposition to each other kept them in the air. The *Dauphine* was no exception. A thirty-nine foot rotor carried it through the air at a cruising speed well over a hundred knots. The shrouded tail rotor, built right into the fin, gave it a very distinctive appearance. Even the whining noise it made was different from the traditional helicopter blade sounds. It was an amazing piece of equipment with state-of-the-art technology.

Frankie was madly in love with it.

She had nicknamed their helicopter Zena and it took all of her limbs to make the helo behave as it was intended. Her right hand held a stick called a cyclic that rose vertically from the floor between her legs. Her left hand gripped the collective, an oversized stick-shift controlling the pitch of the main rotor blades. Her feet rested on a set of pedals that governed the tail rotor.

Hanging judiciously from the overhead console was her good luck charm...her dad's Marine Corps dog tags.

To her left, she was aware that Gage was now talking to their flight mechanic in the rear of the aircraft, double-checking strategies. Chief Warrant Officer Quinton Herriman's accent, low and distinctly Australian, hummed in her ear above the roar of twin engines. As crew chief, everything that went on in the back of the helo was his responsibility.

Damon was their rescue swimmer.

That morning had started out as absolutely glorious. Sunny, with a light northwesterly breeze and exceptional visibility. A few wispy cirrus clouds floated high in the atmosphere. Every seaworthy vessel in New Harbor's marina had launched, sometimes squeezing three abreast on their way out of the bay.

Frankie arrived a few minutes early, received a concise report from the off-going pilot and wandered out to check on the helicopter. She was seated on a grassy knoll bordering the perimeter of the circular helipad, a pair of binoculars resting in her lap, when her pretty-boy crew rambled in.

Damon had a maniacal grin on his face.

"Good morning, boss!" he yelled out to her.

"You're too happy for this time of morning," she answered. "Do I dare ask what you've been up to?"

His reply was a wicked smirk.

Quinton came in seconds later holding a large foil-covered pan.

"Mornin', Chief," Damon called to him. "What's in the pan? I'm starving!"

"Lasagna's not for breakfast, mate. Isabelle made us this for dinner."

Gage was the last to roll in and was more surly than usual. Instead of spending a few moments teasing her, he swept past with a gruff "good morning" and immediately went to work placing a call to the National Oceanographic and Atmospheric Administration for the latest weather and seismic activity reports.

Two hours later, the emergency call for assistance came. A thirty-foot motorboat struck a rock and was sinking fast. Her water pumps could not keep up with the inflow of sea. Keeping her eyes on the horizon, ahead in the distance Frankie saw the trailing red pattern of a civilian flare.

"I have two confirmed in the water," came Gage's no-nonsense advisory moments later.

Frankie angled down. She eased Zena forward, hovering at a set altitude from the surface and listened for Quinton's instructions.

The Voice began calling out distances.

"Left five, right three, forward five."

Beside her, Gage mirrored the instructions with his outstretched arm in a clipped series of hand signals. He was a firm believer in redundant systems and left nothing to chance. If radio communications went out, they could still get the job done.

"Hold."

With slight flicks of her wrist, Frankie countered the tendency of the helicopter to drift left. She kept them stable at a fixed distance from the victims. Helicopter backwash could be overwhelming. The coastal waters at their latitude were bitterly cold even in late summer. Anyone forced overboard wouldn't last long in the frigid water before succumbing to hypothermia. If the survivors could not swim to the rescue basket and enter it of their own accord, Damon would be deployed to assist.

"Hatch open. Request hoist power."

"Roger."

She had an alpha crew, Frankie thought with satisfaction while keeping their position steady. Nothing ever rattled them. All three had military training and Damon had gone on to become a paramedic. Gage was a former PJ, a pararescueman with New York's elite 106th. Quinton had been with Australia's Special Air Service Regiment before moving to the states. Her crew was competent, diverse. They made her proud.

"Right three. Hold."

The wind had picked up. Gusts buffeted the aircraft. Frankie quickly corrected. She glanced down. The people in the water clung desperately to one another but showed no sign of swimming to the rescue basket.

"Take us in for extraction."

Frankie toggled the controls.

Damon gave a thumbs-up and plunged into the water below. He swam rapidly towards the two and signaled for the basket.

"Forward five. Hold," the Voice instructed.

The first survivor pulled in was a woman. She was abnormally quiet, shaking uncontrollably. Quinton rapidly checked her for any obvious injuries, wrapped her in a warm blanket and sent the basket back down.

GAGE WATCHED FRANKIE DEFTLY maneuver the controls to keep them in a stable hover. She almost made it look easy. Her "control touch" was the best he'd ever seen in a pilot. For a moment he had a fleeting fantasy of those same hands running down the small of his back and gripping his naked hips as she took him inside her tight body. Gage shook his head to clear the unwanted image. Thoughts of sex with her assaulted him from time to time, often at the most ridiculous moments.

Gage studied her face. Under the formidable helmet was a cool, decisive head. She never cut corners, never did a half-assed job, no matter how extreme the fatigue. That she was particularly easy on the eyes didn't hurt matters either.

When she'd first transferred to their crew, Gage was vocal about his reservations. She was green, untested and he let her know about it. "I hear your previous flying's been limited to mail runs," he had accused.

"If shuttling parts around the East Coast with an occasional maintenance flight thrown in for good measure was all I ever did, I wouldn't be here," she spoke quietly.

"You only have six months of actual rescue piloting to your credit," he reminded her.

"Enough to get this job."

Not nearly enough to his way of thinking. Gage badgered her constantly, easing off only after hearing through the grapevine that her sister was dying of cancer.

Gage's attention focused back to the water.

The second victim crawled into the basket. Damon clung to the line above the basket and made the journey alongside, as Quinton hoisted them up.

"Boom stowed. Ready for forward flight."

"Affirmative."

Gage gave Frankie the sign. She worked the anti-torque pedals at her feet, banked thirty degrees starboard and headed back to base with a hundred gallons of fuel still left in the tanks.

SAFE AND SOUND IN the rambling white mansion known as Air Station Harmony Bay, the rescued couple snuggled together under warm blankets, sipped steaming cups of hot coffee while awaiting their ride to the airport.

The estate at Harmony Bay was purchased when it became clear that the New Harbor cutter station needed air support. The two-story structure was built in the late nineteenth century by a wealthy lumber mill owner as a

11

summer home for his family.

Boasting a large stone fireplace encased in the south wall and rows of enormous windows looking out over the helipad and ocean beyond, the air base was a mix of old and new.

Maps of the northern Pacific region, bulletin boards, detailed topographical charts and tide tables adorned most of the wall space. A bevy of radios, flight suits and assorted electronic equipment joined the melee of what had once been a sprawling living room for a rich family.

"Ira Bergmann?" Frankie spoke with awe. "Ira Bergmann the movie producer?"

Frankie stuck out her hand and gave his a vibrant shake. His head bobbed. Sprigs of gray hair swayed under the force of her handshake.

"I am soooooo pleased to meet you."

"I'm very pleased to meet you too, young lady," he answered. "Thank you for saving our lives."

Frankie smoothed her hands down her flight suit, dragged a chair across the floor in front of them, swung it around backwards and straddled it.

"How are you feeling, ma'am?"

"Better," the older woman answered in a shaky voice.

"Ma'am, I am Captain Moriarty," Frankie officially introduced herself. "Would you like more coffee?"

She shook her head no. "Please, call me Lonnie."

"Lonnie, I am required to file an incident report anytime we answer a distress call. I was wondering if you and your husband feel up to answering a few questions?"

Lonnie glanced nervously at her husband.

"We'll try."

Ira Bergmann took a long sip of coffee and steeled himself to account for the boating accident.

"Everything happened so fast that I'm a bit sketchy on the details."

"Understandable," Frankie said softly.

"Lonnie and I were relaxing in the cockpit, enjoying a cocktail. We were talking about our new grandchild. The autopilot was on when we heard a terrible wrenching noise from below deck. The boat came to a jarring halt. I was thrown to my knees. Then we started taking on water." He blinked back a tear and cleared his throat with a cough. "What else can I answer for you?"

Frankie flashed a genuine smile and hesitated before speaking.

"It must have been very frightening for you."

"Oh, well, yes it was."

Frankie tried to lighten the moment. "As stressful as working with actors and directors?"

"Almost," Bergmann smiled.

"They must really test your patience."

Bergmann relaxed a bit. "Yes, they can also be exceptionally good at testing my checkbook."

Frankie chuckled. "I watched the last movie you co-produced with Vin Diesel, three times. What a great action flick. I hope you plan on doing a sequel."

Bergmann nodded.

"So, is his last name really Diesel?"

"Uh, no."

She contemplated his answer a moment, eyes gleaming with excitement.

"Do you happen to know if he could use an extra stunt pilot?"

She heard someone exhale a loud grunt.

"I don't know," Bergmann answered.

GAGE WATCHED FROM a corner chair while he polished his scuffed boots. What was wrong with Frankie? Instead of questioning Bergmann about the boating accident, she was steering the conversation towards movies and some actor. What the hell was going on? He glanced over and met Quinton's perplexed look from across the wide room. The big Aussie shrugged.

"Captain?" Gage interrupted. "Don't you have a report to write?"

"Yeah, in a minute," she answered and turned back to Bergmann. "Would you like more coffee, sir?"

"No thank you. I'm jittery enough as it is."

"I was wondering," she paused in mid-thought. "Do you know how I could get an autographed picture of Vin?"

You would think she's a damned groupie or something, Gage thought bleakly. For some reason, listening to her so jazzed about some guy got his hackles up. She was a Coast Guard rescue pilot, for God's sake. One of the finest he ever worked with. What was the deal? Was she taking a second stab at puberty?

"Captain?"

"Lieutenant?"

"Would you like some help rinsing down the helicopter?"

"No thanks. I'll do it in a moment."

Gage tried again.

"Captain, we need to refuel."

"We have plenty of fuel. We'll top the tanks off later." She turned back to face Bergmann. "I read an article in the local paper last week. Is it true that Vin does all his own stunts?"

Enough was enough.

Gage couldn't sit there and listen to one more second of her babble. The next thing she'd want to know was if the guy slept naked. His eyes narrowed. He jumped up and stormed off through the kitchen, slamming the garage door behind him so forcefully that the entire house shook.

FRANKIE KNEW THEIR VISITORS were worn out from their harrowing experience but she couldn't help herself. Opportunity was knocking. She might never get another chance like this. She had lusted after Vin Diesel since she first set eyes on him. Frankie had sat there in the theater, ignoring her buttered popcorn and soft drink, while waves of drooling desire swamped her.

He was not the typical pretty boy.

In fact, he was downright sinister. Yet there was something about him that made her want to do all the kinky things her friends in the Sisterhood talked about.

Frankie jumped at the sound of the garage door slamming and glanced up. The massive windows hummed with vibration under the force. Quinton was standing by the fireplace, looking sheepish. Damon was smothering laughter behind his large hands and Gage was nowhere to be seen. Her face warmed to three shades of red in rapid progression.

"I'm really sorry going on like this. You must be tired and hungry. I can't seem to stop myself. I'm very sorry." Frankie stood up. "Let me get you a sandwich." She flashed Ira a sly grin and whispered under her breath, "Maybe after you're rested we can talk some more about Vin?"

"DAMON? HAVE YOU BEEN doing the laundry again?"

From somewhere in the kitchen she heard, "How did you know?"

"A lucky guess. Quinton won't be happy with these socks. I think you've invented a new color for the crayon box."

"Hey, I always wanted to be famous."

14

"Would you settle for infamous?" Quinton lobbed the remark from his perch on the stairs leading up to the second floor where he was busy with pencil and ruler, sketching a proposed room addition to his house. Frankie glanced over at him and smiled. His voice soothed her raw nerves like a bath in warm honey. Vin Diesel excluded, if someone asked her the dictionary definition of stud, Frankie would have to smile and point her finger at Quinton. Six foot three, with the broad shoulders and build of an athlete, The Voice was not only gorgeous but he knew how to listen.

"I've got a question for you, Almighty Swordsman." Frankie spoke to Damon in a loud, supercilious voice. "Which one of the Sisterhood is going to be your next victim?"

"Victim?" His nappy blonde head appeared around the corner of the laundry room. Devious brown eyes flashed with amusement. "That's a harsh word to use for the services I provide."

"If the perversion fits…"

"Actually, I was thinking about taking on an extra credit project."

"Extra credit?"

"Yeah."

"I don't like the sound of this."

"Can I get Lauren's phone number from you?"

"Lauren doesn't like boys. Who are you really after?"

Gage suddenly materialized beside Damon, sweaty from running the beach. "He's going after Claire."

"Why Claire?" she asked.

Damon was giving her a cheeky grin. Frankie shook her head. The carefree youngest member of their team was a superb specimen in the prime of life. His six-pack abs and tight, round ass sent cars drifting off the blacktop while their drivers strained to get a better look.

"The other one," Damon gestured in the air, trying to come up with a name.

"Sophia?"

"Sophia," Damon confirmed. "Well, I saw her at the grocery store in Fairhaven last week. I was picking up some burgers for a barbecue my buddies were having."

"Yeah, sure," Frankie interjected.

"Honest. All I did was say hello. She started backing up and dropped a big sack of potatoes." Damon shook his head. "The way she overreacted, you would've thought I was some flasher in a trench coat." He took a deep breath.

"She's gonna take some work so I'm saving her for last."

Frankie smiled.

Virgins always were a tad skittish, especially when confronted by a known predator of Damon's caliber. Sophia was Frankie's trump card, the polar opposite of the twenty-six year old facing her now. If anyone in the Sisterhood would foil him and allow her to win the bet, it would be the judicious Sophia. Across the room, Quinton was grinning devilishly. Frankie gave him a wink.

"You think Claire will be easier to score with than Sophia?" she asked.

"Let's say that some women have trouble dealing with physical attraction. I think Sophia might be one of them and I want to devote plenty of time to help her get past that phobia."

Frankie tried to look serious. "Are you sure? Maybe she's not interested in what you have to offer. I know the thought has never crossed your mind but not every woman on earth is interested in coupling with you," Frankie said flatly.

Damon was instantly suspicious. "You haven't broken one of the rules of our bet, have you, boss?"

GAGE BROKE UP THEIR chatter with a bitter outburst. "Frankie, what was that crap about Van Diesel earlier today?"

Her mouth fell open.

"Vin," Damon corrected.

"Right." Gage gave Damon *the look.* He was tired and irritated and didn't need a dose of the kid's righteous shit right now. The thought of Frankie turned-on about some stranger really pissed him off.

He had gone running on the beach to work off his aggravation yet the foul mood remained. The Bergmanns were long gone, probably relaxing in their Malibu mansion by now, and he was still smoldering. In the years that she had been their pilot, Gage had never seen Frankie show a speck of serious interest in the opposite sex. She was sassy as hell and could yuck it up with the crudest of them, yet she never openly flirted with any man. Like a big brother, Gage covertly kept track of her activities. To his knowledge, she didn't date. He was relatively confident she didn't swing the other way and as far as he knew, nothing out of the ordinary had been going on in her life lately. Was her lapse in sanity one of those freaky, biological time clock moments that single women her age were occasionally afflicted with? Why hadn't she told him she was in need of some companionship? He ran a hand through his wavy brown hair and watched while she calmly folded his underwear. "You were supposed to be questioning them about the boating accident," he spurted.

Damon's eyes opened wide. Sensing trouble, he quickly retreated to relative safe distance.

"Are you going to answer me?"

"About what?"

"The Bergmann couple and Vin Diesel."

"Sure," she replied brightly.

Frankie puffed out her lower lip and squinted.

"Today?" he encouraged.

"I'm thinking about it."

After four years, everybody had pretty much figured out which emotional buttons to push for the biggest reaction. Frankie was deliberately pushing his right this moment and it made him feel as though he'd been brained with a frying pan.

"Did I embarrass you?"

"No," Gage flinched. He rubbed the ache between his eyes and glanced up in time to catch Frankie giving Quinton a sly grin. He was instantly enraged. "You were acting like a horny teenage groupie," he snapped.

"You got a problem with horny teenage groupies?"

"Only when they affect the smooth running of this station."

Her jaw clenched and spine went ramrod straight. Her slim nose shot up defiantly above a ripe mouth pressed sliver-thin. Big gray eyes sparked with anger.

"In what way did my behavior affect the smooth running of this station?"

Gage wasn't ready to admit the truth. He knew she had more than enough information for the report but he wanted her to stew awhile longer. As the old saying went, *misery loved company.* Yet for some strange reason, raising her hackles wasn't nearly as gratifying as he thought it would be. Air Station Harmony Bay had an unwritten rule. If an argument had the potential to turn nasty, those involved were left to work it out themselves. No intervention from the rest of the crew was allowed unless the fight escalated to bloodshed. Gage heard Damon clear his throat and knew the kid was about to violate the non-interference rule.

Just then, the VHF radio crackled and Coast Guard Station New Harbor hailed them with an emergency call.

Everyone sprang into action.

Gage momentarily blocked Frankie's exit from the laundry room, towering

17

over her. Frankie's clipped words were frigid. "This is not finished, mister. Now get out of my way."

THE CALL WAS A tragedy finished long before they arrived. Secret Beach was anything but a secret. Despite a plethora of warning signs, kids still plied their luck in getting down the steep shale escarpment to the isolated beach two hundred feet below.

Especially dangerous after a hard rain, sections the size of a house could shear off, plummeting to solid ground, carrying anything unlucky enough to be nearby. A local fisherman had seen the accident and radioed the Coast Guard.

Two lives had been snuffed out in a moment of seemingly harmless adventure.

Gage knew the dead girl reminded Frankie of her sister. Hell, they all knew, even though she never uttered a word about the resemblance. Frankie insisted on making the next-of-kin calls herself and then shut herself in the pilot's quarters. She skipped supper and ungraciously told Damon to screw off when he tried to pry her out of the room with jokes, insults and an offer to share his pistachio ice cream.

Gage grabbed a book he had been meaning to read for months and relaxed on the recliner opposite her room. If she came out and felt like talking, he wanted to be there.

He needed to be there for her.

FRANKIE TOOK A DEEP breath and shook herself out of a brooding funk. Seeing the broken body of that young girl had been an emotional jolt that brought back too many heart-wrenching memories and she'd allowed herself the luxury of a good sulk in solitary confinement. For most of the evening she studied oceanographic charts and flight reports until her eyes burned. The distant memory of her sister's voice rang true.

"Don't dwell on it, sis. You can't save them all."

Her pilot's quarters were nothing more than a large bedroom/bathroom and office alcove. A malevolent file cabinet lived under the office desk, its sharp edge at perfect knee-banging height. Frankie looked at the reams of government-issued papers scattered across the bed and decided she couldn't sit in the room a moment longer.

She was suffocating.

It was time for some therapy…a long swim followed by a hot bath.

Her neoprene wetsuit hung in the closet. Frankie tugged it on, strapped a waterproof pager tight to her wrist and slung her diving bag over her shoulder. Slipping out of the room through a side door, she paused long enough to get Gage's attention. His nose was glued in a book. She waved at him through the big windows and gave the hand signal to indicate her intentions. He nodded back and continued reading.

The air smelled fresh, clean. Harmonic crashing of waves against the shore called her forward. Like a black wraith, she skirted the wide swathe of trimmed lawn around the lighted helipad and found the long set of concrete stairs that led down to the sandy beach.

"It's easy to get turned around at night," she remembered the words of an old boyfriend. "Never lose track of the shore. The ocean can kill anybody dumb enough to think they can fight it, so use its power. Let it work for you. Conquer your fear."

When she had first begun swimming at night, it was at the urging of an old lover. He'd been the first to show her a lot of things, all of them disappointing.

Except for swimming.

Stroking through chilly waters took her mind off her problems and slid everything into perspective. The terrible images assaulting her in Technicolor clarity began to disintegrate into clouds of dust. Minutes stretched and compressed until time lost its meaning.

GAGE FINISHED THE LAST chapter and slammed the book shut. He looked up at the wall clock and frowned. He was a fast reader, especially when the book was good. Front to back had taken almost two hours and he had been completely absorbed in the story. In the fireplace, a log snapped. He yawned, rubbed the kinks out of his stiff neck and listened to the house noises for a few moments.

Quinton was in the garage helping Damon retrofit his Ducati motorcycle. The sleek, black crotch-rocket had set the kid back a few grand.

Country music and the noise of male conversation filtered in from the open screen door. Damon made a bawdy comment about the female gender that should have incited a smart-assed response had Frankie overheard it. Quinton's lewd reply was the only answer.

A sudden wave of dread swept over him.

Gage vaulted to his feet, all instincts screaming trouble. He crossed the living room floor in giant strides. Worry made his voice harsh.

"Is Frankie back from her swim?"

Damon and Quinton jumped at his outburst. They shook their heads in bewilderment.

"When did she leave?" Quinton asked.

"About two hours ago."

Gage did a quick about-face, the other men were right behind him as they sprinted the distance across the house and flung open the door to her quarters.

"Frankie?" Damon called out.

The room was a mess. A picture of her sister sat on the bed beside an empty box of tissues. Gage took a few steps inside and panned the room. His gaze came to rest on a mahogany dresser. Under a loose stack of correspondence, he caught a flash of her titanium diver's watch. Gage let loose an ugly curse.

"We've got a problem."

Chapter 3

A NEW ATTITUDE

"**P**AGE HER AGAIN," GAGE BARKED THE ORDER TO DAMON WHILE HE AND QUINTON suited up. "Page her every two minutes until you get a response and call New Harbor. Tell them we're on divert due to a helicopter malfunction until further notice."

"Affirmative," Damon nodded.

Quinton grabbed a pair of night vision goggles.

"If New Harbor wants details, stall for time. Tell them I'm busy working the problem and will give an update as soon as possible," Quinton said.

"Got it." On the floor in front of the fireplace Damon began to prep a large sleeping bag with chemical warmers. "She'll be mad as hell if she wakes up in the hospital."

"Let's find her first," Gage advised. "We can worry about her temper later."

He and Quinton raced out of the station, their long black-covered legs striding powerfully across the lawn. The sound of rubber booted feet taking the concrete steps four at a time reminded him of a horse stampede. Or maybe all that galloping was the pounding of his heart?

Frankie was upset, not thinking clearly. They had all been there at sometime during their career. Everyone who worked with her was aware that Frankie could function through hypothermia, unaware of its progression right up to the point she keeled over. She had let him know that she was going out for a swim. She had stood by the window and made eye contact with him.

They had to find her!

With each agonizing moment, Gage mentally beat himself up. A debriefing shrink had once told him there was a list of things that could stress emergency workers to the limit. The team was a family, their lives dependent on one another. Ranked in order of seriousness, the worst was to lose a member of

21

your team in the line of duty. According to the shrink, the only thing making that loss worse would be if you thought his death was your fault. The doc had been right.

They paused at the base of the stairs while Quinton secured the night vision goggles to his face and began a grid-like scan of the beach and fog shrouded water.

Frankie normally swam a U-shaped pattern, taking advantage of the surf and currents to aid her movements. Quinton adjusted the search accordingly.

"Over there." He pointed to something a hundred yards down the beach. Gage strained to see. A second later, the unmistakable tones of a pager echoed across the water.

Gage burst into motion.

Frankie had made it up the beach, partially shrugged out of her suit before she collapsed. Ice-cold and incoherent, curled in a fetal position, her hair was entwined with seaweed and sand. Gage dropped to the sand beside her. His big hand cupped her cheek.

"Frankie?"

She blinked and stared up at him, disoriented. Her bloodless blue lips opened to speak, closed and sputtered, "When's the flight?"

"We're boarding right now," he answered nervously while rapidly running his hands over her, checking for injuries. Her eyes fluttered shut.

"Wake up, Frankie," he urged. "Stay with us."

"Stop yelling," she mumbled.

"Only if you keep your eyes open."

Quinton reached them and immediately bundled her into a blanket.

"Is she injured?" he asked.

Gage shook his head. "Just hypothermic."

"I'll carry her back to the station," Quinton spoke.

"No, I'll do it."

Gage tossed Frankie over his shoulder and stood in one swift move. Together they sprinted back to base.

"WHAT'S SHE AT NOW?" Quinton was in the kitchen heating a kettle of water.

Damon took Frankie's temperature for the umpteenth time in an hour. It ran up and down like a yoyo. Each time they warmed her enough to give cautious sips of hot chocolate, her temp did an about face and plummeted. The fireplace was roaring. The decrepit brick furnace in the basement was cranked to the max.

"Ninety-four."

"Damn it."

Gage stopped his ferocious pacing and was perched on the edge of the sofa, watching from a grim world of self-persecution. They had stripped Frankie naked as soon as they got back to the station. Working in unison, they dried her off with heated towels from their blanket warmer and placed her in a toasty sleeping bag. Her alabaster skin was parchment gray except for the dark circles rimming her eyes. She mumbled a few incomprehensible words before she drifted off to sleep. Across the room, Damon's cat Stewie gave her a malignant glare, unhappy with the amount of attention she was receiving.

Gage rubbed his bleary eyes and hissed out a curse. He knew that most of the body's energy was spent in maintaining a stable inner temperature. When calculated in degrees, it was a narrow window of operation. He also knew that Frankie's metabolism ran her a full degree hotter than the norm. Sludge-thick blood was oozing through his precious captain's vital organs.

"I think it's time for a Reuben," Quinton spoke the words softly and stared meaningfully at Gage.

Damon's head jerked up in confusion. "What are you talking about, man? You can't feed her now," he blurted. "Are you out of your mind? Look at her." He ran an agitated hand through his tousled hair. "She can barely swallow."

"Damon," Gage answered quietly. "Strip off your clothes."

"What?"

"You heard me." Gage was standing now, peeling his navy blue uniform right down to bare skin. "Take off your damned clothes."

Damon blinked once, twice, and then his large brown eyes opened wide in understanding. He stood slowly and mimicked Gage's actions. Together, the two men crawled inside the spacious sleeping bag and effectively sandwiched Frankie between the flesh of their warm bodies. She squirmed, twisted, frowned in her sleep and tried to push and kick Damon as far away as possible.

"It figures she'd be a bed-hog," he groused, after taking a nasty punch in the ribs.

"Shut up and deal with it," Gage ordered. He reached out and pulled her chilly body in close to his own. He could feel her cold muscles twitching uncontrollably. After a few moments of being tightly held, Frankie stopped flailing and relaxed against him. She was a perfect fit, curled up firm and tight against his hypersensitive skin. And when she moved against him, his primal

23

response was hot and immediate. His eyes opened wide with realization. *He wanted to fuck his precious captain.* Right then, right there, as hard and deep inside her as he could get.

Frankie moaned in her stupor and gave Damon another sharp kick.

"Ouch!" Damon yelped. "The things I have to do in the name of teamwork."

Quinton bent down. "Stop your bitching, mate, and behave yourself."

"What do you mean behave myself? I'm the one getting clawed here."

He squirmed and grunted. Quinton rolled his eyes and migrated over to the sofa. He picked up the remote control and started channel surfing.

"Damon, settle down and keep a check on your dick," Gage snapped.

"What? Are you insinuating that I might try to slip it to her while she's in a near comatose condition?" Damon asked imperiously.

Gage gave the younger man an over-the-eyebrow look. "Those scars on your back aren't from Stewie," he answered dryly, more than ready to strangle the kid if his hands wandered anywhere on Frankie's body that they shouldn't.

"Ha, ha. Very funny," Damon deadpanned.

Frankie stirred and began to thrash again. Gage wrapped his arm around her midsection, pulling her closer into the curve of his body. She exhaled a soft sigh and relaxed against him. Her small foot connected with Damon's shin.

"Do I get hazard pay for this job?"

"Cowboy-up and move in closer. You're too far away to do any good."

Damon muttered something nasty under his breath.

"What's your problem, mate?" Quinton demanded from across the room. His steely blue stare spelled trouble Damon didn't need.

"My problem? Let me see, where should I start? How about with the fact that I've never been in a sleeping bag with a man before."

"It doesn't mean I want to have your baby," Gage retorted, relishing the feel of her soft skin against him.

"Although you do have a nice ass," Quinton heckled.

"He's right," Gage joined in. "Your ass *is* your best feature."

Damon shivered. "Does the fact that I'm having some trouble lying next to this naked woman mean anything to either of you?"

"That you want to keep her from freezing to death?" Gage answered, trying hard to keep his voice stern and mind on the task despite Frankie's incessant wriggling against his groin.

Quinton piped up. "Knock it off, you wanker. She's like your sister."

"My sister does not have tits like this."

"Shut up, Damon," Gage ordered.

"I'm serious, LC. They're a perfect handful! And those nipples? They're big enough to hang my hat on!"

Gage let out a pained groan. He was well aware of what their youngest crewmember was yapping about. His fingertips had accidentally brushed against her erect nipple. He'd felt the jolt of that tactile surprise all the way to his aching cock. He tried to think about something else.

Anything else!

Damon kept on blabbing. "Did you see that little tattoo on her ass? What's that about?"

Gage closed his eyes and tried to keep his mind on the sole task of warming Frankie's core temperature. *Please don't let her slip away from me!* His inner mantra was interrupted once again by Damon's complaints.

"Quinton, please! No more reruns of the home improvement channel. I'm begging ya, man. I can't take it anymore. Tune in to ESPN or a sitcom or something."

Gage began to chuckle. "For once I agree with the kid," he said.

Quinton let out an exasperated huff and began channel surfing again. Stewie ambled over to the big Aussie, jumped onto his lap and began bathing himself in earnest.

Damon let out a sudden yelp of pain. Gage was almost afraid to ask.

"What is it now?"

"Dude, that better not be *your* hand."

"Damon, give it a rest." He reached out and pulled Frankie's hand away, intertwining her slender fingers between his larger, warm ones. Uncontrolled shivering still racked her body. Gage could feel every tremor.

"Why don't you take her front side for awhile, LC? This isn't right. It's going to ruin me for life."

"Damon?"

"I know, I know. Shut up."

This time the silence managed to last almost fifteen minutes. An explosive rumble sounded from under the covers. Gage gagged and pulled the sleeping bag into a tight collar around his neck.

"Damn it! What the hell have you been eating?"

"Frankie did it."

"It wasn't Frankie."

"How do you know?"

"Because I'm in back and I know she didn't."

Quinton broke into laughter. Frankie sneezed, twisted in Gage's embrace and firmly planted her knee into Damon's testicles.

MORNING LIGHT FILTERED THROUGH pane glass windows. Frankie moaned and made a weak attempt to struggle out of a deep slumber. She was securely held in place. Something hard, smooth, and warm was curled up behind her. She wanted to open her eyes, cast off the strange dream, but couldn't muster the energy. Whatever had attached itself to her backside felt good. Really good. Comforting in a yummy way she didn't want to wake up from. Her nipples tingled and ached. She squirmed and wriggled, trying to push closer to the delightful sensation rubbing against her ass. Her lips parted, she let out a soft sigh and whispered, "I want to see spots," then promptly fell back to sleep.

GAGE ADAMS CAME BRUTALLY awake at the lusty sound of a moaning female. He was sporting a raging, almost painful, erection. The kind of diamond-cutter he hadn't had for years. Warily opening his eyes, Gage found to his marked horror that he was lying on his side with Frankie curved to his body like a spoon. She was cleaved so tightly against him he was damned near inside her.

That wasn't the worst of it.

She wiggled her sweet little heart-shaped butt. God save him. He almost slid right into home base. Gage held his breath and counted to ten, then slowly, cautiously, slipped from beneath the blankets.

Padding quietly across the wood floor, he tiptoed up the wide staircase to the second level and eased past an open door. Quinton was still in bed, snoring softly with his head tucked at an awkward angle.

Gage closed the door to his room. When he found the nerve to start breathing again he took a quick cold shower and dragged on a sweat-suit and running shoes.

The house was silent as he stealthily crept back down the stairs. He turned and took one last look before exiting. Damon was stretched out on his stomach with Frankie's arm draped over him.

HE RAN UP AND down the sandy beach for almost an hour and still couldn't find *the zone.* His mind and body were frustratingly out of sync. Running always brought him a measure of relief from whatever was troubling him, some temporary peace of mind while listening only to his body. His senses would blur and the miles drag on.

Frankie.

She was the problem. He had gotten a boner over his captain and he was way beyond distracted. His body screamed over the clamor in his head. He tried to regulate his breathing, make his running movements smooth and fluid but his body wasn't responding. The only high it wanted was to have sex with her until it passed out from sheer exhaustion. He tried to divert his mind to other, less pleasant things.

Like Robin.

The thought of what she did always put him in a bad mood.

Or Greg.

Greg would still be here if Gage hadn't fucked up and gotten him killed.

He pounded past the tourists who were flocking to the shore like migratory birds. His feet sank into the dampened sand then pulled free. He stared straight ahead, ignoring the bikini-clad females ogling him.

The morning sun beat down on his exposed skin. He stripped down to running shorts and insignia shirt. The pager at his waist slapped against his hip with each jarring step. Gage wiped the sweat from his eyes and angled a path through the edge of the water in deliberate attempt to get his shoes wet.

Wet.

Gage bit down painfully on his lip. His mind would not let it go. Frankie had been arched and shuddered against him that morning, inviting moisture seeped from between her legs while she moved in a sweet, stroking rhythm to coax him inside. She wanted sex. If he hadn't caught her hips in that last moment of sanity, Gage would have done the unthinkable.

Military training had helped school him to minimize and control his reactions. Fucking her was all he could think about at the moment and not a damned thing seemed to change that.

He scowled and picked up the pace.

SHE WAS NOT BY nature a morning person. Dragging herself upright without the adrenaline-rush that a rescue call brought was a challenge. Frankie pitched into wakefulness in total confusion. She sat up, rubbed her stiff shoulders and looked around. She was naked and alone under a big bedroll in the middle of the living room floor.

"What the hell?"

The house was silent. She sniffed in the scent of Damon's after-shave and sneezed. Mingled odors permeated the air and tainted her skin. She smelled like salty ocean, hearth smoke, the rich aroma of chocolate and something else. A musky female scent combined with the delightful essence of…

"Gage?"

Her mouth tightened into a thin line. Her recollection of the night before was punched full of holes. She sifted through fragments of vague recollection.

Swimming.
Fighting a strong current.
Numbing cold.
The face of her dead sister.
The worried tone in Gage's voice.
Damon's nagging.
Swatting at a temperature probe.
Quinton's reassurance.
Drinking something too hot and sickeningly sweet.
Naked flesh next to her own.
Warmth and security.
More naked flesh next to her own.

Frankie rocked back on her heels, feeling suddenly queasy.

"What have I done?"

She took another wary glance around the room and tried to stand. Her legs were wobbly. Moving with trepidation, she scooped up an armful of bedding and staggered off. No matter what had happened, Frankie reminded herself, she was still the senior officer of the station with duties to perform. Or at least she hoped that was the case. She stumbled on a trailing edge of blanket and banged her knee.

Her mind swirled with images while she showered, dressed and worked up the courage to seek out Quinton. She found him on the far side of the helipad. A braided steel cable had been played out to its full, three hundred-foot length. Quinton was running it slowly through his ungloved hands, checking for any frayed strands. The sturdy metallic rescue basket and Stokes litter were on the ground beside the helo.

He looked up at her approach and motioned her closer. Intense blue eyes sparkled with genuine warmth.

"Feeling better?"

Frankie gave him a sheepish grin. "It depends."

"On what?"

"On how big an ass I made of myself last night."

He let out a deep rumble of laughter that warmed her heart.

"Fuzzy on the details?"

"In a major way." She was cautiously finger-drying her wet hair. "I bet Gage is ready to strangle me."

Quinton shook his head negatively. "You gave us a scare."

Frankie looked away. She couldn't bear the thought she'd disappointed him.

"It'll never happen again, Chief. I promise."

"I know that," he answered solemnly. "Gage needs to hear it from you. I've never seen him like that."

"Seen him like what?" she asked, confused.

"He blames himself for not reaching you sooner," Quinton answered matter-of-factly.

"It wasn't his fault," Frankie whispered. She shook her head, trying to clear away all the panicky thoughts.

That Others May Live.

To Gage they were more than empty words. The PJ motto continued to shape his behavior. He always put the welfare of others before his own safety.

Quinton stopped working the cable and watched her closely. His soft brown hair, lightened by the sun, curled in a corona around his angular face.

"He was frightened for you. Scared shitless, in fact. We were all worried."

"Where is he now?" she asked.

"Running the beach."

"Where's Damon?"

"Taking Stewie to the vet."

"What's wrong with him?"

"Him is about to become an IT."

She grinned widely. "Serves the little monster right." Frankie stared across the blue-gray ocean at a distant speck. A cargo ship with a heavy load, she thought automatically.

"I wonder if it will improve his attitude?"

The gnarled alley cat Damon had found wandering the woods had a deep lack of affection for Frankie, it spit and hissed except when she came bearing gifts of food.

"If neutering works on Stewie, we should send Damon in for the same treatment," Quinton joked.

Frankie listened, attentive to the way the big man spoke and wondered if God was feeling exceptionally generous the day he created Quinton's vocal cords. Something nibbled at her subconscious that didn't quite make sense.

"Quinton?"

"What?"

"I need to know something."

"I'm listening."

"Who was in the sleeping bag with me?"

She brought her curious gaze up to meet his. His only reply was a sly grin showing the faintest hint of a dimple in his right cheek. She closed her eyes on a curse and wandered back into the house.

HANGING OUT WITH THE boys was part and parcel of life in the Coast Guard. Chores and maintenance were done while keeping an eye on the prevailing weather patterns.

Frankie was making potato salad and sandwiches for lunch when Gage came back from his run. Turning to the sound of the sliding glass doors, one look at him almost stopped her heart.

Pale, drenched with sweat, guppy-breathing, he had hit the wall, literally running himself into the ground. He made direct eye contact with her, turned slowly and dragged himself upstairs to his room.

Frankie dropped the paring knife onto the counter and followed. She gave him a few moments of privacy, waiting for the tinkling spray of the shower, then opened the bathroom door and stepped inside.

"Gage?"

"What the hell are you doing in here?" he barked.

"I'm the boss. I get to go anywhere I want. Remember?"

His mumbled reply was unintelligible but Frankie got the gist. The man could be so damned testy. Something vicious weighed on his mind and it got worse every year around this time. After four years of working together, she could usually decipher his mood but rarely understood what powered it.

"What do you want?" he growled.

She took a deep breath and tried to stay calm. Gage always responded better to honesty. "I want to thank you for helping me last night," she replied nervously. He'd always affected her more than she liked to admit. The thought of disappointing him weighed heavy on her mind. "I also want to apologize for my irrational behavior."

"It wasn't irrational," he snapped.

"Yes it was," Frankie answered. "I made a stupid mistake. It won't happen again, I promise."

Gage leaned his forehead against the cool tile of the shower and closed his eyes. Warm water trickled down his spine. He could tell by the way her voice carried that she was standing not more than three feet away from the opaque shower stall. Good thing there was a glass door and some distance between them, he thought. Because he felt an inexplicable need to hold her.

"I have to ask you something. One question and I'll go away." Frankie cleared her throat. "Exactly where were you this morning?"

"Running the strand," he rasped, winced when his burgeoning cock struck the shower wall.

"That's not what I mean."

"Then say what you mean, captain," he enunciated each syllable. "I can't read your mind."

He was going to make her spell it out.

"Were you in the sleeping bag with me last night?"

Frankie thought she heard him pound his head against the shower stall.

"Are you going to answer me?" she asked.

"No."

"No? You weren't in the sleeping bag or, no, you're not going to answer me?"

She bit her lip in exasperation and tried not to get pissed off. Why all the secrecy? Where was the straight answer from these guys? She had a simple request and they acted like it was a need-to-know case of national security. She was a big girl. She could handle it. At the very least, she could pretend she did. His silence only added to her suspicions. Had she made such a big fool of herself that he couldn't even talk about it? How could she be embarrassed without any cold, hard facts?

"Yo, Captain." Damon, silent and sneaky, had returned to the base and was lurking just inside the bedroom door. "Glad to see you're feeling better."

Frankie grimaced at the sound of Gage's exasperated groan. Maybe she could get some answers from their resident frat-brat.

"How's Stewie?"

"Sore down-under," Damon answered with a frown. "They're keeping him overnight for observation."

Frankie tried to hide a perverse grin.

"Hey," Damon protested. "It's not funny. My cat is great. He's the perfect pet."

"He's perfect all right," she deadpanned. "Stewie would fit perfectly on the barbecue."

"You're a sick woman, Moriarty."

"You're a fine one to call *me* sick." She rolled her eyes and looked to the heavens. "Why couldn't I have been assigned a junior crewman who likes reptiles or birds?"

"No way," he shook his head.

Frankie continued to harass him. "How about a big green parrot who likes to shit down the back of your shoulder? Now that's a pet I can identify with."

"Any animal that has a can opener for a mouth isn't my idea of a pet," he sneered. "All loving and snuggly one moment and the next, the thing's taking a DNA sample from your finger."

Gage suddenly spoke up. "Do you two mind taking this discussion elsewhere? I'm trying to shower."

Frankie ignored him.

"Damon, I've got a question for you."

"Yeah?"

"I want to make it clear that your entire career is hanging in the balance, so think carefully about your answer."

His full upper lip curled in petulance.

"Roger that," he answered wryly.

Frankie could barely keep a straight face.

"Exactly where were you last night?"

A slow conspiratorial grin spread across his baby-face. He arched a blonde eyebrow. "I was the one keeping your breasts warm."

She had to give him credit. The boy's reflexes were superb. He spun so quickly that she barely had time to lob a toothbrush in his direction.

"By the way," he yelled from down the hall. "You really ought to shave your legs more often."

Frankie could hear a pathetic groan from the shower as she let out a howl and sprinted after Damon.

THE CIVILIAN PUBLIC WORKS scanner, monitoring activities around New Harbor, crackled with static and went silent. Frankie eyed Gage over the top of a roast beef sandwich. All his attention seemed riveted on his meal. He hadn't said two words to her since the shower incident. His eyes were hooded and wary. Across the wide kitchen table, Quinton studied them both like they were some freakish lab experiment gone wrong.

"So, boss," Damon asked. "What's the significance of that tattoo on your butt?"

Frankie bit the inside of her lip and glared at him. "You're the second person to ask about my tattoo this week."

Gage's head snapped up. "Who else asked about it?"

Lauren, she mouthed.

All three men asked simultaneously, "Lauren saw your tattoo?"

Frankie nodded.

"Isn't she a—" Gage paused.

"A lesbian?" Frankie finished the question.

His brilliant green eyes flew open in what Frankie recognized as worry. This was the most talkative Gage had been all day and she wasn't about to let the opportunity slip away.

"Yes, she's a lesbian and very popular with that crowd too. Did I mention that she is currently single and back on the dating market?"

Gage shook his dark head.

"What happened to her last girlfriend?" Damon asked.

"I'm not entirely certain but I know they haven't seen one another for months." Frankie paused to take a sip of water. "I think Denise might have been too butch for her."

"Doesn't Denise work for the fire department?" Damon asked.

Frankie nodded her head. "She's the director of their emergency medical services. Book smart, street dumb."

The three men were strangely quiet.

"I heard things got ugly between them. Denise started to harass Lauren at work, circling the ER's ambulance bay on her big red motorcycle until the hospital security staff called the cops. Lauren was mortified. She even took out a restraining order."

"Motorcycle?" Damon perked up. "What kind of motorcycle?"

"I don't know. Lauren is coming over for dinner next weekend. I'll ask her."

"You're having dinner with Lauren?" Gage's firm jaw twitched. "The two of you?" He leaned over the table. "Alone?"

"Of course," Frankie lied. "She has something she wants to discuss with me in private so we're going to order Chinese take-out, rent a movie and have a relaxing evening."

Quinton began to cough. Beside him, Damon was speechless with shock, leering at her like she'd morphed fangs and needed blood to survive.

GAGE FELT LIKE THE top of his head was about to fly off. *Lesbian?* Was Frankie thinking about starting a relationship with Lauren? He stared down at his empty soup bowl and saw his raw reflection. Hell, maybe he needed to call that shrink after all. At this rate he would be a raving lunatic before the week was out.

"Lauren volunteered to help me re-wire my spare bedroom. I've been meaning to put another electrical outlet in there for my new computer." She reached over and poured herself a glass of water. "She's very handy to have around the house. She also offered to help repair the screen on my front door. I was going to ask Quinton but I want the job done sometime this century and Isabelle's got him booked solid with the remodel job."

Gage rubbed his aching temples while Frankie talked. "I'll do it for you," he blurted. "I've got all the tools you need."

"Are you nuts?" Damon blurted.

Quinton turned to give Gage a curious stare and bit of advice. "This time, don't forget to hook the wires together *before* you close up the wall, mate."

Damon chuckled. They all knew what a marginal electrician Gage was.

"Are you sure you want to tackle it?" Frankie asked. "I know how much you hate that kind of stuff."

"Yes," Gage replied. "I'll do it first thing Wednesday morning."

"Okay, if you're sure," Frankie agreed. "Give me a list of what you need for the job and I'll pick it up from the hardware store."

Gage took a deep breath and eased back in his chair. Frankie was spouting off some blather about Lauren's reported prowess in bed. Gage eyed her warily and wished for a couple of aspirin.

"Hey, boss," Damon said. "Do you think Lauren would be game for comparing notes on oral technique?"

Gage clenched his fists until his knuckles blanched white. The thought of anybody, male or female, giving Frankie that kind of pleasure infuriated him.

By the time lunch was finished and the other two men wandered from the kitchen, the slow simmer of his anger had cranked up to full boil. He helped clear the table while Frankie loaded plates into the cramped dishwasher.

He crept up behind her, blocking any path of retreat. He could smell her lilac body lotion, hear the soft intake of her breath. The recessed fluorescent lights of the kitchen cast sparkles of gold in her curly red hair. He wanted to run his hands through every strand, hold them against his face while he pummeled her cervix with his cock.

"It would be a really stupid thing to do," he whispered through clenched teeth. "She's not right for you."

Frankie stiffened but continued working.

"What are you talking about?"

"You and Lauren. Don't do it."

Silence.

"What's really eating you?" she asked quietly.

Nothing.

Everything.

"Are you mad because I forgot to wear my watch? It was an accident, Gage. I was upset. I promise it will never happen again."

"You're right." He dipped his head low. The need to protect her was so strong it almost dropped him to his knees. "That little stunt was a one-time deal and you won't be swimming again at night unless I'm with you. Is that understood?"

Frankie whirled around and stared directly into his chest. She swallowed hard and put her hands up to shove him away. "I don't need a babysitter."

A muscle in his jaw twitched. He bent down and whispered in her ear. "Is that so? I'm not so sure." His voice was pitched low and dangerous. "Not anymore." Her breath hitched as his lips raked across her earlobe. He could hear her heart beating double-time. He stared at her lips for a moment longer then turned and walked away, leaving her trembling in the middle of the deserted kitchen.

Chapter 4

HE WHO DARES, WINS

"WHEEL BRAKES?"

Gage began the verbal pre-flight procedure they had been through countless times. Every crewmember had an assigned task and was relied upon to perform it efficiently.

"Set," Frankie answered.

"Aft cabin door?"

"Secured," Quinton replied.

"Fuel flow control levers?"

Frankie panned the center of the roof. "Levers forward," she answered.

"Low RPM lights off?"

"Check."

Frankie flipped the engine control to the on position.

"Starting."

Twenty seconds passed.

"Rotors at one hundred percent," Gage announced.

"Ready for take-off."

Zena was airborne.

Frankie pointed them into the wind and started a climb towards the airport to refuel. The vista took on a different perspective. Five minutes later, a red light on the forward console demanded their attention.

"We've got a chip light," Gage stated coolly.

"Roger that."

"ETA to airport, five minutes," Gage responded.

"Roger that," Frankie responded. "We'll land and do a burn there."

With hundreds of rescue missions under her belt, Frankie knew an "oh shit" moment when one came along. A piece of metal was trapped in the filter designed to catch it. Nevertheless, she kept a close eye on her instrument panel for any further signs of trouble. In the dual-control seat beside her,

Gage scrutinized engine power percentages and confirmed her findings.

Plenty of time.

She carefully scanned the surroundings for obstacles. They flew past the airport in the downwind direction, turned and made a final approach. Gage barked out the landing check while Frankie made a shallow descent.

They touched down on the tarmac and slowly taxied to an open hangar. With the rotors still spinning, she reached up to the overhead console and flipped the "chip burn" switch.

"No joy," Gage called out moments later.

Frankie repeated the function twice. Gage shook his head.

It was up to Quinton now.

Their crew chief removed his helmet and went to work. Within minutes he had delivered the bad news.

"We don't fly until I can get a visual inspection of the filter," he informed them.

"Okay," Frankie agreed. "How do we expedite that?"

"With the proper equipment and a second mechanic to assist, I can handle the job."

"The nearest Avionics Technician and APU are in Portland," Frankie advised. "It will take at least two hours to get them here."

"Then we've got some time to kill." A thin stream of sweat trickled down Quinton's forehead. He swiped at it with a gloved hand. "I can't do the right job without the right tools."

"I'll radio Station New Harbor and notify them of the situation," Gage volunteered.

Quinton shut the compartment hatch and passed a distracted hand through his hair. "Sounds good, mate. I'll make the call to Portland."

The airport terminal was little more than an oversized shack with a receptionist who catered to private planes and the occasional Coast Guard helicopter. Frankie listened without a word while Quinton made swift work of the arrangements and Gage dropped the news on the commander of their cutter station.

"Why don't we walk into town for lunch?" Damon suggested. "We've got a couple of hours. No use hanging around here."

"Sounds good to me," Frankie replied.

Quinton and Gage nodded in quick agreement. Frankie reached for a pen and paper from the receptionist and scribbled down their pager numbers.

"Would you let us know when our technician arrives?"

The woman smiled up from behind large blue eyes. "I'd be more than happy to."

With Damon leading the way, the four of them struck out by foot across the warm pavement. The airport grounds quickly gave way to a residential district of vinyl sided homes. Frankie pulled her baseball cap down low on her forehead and pushed up the sunglasses that kept sliding down her nose. As the four of them walked single file down the narrow sidewalk, she had an unpleasant sense of déjà vu. She was propelled back to her first few months of assignment at Harmony Bay. Earning the respect of her crew meant she suffered through numerous petty cruelties. Their practical jokes had run the gamut from mean-spirited things like rimming the eyepiece of her binoculars with black shoe polish, to more sophomoric tricks such as turning off the hot water in mid-shower and putting a whoopee cushion under her cockpit seat.

On a daily basis, without respect and the credibility accompanying it, superior rank was worthless official bullshit. Frankie swallowed hard.

Had she lost Gage's trust?

Her mind clouded with possibilities. All the errors she'd ever made returned to haunt her. Frowning, she blew several long strands of hair from her face. Undoubtedly, the last twenty-four hours had been some of the strangest of her life. She'd managed to score a few solitary moments with Quinton the night before. Frankie replayed their conversation over in her mind, but it didn't get her one bit closer to really understanding what was going on in her co-pilot's gorgeous head.

"Quint, can I talk to you?"

"Anytime," he had replied.

"There's something weird going on with Gage."

"I noticed."

"You did?"

"Hard to miss."

"What should I do about it?"

"Whatever feels right to you."

A swing and a miss. Quinton gave her nothing solid to grasp. His ability to keep a confidence was a double-edged sword sometimes. Frankie bit her lip.

Time for Plan B.

She was going to have to go straight to the source for answers. Right now, that source walked in sync behind her; so close that if she stopped suddenly she'd be wearing him like a shawl.

Life had been that way all morning. Every time she turned around, Gage was there. She shut a door for privacy. He opened it. She wandered out to the gym for a workout on the treadmill. He followed. Gage had slipped back into his surly, brooding mode, with one distinction:

He had become a stalker.

Despite the warmth of the day, Frankie shivered. She picked up her pace. Gage increased his steps to match hers. Damon led them through one of New Harbor's suburban areas. A middle-income neighborhood of identical brick houses mirrored one another on either side of the narrow street. Across the bay, Frankie could see the town's landmark. The enormous concrete bridge, built in the early forties. They turned left at the corner and spilled out onto the busy main drag.

"You're gonna love this deli," Damon made a kissing sound and smacked his lips. "Primo."

"Does that translate into 'I've scored with the waitress'?" Frankie quipped.

Damon didn't bother to respond. A van full of soccer kids coasted by them, driven by a perky blonde whose head was craned in their direction.

"MILTF alert," Damon spoke excitedly.

Frankie gave him the evil eye.

"Do I even want to know what MILTF means?" she asked.

Quinton turned and spoke matter-of-factly, "It means a Mother I'd Love To Fuck."

"Okay, okay, I got it." Frankie waved her hand in the air and almost smacked Gage on the nose.

Halfway down a commercial block of gift shops and specialty kite stores, Damon ducked into a small restaurant. The others followed.

The deli was an eclectic hole-in-the-wall with a circa sixties hippie feel to it. Their waitress, a homely girl in her twenties, ushered them to the back patio and proceeded to stumble over chairs, tray tables and a few less fortunately positioned patrons in her rush to serve.

Frankie had learned it was always like this when the four of them were in public. She was surrounded by three of the most gorgeous guys in the Coast Guard, made irresistible by their uniforms. Frankie shook her head and grabbed a menu.

"What are you having?" Damon asked each person in turn.

"Prawns," Quinton answered.

"Burger and fries," Gage growled.

Frankie wrinkled her lip in contemplation. "I was thinking about having a Rueben. For some strange reason I've been craving one all day."

The pin-dropping silence made her look up. Three toothy grins stared at her in a way that made the short hairs on the back of her neck stand straight up and scream conspiracy. A mischievous chuckle started. Frankie leaned forward and hissed in a voice pitched low, "You've got two seconds. Spill."

GAGE BROKE EYE CONTACT and took a deep, shaky breath. He could feel himself breaking into a sweat. His cold, dead heart felt strange, tender things. She sat there, making empty threats with her chin thrust out and lip curled in a pseudo-snarl. Why hadn't he ever noticed the blue highlights in her gray eyes, or the way her nose flared when she was riled? He choked on a strangled cough.

He was in trouble, all right. Big time.

A leak had sprung in his emotional dam. The tiny hole seemed to expand with every hour and threatened to let loose something that he wasn't ready to face. He pinched the bridge of his nose, trying to ward off the beginnings of another stress headache.

"A Reuben," Damon took the honor of explaining, "is the code name for the naked warm-up you don't remember participating in the other night."

Frankie's expression remained neutral.

"Is that so?"

"Honest." He held up his hands. "I'm still scabbed over from all those razor-stubble wounds you gave me."

She glanced from Quinton to Gage and back. Both of them were doing a miserable job of keeping a straight face.

The waitress returned.

"What can I get for you?" the girl asked sweetly

Frankie was scowling now and Gage could tell she wasn't going to let anyone get the best of her. Clearing her throat, she evenly announced, "I'll have the tuna special."

The group exploded into laughter.

"SMALL CRAFT ADVISORY WITH winds north-northwest at twenty to twenty-five knots. Swells four to six feet, increasing to six to eight feet by late afternoon. Barometric pressure thirty point ten and falling."

Frankie listened to the background noise of the weather forecast and glanced surreptitiously at her three poker-playing crewmen. How many small boats would ignore the warning? How many desperate fisherman or foolhardy boat owners would venture out to sea tomorrow?

Quinton and his apprentice had taken nearly three hours to get the helicopter up and running again. She and Gage helped the two aircraft mechanics as much as possible, never missing an opportunity to learn more about Zena's inner workings, especially with Quinton's recent reservations about Zena's overall health. He couldn't put his finger on anything specific yet something about the helicopter was creasing his brow more and more lately.

Damon used the downtime to shuttle a mewling Stewie back to the air station where the pathetic cat spent the rest of the afternoon curled up on his favorite pillow. With his duties as responsible pet owner appropriately dispatched, Damon returned the borrowed airport vehicle and walked down to the cutter station for some hobnobbing with his lecherous buddies.

Damon had been the one to suggest they squander their evening with a game of naked truth poker. Playing with matches instead of money and a few unconventional rules, a winning hand presented the victor with an opportunity to ask a singular question of anyone at the table. The loser was faced with a troubling choice—tell the truth or relinquish an article of clothing.

The fact that Gage jumped on the idea of a poker game like the call to reveille, should have set off all of Frankie's internal alarms. She had never caught him cheating. Yet, as she sat on the edge of a dining table chair, clad only in her underwear and a thin cotton chemise, Frankie decided that there was a first time for everything. Gage was slaughtering her.

Frankie chewed on her lip and thought about how she'd gotten herself into such a pickle. *Should have opted for a few rounds of pinochle.* The first two questions posed to her had been easy, no-brainers.

"Do you have a vibrator?" Damon asked mischievously and leaned closer, intent on her words. Her unequivocal "no" clearly surprised him.

Gage asked the next question. "What is the significance of your tattoo?"

Another no-brainer. Fully clothed, Frankie answered triumphantly, "Pretty boys are a mental health menace."

Gage's eyes narrowed at her revelation.

Damon and Quinton shook their heads and folded simultaneously with the next round. Gage upped the ante.

"I'll see your match stick and raise you two."

Frankie took the bet.

"I'll call your two," and showed her hand. A pair of nines. Gage calmly fanned out his cards face-up on the table.

Three sevens and question number three.

"Where is the wildest place you've ever had sex?"

That one set her back a little.

In the years they had been playing the game, it had never escalated to such a level of intimacy. Frankie removed her flight jacket rather than admit to the dismal fact that she hadn't had wild sex anywhere with her previous partners.

The next hand belonged to her and she asked Gage the same question. Without hesitation he removed his shirt. When she won her second hand in a row, Frankie directed the exact question to Quinton. He made some vague reply about 'bush in Tasmania'. The way he was snickering, Frankie didn't dare ask for clarification.

They could all see that Damon was dying for his turn to answer, but nobody was willing to waste a winning hand on something he would gladly tell them anyway.

Damon won the next hand, his question directed back to her.

"What is your favorite sexual act?"

She kept her face blank while considering the question and her limited options. How many sexual acts were available to choose from? None of the few she'd tried could be considered favorite. She didn't know how to answer and opted to remove her boots.

The favorite sexual act question was a keeper. For the next three rounds, everyone at the table was given the opportunity to answer it.

"I prefer to back my woman up against a wall and take her in public," Quinton admitted. "Getting nicked makes it more exciting."

"Getting nicked?" Frankie gave him a sidelong glance.

"Caught in the act," Gage answered for Quinton.

Her eyes opened wide at the thought. "Are all Aussies such perverts?"

He shook his head and grinned. "Win the next hand and I'll tell you."

Damon spouted off some number from the *Kama Sutra*, claiming it was his all-time leading score. Frankie had no earthly idea what he was talking about.

Gage was last to answer. He leaned across the table and stared directly at her until she broke his bold eye contact.

He matter-of-factly replied, "Spelunking."

"Huh?" If Damon's answer was bizarre, Gage's was completely out of the solar system. "Spelunking? As in cave exploration? I don't understand. Your answer has to make sense to the winner. Those are the rules."

"Oh, it will," he grinned.

All three men were smiling. Quinton was actually whistling the tune from

Jeopardy. Stewie, asleep on the couch, perked up at the noise and came running over to demand his rightful place on Damon's lap.

Frankie pinched her lips into a grim line. Gage was being evasive and she didn't like it one bit. Her quest for understanding overrode any shame over being naïve. She wanted answers, not malarkey.

"Well?" She held her hands up. "What are you talking about?"

Dark eyebrows arched. His droll gaze traveled slowly down her body, halting at the juncture of her thighs and remained there. It took a few moments before she understood why Gage was staring at her crotch. She sucked in her breath, felt the heat rise to her cheeks and gasped. "Smart ass," she snapped, hoping no one noticed her lick the perspiration from her upper lip.

Damon's next winning question was directed to Quinton.

"Have you ever cheated on someone you were dating?"

The big man responded by quietly removing his shoes.

That one shocked her.

"When is your date with Lauren?" Gage inquired with his next win.

Frankie sincerely wanted to lie and say "next Friday", but shed a sock instead. When she finally won a round, things got ugly. Tired of being the focus of twisted attention, she went for the jugular—- Gage's jugular.

"What is the significance of March? You always get so pissy around this time of year. What gives?"

He stared at her, jaw twitching, eyes darkening. He opened his mouth, closed it. His eyes bore through her as he very quietly removed a boot. Quinton and Damon exchanged a quick, worried glance. Frankie puckered her lips and pondered his bizarre reaction. She was not getting the information she wanted.

Now what?

She was contemplating her next question when Gage won the next hand. Staring intensely, he casually asked, "Have you ever had an orgasm?"

Frankie kept a blank face but the rapid pulse at her throat was a dead giveaway to everyone at the table. She reached down and pulled off her other sock.

"Never?" Damon blurted with undignified horror and muttered an expletive. She shot him a scathing look. Quinton sucked in a breath.

"You've never had an orgasm?" he repeated dumbfounded. "I can't believe it. Why didn't you tell us sooner? I've got some buddies who'd love a chance to fix that for you. They're always asking me to introduce you to them."

This time it was Gage who gave Damon the dirty look, then he gazed back at Frankie and stared as if seeing her for the first time.

"Gage, did you hear me?" Damon blurted.

"What?"

"We need to find someone to remedy this problem for her," he stated.

Gage stared numbly at him. "Don't you have enough on your plate?"

"Not me personally, LC. I mean, she has nice breasts and all."

"Knock it off," Frankie jumped in with indignation. "You could at least wait until I'm not sitting right here next to you."

Damon rolled his eyes at her.

"It's Quinton's turn to deal."

The next round that Gage won cost Frankie her pants rather than confess she had never been tied to a bed during lovemaking. She scowled and flung her shirt across the room when he won the third hand in a row and asked how many lovers she had been intimate with.

"One? Two?" Damon slowly started counting, hoping to get a reaction despite her refusal to answer. "Three? Four?"

Frankie broke into a cold sweat. Surely they knew her well enough to realize what an abysmal sex life she had. She took a deep breath and continued to play, winning a small reprieve when Quinton was victor of the following round.

"Hey mate, have *you* ever tied a woman to a bed during sex?"

"Yes," Gage answered, never breaking eye contact with Frankie. She swallowed hard.

By now they had all figured out that in reality, only two people at the table were playing this game and one of them had a definite agenda.

Frankie was in deep shit and she knew it. She blinked back to the present. Someone was speaking to her.

"Question, Captain." Gage aimed his intensity upon her. "What did you mean when you said you wanted to see spots?"

Everything happened at once. Damon spewed a mouthful of coffee. Stewie did a stunning aerial loop and took off for high ground. Quinton grunted with surprise. Frankie lost her composure.

"Whaaaa?" Like a crimson tide, the blush crept right up to her scalp.

"You heard me," Gage replied.

"When did I say that?" Her mind raced to come up with a time she would ever say those words in the presence of him and came up empty.

The rules of naked truth poker were simple. Respond truthfully or refuse to answer the question thereby forfeiting another article of clothing she couldn't afford to lose.

What to do? What to do?

"When did I say that?" she repeated.

"I'm the winner of this hand," Gage smirked. "I get to ask the question."

She opened her mouth to speak and nothing but air whooshed out.

"Answer the question," he urged, "or start stripping."

He waited.

They all waited.

"Well," she twitched and shifted in the chair. "I think I was probably wondering about something that one of the Sisterhood mentioned last week." She shook her head. "More than likely, I think," she jabbered on. "At least, I seem to remember some, some mention of that."

Seconds passed.

The overhead light fixture flickered.

The radio crackled with static.

Gage arched an eyebrow and hid his smile.

All three men stared expectantly at her, silent hostages to their own curiosity. They waited—three hovering vultures circling fresh kill.

Frankie blinked and cleared her throat. "Umm," she continued. "One of the girls mentioned an incident and I was curious to know what she was talking about, you know. I mean, it didn't make any sense and I've been wondering about it for days. It was probably some subliminal thing that slipped out while I was delirious."

"No." Gage shook his head. "Your exact words were, 'I want to see spots'." His eyes dared her to tell the truth.

Her mouth formed a perfect O.

Above the roar in her ears, Frankie could hear the little hitch in the back of Quinton's throat that always preceded his raucous laughter. No help would be coming from his direction. Unfortunately, it was Damon who jumped to her rescue. "She's talking about sex, LC. That was something that happened while Kristen and I were doing the wild thing."

All heads turned his way.

"She almost passed out on me, dude. Said something about seeing spots and then her eyes rolled back in her head. I thought I'd shagged her to death."

Frankie let out a pitiful squeaking noise. Damon kept talking.

"I was sure the neighbors were going to call the police and haul my ass off to jail." He took a deep breath. "What a set of pipes that woman has. My ears were ringing for a week."

Gage watched her every move as Frankie put her hand over her face, stood and quietly walked to her room. She heard Damon ask if the game was over and Quinton answer, "That's affirmative, mate."

"My life is going to hell."

With squared shoulders, Frankie wrapped a big terrycloth towel tightly around her torso and carefully stepped out of the misty shower stall. Billowing fog rolled out in her wake.

Some serious strangeness was afoot at Air Station Harmony Bay and the more she thought about it, the more her head pounded. Earning the respect of her three crewmen had taken months of hard work and endurance.

She paid her dues.

Now, after one reckless incident, Frankie feared she was plummeting straight back to square one. She should never have gone off swimming that night. None of this would have happened if she'd only kept her cool.

The melodic voice of the ten o'clock newscaster sifted in from behind the closed bedroom door. She heard Damon's hearty complaint about the superficial stories thrown up as important national news. The kid was more than a pretty face, she thought, he was politically astute.

Her team. Her wonderful crew.

She had let them down.

Frankie closed her eyes and chewed on her lower lip. She was in over her head. She needed a plan.

The night was still young enough to give one of the Sisterhood a call. Her landscaping problems would be a great excuse to make contact and maybe she could work up the courage to confide what was really bothering her.

Andie Daniels would know exactly what plant would thrive in the empty planter box on the east side of her house. Andie might also have some words of wisdom to help Frankie get through this latest personnel crisis.

Frankie reminisced about the naval academy and subsequent years as she'd clawed her way to the top of the rescue-pilot ladder. She tiptoed from the bathroom, turned to the dresser in search of a comb, took two steps and walked square into a towering, hard body. Her chin shot up.

"Gage."

He stared down in a way that totally unnerved her. Her knees almost buckled. She took a small step back.

"Do I have to tie a bell around your neck to know where you are?" she asked.

His strong arm shot out and pulled her so close she could feel him against her belly. Large. Hard. Hot. She tried to look anywhere but down *there.* Her body tightened in anticipation.

"What are you doing?"

His voice was a harsh caress, "Serving notice." His long fingers slowly untied the flimsy towel and held it open while his molten gaze roamed her body possessively.

Frankie gasped. This man she trusted with her life helped himself to an eyeful. She was frozen with shock. Waiting. Her bare, goose-fleshed arms hung at her sides.

Her voice cracked. "Notice of what?"

"The last time I had a woman tied to the bed," he whispered in a husky voice, "she saw spots."

His blazing eyes raked her up and down for what seemed an eternity. Frankie was paralyzed. Her nipples tingled under his scrutiny and beaded into tight, hard pebbles. Her breath came fast and shallow. Little sparks of excitement shot down her spine. Moisture slid down her inner thigh.

Gage bent his dark head and brushed a gentle kiss across her trembling lips. His warm hand spanned her chest. "Spots," he whispered against her overheated flesh. "I can make you see them too. All you need to do is ask."

Without warning he pushed himself away, turned and left her standing there.

Naked.

Aroused.

Blown away.

Frankie's scorched brain fired a few erratic electrical impulses.

"Holy shit."

Chapter 5

DECISIONS, DECISIONS

"THAT IS THE STUPIDEST IDEA I'VE EVER HEARD."

"Wait, finish hearing me out."

Frankie looked around for something to throw at him. They were squared off in the middle of the garage with wrenches and hammers. Damon had taken cover on one side of a forty horsepower outboard, ready to dodge either way should she attack. Frankie angled toward a greasy rag draped atop an oil can.

"Before you decide to dabble under the covers with Lauren, I think you should give the XY chromosome one more chance." He shrugged his shoulders. "You can't hold the entire male population responsible for your non-orgasmic experiences with two useless dudes."

"Wanna bet?" she answered. "For the record, they weren't useless. One of them was a fireman and Brian is a successful investment banker."

"An investment banker, huh? Now there's a life-saving public servant for you," he scoffed.

Frankie took a step closer to the rag.

"I don't care how successful they are during the day. If they can't get their women off at night, what good are they?"

For a moment her vision blurred to near blindness. "The answer is still no."

"Give it one more chance. Please? I've gone to a lot of trouble to find a guy you'll like. Give him a chance." He peeked around the outboard motor.

"Maybe in my next life." She was only an arm's reach away from the rag. She talked, hoping to distract, goad him into making a fatal directional error. "You know, Damon, I was thinking about reincarnation the other day and the possibility of coming back as someone like you. I would want a much larger set of jewels, of course."

"It isn't right." Damon took a step backward, cleverly keeping himself out of striking distance. "Who knows, he might even be able to get you off."

There.

She snatched the rag into her hand and then realized what it was—a ratty pair of old jockey shorts covered in motor oil and God only knew what else. She dropped them with a curse.

"My getting off is not a topic for conversation," Frankie snapped.

Damon continued, undaunted. "But boss, he is seriously attracted to you. He's a pleaser. He'll do his best to give you a good time. I'll even provide a few insider tips beforehand. Prime him, so to speak."

"No way," Frankie insisted.

"Haven't you noticed how he disappears to rub one out whenever you're around? He wants you."

"That is way too much info."

Frankie faked right and went left. Damon compensated.

"He's a straight-up dude, boss."

"Seaman George at New Harbor? He's just a baby."

She stomped her foot dramatically.

"Then you *would* be interested in doing him if he wasn't so young? Is that it? The age difference is a problem for you?"

Damon almost hopped up and down with glee.

Frankie gave him the evil eye. Maybe pitch that little bowl of rusty bolts and spark plugs that sat on the edge of the workbench. Not a bad idea after all. If nothing else, it might shut him up.

"My 'doing him' would be tantamount to statutory rape."

"So the age thing is the problem." Damon swerved to grab the bowl before she could reach it.

"What if I told you he's much older than you think he is?"

"What if I told you that you're wasting your time?" She tried to edge closer. A few more feet and she could tackle him to the ground and tickle-pinch him till he screamed uncle. Damon took a cautious step toward the side door.

"Great sex is never a waste of time," he warily replied.

Frankie closed her eyes, held her hand high in the air, touching her temple. "Wait a minute. I think I might be having an epiphany." She paused and sucked in a dramatic breath. "How much did you bet your perverted psycho buddies that you could get George and I together?"

"What makes you think that?"

"You're not denying it?"

Damon was up on his toes, ready to spring in any direction.

"It's just a small bet."

"How much?"

"One Ben Franklin, two if he gets in your pants on the first date."

"No way," she snarled.

"I'll give you half."

"Does your mother know what a monster she created?"

"Come on, boss," he begged. "Take one for the team."

FROM HIS SEAT AT the kitchen table, Gage heard every word. His broad shoulders were rigid. One more comment about Frankie having sex with that pimple-faced, dumb-ass kid at New Harbor and he was going to blow a head gasket. Thankfully she had more sense than to get mixed up in that kind of no-win situation.

Reality jolted his senses.

He was jealous! Gage wanted Frankie for himself.

Gage launched himself to his feet and stormed off toward the helipad. Stewie caught sight of him and padded across the floor on an intercept course. At the last moment the cat sensed his foul mood and sidestepped to avoid a fatal collision.

George Harvey was a threat.

In painful fact, George was a highly intelligent, clean cut, all-around nice guy in his late twenties. He would go far within the ranks of the Coast Guard. Right now, however, he was the newbie, low on the food chain and object of scorn. A woman's compassion, her pity, was a powerful tool in a man's seduction arsenal. Gage knew that Frankie would sympathize with his plight. He wrinkled his face into a scathing grimace. The odds were slim that she might succumb to sleeping with him out of kindness.

Slim wasn't good enough.

QUINTON HERRIMAN WAS ENJOYING the spectacular sunny morning. In the distance, impressive banks of cumulus clouds were spreading east. According to NOAA predictions, an atmospheric low-pressure system was heading their way. The promise of stormy weather did nothing to dampen his high spirits, however. Sprawled out on an orange plastic deck chair, he was clad solely in white boxers and a wide grin.

His wife was coming for a visit.

Isabelle was going to bundle up the girls and make the long drive to spend a few hours hanging out at the station with her husband and his coworkers.

His daughters would crawl all over the helicopter, bombard him with a million questions. Sarah, the eldest, would be seven next month, and was determined to become another Frankie when she grew up.

From the corner of his eye he spotted Gage. One look at his face told him there was more bad weather brewing. Quinton could almost hear the scrape of tooth enamel.

Gage stalked across the helipad, prowled around in the cockpit for a few moments and then proceeded to pace back and forth between the supply shed and the garage.

"Hey, mate," Quinton called to him after his third empty trip to the shed.

Gage spun around and walked over. Quinton squinted up at the brooding co-pilot. Sunlight encircled him with a halo they both knew he didn't deserve.

"What's on your mind?" Quinton held his hands palms-up in a gesture of openness. Gage took a tortured breath and dropped to the grass beside him.

"Frankie." Something flickered behind his fathomless green eyes. "I can't stop thinking about her."

Quinton listened quietly. He'd waited a long time for this particular confession.

"She's in the garage right now, being propositioned on George Harvey's behalf." Gage ran a distracted hand through his short dark hair. "I know that's not what she needs." He centered his rabid thoughts. "He's not right for her. She doesn't need a young stud lover."

"What *does* she need?"

Quinton had known the answer from the first morning Frankie walked brazenly into Harmony Bay. That Gage might have finally come to the same realization and be ready to discuss the fact with him, would be a real breakthrough.

"She needs someone who will accept her for the exceptional woman she is; not just sleep with her and leave," Gage replied without hesitation. He shook his head despondently. "I don't know what the right thing to do is anymore. Everything used to be so clear-cut. Black and white. Right and wrong. The rules have changed."

"What rules?"

"The rules of professional behavior," he blurted. "I can't keep my mind off her. The curve of her waist, the shape of her legs, the dip of her shoulders and slope of her breasts. That stubborn angle of her jaw when she's fighting strong winds." Gage paused and stared across the helipad. "I think I'm losing it, man. She's always been like a little sister to me. It's different now."

"Different, how?"

"I want her," Gage whispered and watched a solitary white gull flap across the sky. "I want her to want me." He took a deep breath and stared out across the horizon before continuing. "I must be going crazy. She'll never agree to take me as a lover. Maybe I should consider that full pilot opportunity in Washington and get away from here for awhile."

Quinton sighed. A storm of emotions raged around them both. "Life is about five percent what happens to you and ninety-five percent how you react to it. Don't run away from this. Give her a chance. Show your hand and let her catch up."

Gage's head snapped around. "What do you mean?"

Quinton gave him a grin. A long moment passed between them before he spoke. His voice rumbled across the open space. "I knew someone like you once. He was afraid of getting involved with a lady he thought was untouchable, above him. So he did his best to ignore her because he was such a clumsy ass around her. He didn't think he could ever be worthy of her." Quinton paused for a moment, leaned back and swatted at a fly. "It turned out that the lady wanted him so much she was willing to risk everything to have him. Even her life." He paused, blinked against the sun and considered how much more he should divulge to Gage. "Communication of her own needs was a problem for this lady," Quinton continued. "She didn't have much experience with raw emotion. Her life had been carefully constructed. Real intimacy wasn't an option but she managed to find a way around it."

Gage looked at him, perplexed. "How did it all turn out?"

"You tell me," Quinton replied with a smile. "Personally, I think she was worth it, even if she hadn't given me Grace and Sarah."

"That lady was Isabelle?" Gage asked, his mouth hanging open.

Quinton nodded. "My advice is, if you want Frankie, fuck the rules. Go get her."

"How?"

Quinton was quiet for a few lengthy moments. "Isabelle wore a pair of sexy black underwear that peeked out over the top of her low-rise jeans," he replied. "You're a smart man, Adams. You'll think of some way to generate her interest."

FRANKIE WAS LOSING HER voice. She rummaged around the catchall drawers in the kitchen for a throat lozenge or two. All morning, she and Damon had been at it. Bickering. Negotiating. The kid seemed to be on a one-man crusade to get her laid.

No, not laid, she thought with irritation, but *well laid.*

Frankie's face pinched into a scowl. If he didn't back off soon, she could always call for an unscheduled training mission and tea-bag him until he got the message. Being repeatedly and forcefully dipped into the ocean while he dangled on the end of a rope would have a sobering effect.

And what the hell was up with Gage? After the peep-show episode, he had literally disappeared off the face of the earth. Not that she wanted him to come back and finish that blistering breach of protocol, of course. No matter how much more she wanted. "It was a fluke," she rationalized. "He's always on edge this time of year."

Frankie chewed her lip. If loss of trust in her decision-making ability was not behind Gage's bizarre behavior, what was?

She shrugged her shoulders and opened the refrigerator door. A cool mist rolled out to envelope her face. She grabbed a pitcher and poured a glass of orange juice.

In the past, her personal boudoir tales had never been on the front line for discussion. Her lack of sexual experience wasn't an issue. Nobody asked. Frankie never told. Damon was doggedly determined to change that.

In the last few hours Damon had made a dozen urgent calls to various acquaintances in his pretty-boys club. He assured her he would find the right man for the job, despite her vehement protests. If she wouldn't accept George Harvey into her bedroom, perhaps he could interest her in someone more her age.

"Trust me," he spoke with all seriousness. "There's got to be some guy out there who's interested in a feisty bed-hog with tiny boobs and hairy legs."

Frankie was ready to throttle him.

She drank her beverage, savoring the cooling effect on her sore throat.

Gage suddenly appeared on the stairwell. Frankie halted in mid-sip, lips frozen to the rim of the glass, staring hard as he sauntered down the stairs and nonchalantly strolled past her. Wearing only a tight pair of biking shorts and his running shoes, his long, powerful legs flexed with each step.

Frankie gulped in a breath. She couldn't drag her eyes away from him.

His body was sculpted to perfection, the personification of male in its purest form. And his legs, oh those legs! They were a masterpiece of nature.

Time slowed while she worked her examination upward, past a butt that rivaled Damon's and a broad chest heavy with layers of honed muscle. Her gaze stopped at the faint scar encircling his lower neck, a grim reminder that someone had once sliced his throat open, leaving him to bleed to death. She studied the play of light and shadow molding his high cheekbones as he strolled past the open kitchen and through the laundry room. He never made eye contact or even acknowledged her presence but she knew that *he* knew she was watching.

And he knew that she liked what she saw.

FRANKIE SPENT THE AFTERNOON helping Quinton give Zena a thorough wash before re-checking atmospheric reports. She tried to keep her mind off Gage's tantalizing body.

Predicting weather patterns was one of the most challenging aspects of her job. Not that bad weather would have prevented Harmony Bay's crew from bouncing through insane turbulence to help others in trouble. She grabbed a thumbtack and posted projected reports on the bulletin board above the radio frequency scanner.

Damon walked up behind her and started to complain. "Disgusting losers. It's un-cool to leave a woman not so high and very dry."

"It's no big deal," she answered, stumbling as Stewie weaved between her legs.

From across the expansive room Gage and Quinton pretended not to listen. Frankie shot them a surreptitious glance. It was obvious they were glued to their seats at the kitchen table, taking in every word while meticulously cleaning a row of flare guns. Normally they would have been conversing, joking in low, amiable tones; comparing war stories. Their uneasy silence was a waving red flag.

Frankie felt like an idiot.

"Sex is about giving," Damon informed her with a sly grin. "European dudes figured that out a long time ago. Most American guys are too selfish to take the time to understand. You have to learn what a woman needs and then give it to her." He took a deep breath and started up again. "You've gotta do your homework if you want to pass the class."

Frankie looked at the ceiling. "It doesn't matter," she whispered.

Damon sucked in a dramatic breath, stricken with insight. "Is that why you're all hot and bothered to spend some time in Europe? Are you hoping to find some wild Frenchman?"

"Actually, I was looking forward to all those nifty in-flight movies." Her voice was cynical enough to cover the rising humiliation. "Not to mention the wonderful airline cuisine."

Sudden loathing twisted Damon's handsome face into a mean sneer. "You didn't fake an 'O' just to make those dipshits feel better about their performance, did you?"

Her jaw clamped down so hard she almost chipped a tooth. The reverberation pounded through her skull. "Absolutely not."

"Oh, that's right, sorry. How would you know how to fake what you've never had?" Damon squinted and studied her closely. "How long has it been since you tried?"

"Tried what?" she snapped.

"What do you mean, what? Whaddya think we've been discussing," he replied testily. "Getting off. The big O. *La petit mort.*"

Blood roared in her ears. Frankie felt a hot flush creep up her neck. She inhaled a deep breath and buried her distress. From the kitchen table came an angry grunt. Frankie stared at the dimpled beige cork of the bulletin board and gnawed on her lower lip. She really, really did not want to discuss this any longer.

"Can we change the fucking subject?" she hissed.

"Fucking *is* the subject," he announced too loudly. "It's common knowledge that women who are unable to orgasm during sex will eventually lose their interest in it." He paused to stare pointedly at her. "You've given up, haven't you, boss?"

The kid sounded like some crazed sex therapist! Before she could attempt a reply, he launched back into the interrogation with a salvo of questions; wanting to know the whens, whys and hows of what her previous lovers had tried. He was like a moray eel, latched on, unable to let go. How was she going to pry his jaws loose? She let out an audible sigh and stood very still. The best option would be to point out the framed copy of the Uniform Code of Military Justice that hung on the wall. Then she could launch into an unofficial and very private berating.

A menacing voice interrupted her plan.

"Leave her alone!" Gage growled each word with a force bordering on sinister. Both Frankie and Damon looked over in surprise. A muscle in Gage's angular jaw twitched. Damon gave him a crisp salute then leaned in and whispered so softly only she could hear him.

"Don't throw in your cards yet, boss. Third time's a charm. I'll find the right guy for you."

Frankie shuddered.

BY EARLY EVENING, ISABELLE and the girls had arrived and taken over. Stewie rubbed against every available leg. The worthless puss even granted Frankie the privilege of scratching behind his scarred ears.

A warm ocean breeze rustled a stack of papers on the operations desk. She glanced around the room. Isabelle sat so close to her husband on the couch that she might well have been straddling him. Quinton was absently braiding her jet-black hair while feigning interest in the movie that Damon rented for them to watch. Momentarily, he would excuse himself and take his beautiful wife upstairs to the privacy of his room while Frankie and the others were left to baby-sit.

Sarah and Grace, more hyperactive than usual, were sliding down the stairs on a piece of cardboard Quinton had fashioned into a bobsled. The dull monologue of the movie was occasionally interrupted by their shouts of, "Daddy, look. Watch me!"

Frankie curled up in a chair by the west window, pretended that life was hunky-dory and she really wasn't losing her marbles. At least she was partially right. Life was definitely hunky. On the floor a few feet in front of her, Gage sprawled, wearing tight synthetic running pants and nothing else. All day he paraded around the station in next to nothing, flexing his muscles. He looked so irresistible that it sent her spiraling into a cascade of vicious hot flashes. The man had scrambled her brain.

Gage stayed in good physical shape out of necessity, not vanity. Until today, she had never dwelled on what an exceptional piece of eye candy her co-pilot really was.

He dressed to the left.

She let out a tense breath through pursed lips and tried to concentrate on the movie. An impossible task when the show on the floor was so much more interesting. Gage was slurping dessert from a small plastic bowl and there was nothing subtle about the slow way his tongue was working the tip of the spoon. He savored each bite with a decadence that bordered on pornography. Was she the only person in the room who noticed he was practically having sex with a dish of strawberry sherbet? Should he be doing that with children in the house? She glanced over at Quinton and almost fell out of her chair. He was in the midst of a scorcher kiss that had Isabelle moaning softly in response.

Frankie shifted one restless leg under her other and then back again. She shot Gage a wily glance just in time to catch a glimpse of his long, pink tongue dart out to languorously circle and sweep the spoon. All the oxygen was abruptly sucked out of the room. First she was icy cold, then feverish with heat. Frankie closed her eyes and tried to slow her pulse.

No joy.

Her overactive imagination kicked into high gear. How would that tongue feel as it roved across her skin? Would he tease her the way he tortured the tip of that godforsaken spoon? Would he tie her to the bed and make her see spots? She shifted in the chair again and switched her weight to the other hip. She couldn't stop squirming, couldn't get comfortable, couldn't get the naughty thoughts out of her mind. Gage pulled a small dollop of ice cream into his inviting mouth and turned to catch her ogling.

He winked.

Frankie bit down hard on her lip and tasted blood. The static squelch of the VHF radio fractured the strained moment. Seaman George Harvey's distinct voice hailed them.

"Harmony Bay, this is New Harbor. Do you copy?" Startled out of a semiconscious slumber, Damon leaped to his feet and rushed to answer, painfully goring himself on the edge of the couch in the process. He clumsily keyed the microphone while grabbing a pen and paper to take notes.

"New Harbor, this is Harmony Bay, go ahead."

Seaman Harvey cleared his throat with the microphone still keyed and began speaking, "This is notification of a training mission at zero eight hundred hours. New Harbor Station Commander is requesting your participation."

"Copy that," Damon replied and repeated, "Training mission at zero eight hundred hours."

"Expect winds twenty five to thirty knots and seas to twelve feet," Seaman Harvey continued. "Anticipate four victims in water. Full briefing by fax and land-line at zero six hundred."

Frankie glanced over at Gage. The spoon hung loosely between his fingers. He was staring into space, face pinched with what? *Worry?* Frankie shivered. As if in sync with Gage, she felt her own queasy flicker of intuition.

Chapter 6

AN 'OH SHIT' MOMENT

FROM THE RELATIVE COMFORT OF HIS BED GAGE COUNTED STARS, GAZING OUT THE window at their cold perfection; envying their detachment. A muscle jumped at the corner of his mouth. He rubbed the scar encircling his neck and flinched. He had been trying to fall asleep for hours. Instead, he relived grueling memories of pain and betrayal and a Persian Gulf assignment gone horribly wrong. Brutally awake, his mind was ablaze with images of the murderous high altitude, low opening parachute jump and savage hours afterward as a POW.

Their intelligence sources were false. He and his team had dropped right into the jaws of the enemy. Gage shook his head to dispel the ghastly images. He wasn't ready to go there again.

Not now.

Not yet.

Not ever.

The week had passed quickly since the ill-fated training mission that had set a brutal barrage of flashbacks into motion. Gage knuckled his eyes. If only daylight would come soon. A new crew would be there in a few hours to replace them.

Meredith Bishop, tall, quiet and eternally wary, would relieve him of his duties. Maybe then he could go home, take a tranq and get some decent sleep. Gage sighed. No other relief was in sight. At least not the kind he really wanted, definitely not what Frankie needed.

She fought the attraction between them. He shouldn't have expected anything less from her, although there was no doubt he had her attention. At work, he was always there, in her face, by her side at every turn.

Gage rolled to his side and put a pillow over his head. He smiled in the darkness. It wouldn't be long before she was hot and ready to straddle him.

He could almost feel her thighs and legs wrapped around his hips as he pounded into her.

God, he was going to love fucking her!

He wanted to kiss her again, a long and deep exploration that left her pliant. He wanted to leisurely chart the inside of her sassy mouth, run his tongue along her neck, her shoulders and down to those sweet breasts that plagued his every waking moment. His lips twitched.

He wanted to make her come in his mouth.

He was going to love her in a way those other idiots hadn't been able to.

For the millionth time since the accident, he mulled over what had occurred during their routine training mission two days earlier and how quickly the situation turned deadly. He had almost forgotten why they called her Tenacious Bitch. The mission and safety of others would always be her primary goal. He closed his eyes and replayed the training mission.

The winds had been stronger than anticipated that morning, blasting out of the northwest at a steady thirty knots with gusts up to forty. A few hearty souls had gathered on the beach to watch, huddled deep inside their down parkas. *Sakajawea,* the New Harbor cutter, was strategically positioned a few hundred yards offshore to observe, document and assist if necessary.

The sea was angry that day and in a change from their normal routine, Frankie had invoked "Captain's discretion" and insisted all four of them wear their mustang suits.

"Humor me," she had replied when Quinton questioned the order. She couldn't give them a specific reason. Gage shrugged and followed her hunch. Wearing the cold water survival suit for a couple of hours wasn't undue hardship. Erring on the side of safety was simply good sense.

She was as smart as she was beautiful.

Frankie's right hand barely moved as it plied the cyclic stick, adjusting to wind gusts almost before they hit. She held them steady, hovering at a two o'clock position close enough to the off-duty rescue swimmers, termed 'ducks', to keep track of their progress but far enough away not to blast them with the rotor wash. She waited until Quinton gave the go-ahead for extraction.

The winds whipped the ocean into a turbulent froth. The swell of the waves would carry the ducks in their bright orange dry suits, up and up and then plunge them sharply down a twenty-foot trough out of sight.

Each time the ducks disappeared behind a wave, her jaw visibly tensed.

She fretted over their welfare until she could see them again. Her lips puckered into a tantalizing pout that only Gage could see. He took a deep breath and let it out slowly to get his mind off his aching groin and back on the mission.

"The automatic flight control system is at full ops," he reminded, in case she preferred to have the computer hold the helicopter in a stable hover.

"Understood."

From their earphones, they heard Quinton.

"Rescue swimmer ready for first victim."

Frankie toggled the controls. It took mere seconds to close in and hover fifteen feet above the water for Damon's free fall. Gage chanced a look behind him. Damon had moved up and was sitting in the door of the helo while Quinton did a weight check on the hoist.

Every action was by-the-book, executed in a proven right way to do the maneuver. Gage glanced over at Frankie. Her eyes were fixed on the horizon. He looked down at the water. All four ducks were in perfect alignment, ready to be picked up and checked off on the exercise in time for lunch. Over the years, this mandatory training mission was one they performed countless times, in all sorts of weather.

Quinton gave the command to jump. Damon pushed out and down in one smooth move, caught the backside of a six-foot swell and rode it up and over.

"Swimmer away," Quinton advised. "Proceeding to first duck."

A high-frequency vibration slithered through Frankie's legs.

"Gage, did you feel that?"

"Negative."

"Move in for pickup." Quinton gave Frankie the verbal orders that zeroed her in directly over Damon. "Forward ten. Right five. Hold." Gage mimicked his instructions with hand signals.

"Deploying basket." Quinton slowly lowered the basket to where Damon and the first duck waited.

Frankie frowned again. Gage scrutinized the instrument panel. All readings were normal. Nothing amiss.

"Is there a problem, Captain?" he asked.

"A faint vibration. I can feel it rippling up my calves."

Gage concentrated his attention on the pedals but couldn't detect it. The first seaman clambered into the basket. Damon gave the signal to send the basket back down.

"Ready for hoist," Quinton acknowledged.

They worked quickly, repeating the procedure until everyone was aboard and the basket and boom were safely stored.

Zena was thirty feet over the water with Quinton preparing to secure the hatch when all hell broke loose. A loud bang was followed by an accelerating counterclockwise spin.

"We've got tail rotor failure," Gage advised.

Frankie struggled with the useless controls. The anti-torque system had blown apart.

"Quinton," she spoke with icy calmness. "Immediate evac."

There was no time to call a mayday warning. The rescued ducks bailed back out of the spinning helicopter and tumbled into the waves below. Damon followed, immediately setting off an orange flare. Quinton paused long enough to make certain all was clear below before he jumped.

Emergency procedures called for the pilot to promptly back the throttles to the off position to prevent the helicopter from spinning. Doing so would also cause Zena to make a beeline for the ocean below. Frankie wanted a more controlled ditch.

Engine one began sputtering.

"Gage, go. Get out of here!" A fine line of perspiration dotted her upper lip. "I have to ditch her."

"Negative." Gage knew her plan. He also knew there was no time to escape from the five-point harness strapping him to the seat.

"Now!" she yelled.

"No." His hands were on the dual controls, ready to add his strength to hers and take control if necessary. "We're doing this together."

"Get out."

"You need my help."

"I need you safe."

Engine two began to sputter.

"Go!"

"I'm staying with you."

With only seconds remaining, Frankie threw the throttles to the off position. Every light on the control panel lit up like a Christmas tree.

Zena plummeted to the swirling ocean below.

Frankie dropped their nose to maintain the rotor RPM. If she couldn't hold them at the perfect angle, the transmission would tear loose on impact and hurtle through the cockpit window, killing them both. Frankie pulled back on the stick and pulled the pitch of the blades up just before Zena hit the water. She held her breath and looked at Gage.

Sky and ocean blended into salty foam.

The noise of the rotor blades disintegrating combined with the force of impact to knock every centimeter of air from their lungs. The freezing ocean rushed in to claim them.

Gage had seen his share of battle. He had experienced the surreal sights and sounds that were impossible to explain and had lived to lose sleep over it. Their chances for survival now rested on luck and swiftness. Being paralyzed with indecision had never been an option for him and there was no room for it now.

Frankie was fumbling to release the sturdy harness latch when he pulled her loose from the bindings. With all the strength he could muster, Gage pushed her ahead. Frigid water bit the bare flesh of his face. He could feel the sickening roll as the helicopter turned upside down in its slow descent to the ocean floor. Frankie scissor-kicked to overcome the drag of heavy boots. Her father's dog tags floated about the cockpit like shimmering smelt, flickering past Gage's face. He reached out to grab the chain and missed.

They swam through the open hatch door together and let their natural buoyancy pop them to the surface amidst the debris, roaring wind and stinging waves. Frankie gulped in a tortured breath of air. They bobbed a few feet apart, stared at one another.

"You disobeyed my direct order."

"You're welcome," Gage retorted and pulled her close enough to inflate both their life vests. "I appreciate your concern," he snapped, "but you know damned well there was no way for me to get out in time."

Her lips quivered. A tumult of anguish and relief broke across her drenched features. Her arms flew up to wrap tightly around his neck. She pulled him into a crushing embrace. "You scared me to death." The salty kiss she pressed to his forehead quickly rode down to his mouth. She lingered there. Lips warm, wet and soft. Then she ran her tongue across his teeth. It almost did him in. Even in the chilly water, Gage could feel the familiar stir of an erection down below. He glanced over her shoulder and caught sight of Damon swimming rapidly towards them. Two hundred yards to the south, the cutter was pounding through the waves, heading for Quinton and the ducks.

He pushed away slightly and stared at her. Seeing her struggle desperately to free herself from the harness had almost stopped his heart. Gage didn't know what to say so he kept it technical.

"That was a good call, having us wear the mustang suits."

"I can't believe you did that," Frankie gasped, clinging to him as a large swell carried them along. "I can't believe you stayed with me. I was so frightened for you," she choked. "All I could think about was getting you out of there."

Likewise, he thought, too unnerved at the idea of losing her to express the sentiment out loud. All he could do was hold her tightly and give a silent prayer of thanks.

STRIPPED NAKED AND STUFFED into a warm blanket only minutes later, Gage remained mute, staring straight ahead while a grinning medic took his blood pressure. Ensign Shelly Patterson had saved his medical exam for last and she was taking her sweet-easy time. Everyone at the New Harbor base knew the spindly brunette had been lusting after him for years. Gage wasn't interested. Never had been. However, he was getting an interesting response from his snarling, waterlogged captain, so he played along with the groping exam, slowly unfolding his blanket to give Patterson a full frontal view. She exhaled a little gasp and grinned.

There was a commotion from the far corner of the cabin. Gage glanced over. Frankie was shrunk into a tight ball of wet hair, dry wool and silent fury. Snuggled in tight next to Quinton, she scrutinized every lingering move Patterson made with a glare that spoke volumes. Quinton reached over and soothingly patted her knee as Gage lifted his arms. Patterson painstakingly assessed him for any broken ribs, actually repeated the motions twice, "Just to be sure."

Gage heaved a weighty sigh and submitted to her unconventional abdominal assessment. Fingertips dipped low enough to raise his eyebrows. Another commotion stirred in the corner. Angry whispers, the rustle of blankets, a muffled curse.

"Ensign?" Frankie called out.

Patterson's head whipped around.

"Yes, ma'am?"

"I'm feeling lightheaded. Could you take my blood pressure?"

Patterson grabbed a stethoscope and rushed over to the senior officer.

Frankie's voice had sounded remarkably strong for someone who suffered from low blood pressure, Gage reflected wryly. He sneaked another glance in that direction. Quinton gave him the thumbs-up. Gage leaned back and let a wicked smile crease his lips.

After being medically cleared, they were taken by van to Coast Guard headquarters for debriefing. The process didn't take long. All four were back on duty in time to watch themselves on the eleven o'clock news.

Chapter 7

HOMEBODY

*F*RANKIE AWOKE JUST PAST DAWN, RESTED AND BURSTING WITH ENERGY. SHE SPLASHED cold water on her face, dressed quickly and took off barefoot for the sandy beach to look for unusual pieces of driftwood. The tide had been exceptionally high during the night, and pushed debris all the way to the edge of the bluff.

The morning was typically damp and hazy. By afternoon, the sun would rise victorious. A blue heron flapped inland to new hunting ground, its long neck tucked in close to its body during flight.

The water was a darker shade of green today, olive tinged with murky brown. Long strands of kelp twined the beach and marked the highest point of tide. She took a tranquil breath and listened to the rhythm of the ocean.

On the bottom of that vast body of water, Zena rested peacefully. How many lives had their helicopter saved from the chilly waters that eventually claimed her? Frankie lost count. A flood of sadness, followed by marked relief, washed over her.

They had been very lucky that day.

The crash had been a clear case of mechanical failure. Within hours of their accident, a new helicopter was en route from Seattle. No formal investigation, no suspensions, no hint or innuendo of pilot error. The Admiral praised their ability to act in the midst of extreme risk before promptly sending them back to work.

Frankie blinked.

A surfer caught her eye as he rode a wave. She paused to stare. His balanced, aggressive style reminded her of someone else who was comfortable either above or beneath the ocean's surface. She felt a clench of anticipation down low in her pelvis.

Gage.

She shook her head to clear it. Her neighborhood was an ideal locale for surfers. Long, gentle waves wrapped around the north jetty and curved to deposit the rider on the stretch of beach below her house. The fearless surfer dipped low, swaying side to side for a better angle on the wave.

"Nice technique," she whispered.

Her mind couldn't help but stray. What sort of technique would Gage use to make her see the spots he'd promised if she would agree to have sex with him.

What was she going to do?

Her gaze dropped and settled on a stick of driftwood. Stripped of bark, bleached white by the sun and salt, it resembled the reclining form of a nude woman. Frankie smiled. The piece would make a perfect gift for an old friend—Andie. She and her husband and their two enormous dogs were coming by later that evening for dinner.

Frankie tucked the driftwood under her arm. A shorebird skittered over the sand ahead of her as she wandered the beach. The local residents were gearing up to meet the placid Friday morning. A couple jogged past. Frankie recognized them as the town librarian and her husband.

"Good morning," she greeted and scanned the beach beyond them.

Couples.

Everywhere she looked, people were paired off. She walked slowly, enjoying the soft kiss of wind on her skin and considered her own marital status.

Being single was enjoyable, although at times she really missed the comfort of sharing her bed with someone else. She answered to no one, cherishing the ability to come and go as she pleased. All of her passion and creativity was thrown into living a solitary life to the fullest. Besides, with the exception of two, Quinton and Andie to be exact, Frankie hadn't seen any truly happy married couples. The enticing idea of a soul mate was a subject best kept to speculative fiction books. What possessed two people to take a solemn vow and swear allegiance to the bitter end? She had a vague idea.

Loneliness.

A need for companionship.

Too often she had seen undying love wilt into everlasting resentment. Even her globetrotting parents had stayed together more out of habit than for any residual affection. They'd been more than happy to tell her all about their woes—whether or not she asked.

Frankie shook her head.

Finding the best good-provider she could stomach, then spending the rest of her miserable life with him, was not on Francesca Moriarty's agenda. Neither, it seemed, was the ability to have the kind of great sex that her friends raved about.

Frankie had lost interest years ago.

She still listened, however, and took wistful mental notes every time one of the Sisterhood mentioned that esoteric entity called 'orgasm'. The far-fetched concept sounded marvelous, electrifying.

Unobtainable.

Damon thought the problem was with the caliber of her previous lovers. Frankie wasn't so sure about that. Not for the first time she wondered if there was something anatomically wrong with her. A physical defect of some sort?

Frankie forced herself to the present, strolled across the soothing warm sand while her mind wandered where it pleased. Her thoughts didn't take long to zero in on the source of their constant yearning.

Gage. Gage. GAGE!

She couldn't stop thinking of him, couldn't stop wanting him. The wildfire lust in his hypnotic eyes when he held open the bath towel and inspected her nakedness. The stark fear in her heart when he insisted on flying Zena into the ocean with her. The blazing kiss she couldn't control afterward. The feel of his arms holding her tight to his chest while they awaited rescue.

Her mind was a buzz of emotions.

She was drowning in the anticipation that zinged through her nerve endings while she waited for him, ached for him, to touch her again. Gage hadn't made a move on her since Zena crashed. She knew the decision up to her. If she wanted another kiss, she'd have to instigate it.

Always true to his word, he had shown up promptly at eight on Wednesday morning. It had taken him half a day to do the simple electrical project that Quinton could have completed in under an hour. And she hadn't been able to take her eyes off him the entire time he puttered around the room.

"I want to kiss him," Frankie yammered out loud. "I shouldn't want to kiss him. It's poor judgment. Bad call. Never shag your friends. Never, ever, ever shag your coworkers. Remember that, Moriarty," she chastised herself. "Don't be an idiot. You'll spoil everything you've worked so hard to achieve."

Andie had cautioned Frankie against being too inflexible. "Find out his intentions before you jump to any conclusions."

Frankie let out a sigh. A gust of air whipped her cheeks and flowed through her hair.

She knew what Gage's intentions were.

From day one at work, Frankie had laid down the law about her rules on fraternization. The edict had never been at issue.

Until now.

His methods might be agonizingly slow but Frankie was convinced that Gage was trying to seduce her. He was hanging around, being politely irresistible, hoping she'd change her mind on fraternization. Worse—she wanted to. Touching his hard body was all her muddled brain could think about.

As the last few days at work had passed, she realized that it wasn't lack of trust fueling Gage's strange behavior towards her. The real issue was lack of sex.

Her sex to be exact.

He was deliberately tormenting her. Testing her conviction. The thoughts he put in her mind were exciting and terrifying all rolled into one tempting package.

Frankie ran a hand through her hair in frustration. She reached the top of the bluff and walked across a thin strip of cool, soft grass.

Her little bungalow home was bordered by a concrete walkway allowing public beach access. A brick patio, enclosed by a retaining wall, kept stray animals and people at bay. Her special way of saying, "do not disturb" without obliterating the incredible ocean view.

Frankie shoved the wooden gate open with her hip and dropped the driftwood she'd collected on the chaise lounge just as the patio phone rang. She picked it up.

"Hello?"

"Good morning to you, oh-conflicted-one."

Frankie chuckled.

"Hello, Andie."

"Are we still on for dinner?"

"Of course, I'm looking forward to it."

"Excellent. I can't wait to hear more of your tortured secret fantasies."

Frankie groaned.

"Don't expect much. I think I've pretty much shot my secret fantasy wad."

"I doubt that," Andie countered. "Anyway, Max will be cooking. He's got a new recipe he wants to try out on us."

"Max can use me as a culinary test subject anytime he wants. I love his cooking."

"He'll be ecstatic to hear it," Andie replied.

There was a long moment of silence.

"Are you still there?" Andie asked.

"Yes." Frankie grew serious. "Can I ask you a very personal question?"

"Of course."

She cleared her throat. "Before Max came along and stole your heart, how many lovers did you have under your belt?"

"Casual flings or the serious stuff?"

"Casual."

"Only one."

"Only one?" Frankie repeated.

"Don't act so surprised."

"It's, well, it's just that I thought—"

"I know what you thought," Andie chuckled.

Frankie eased down on a deck chair.

"I didn't mean to offend."

"You didn't." Andie's voice grew soft, conspiratorial. "Would you like to know a little secret?"

"I'm listening."

"This is only my opinion so take it for what it's worth."

"Duly noted," Frankie replied.

"No casual encounter can beat the incredible intimacy of making love to the one who loves you. For me, there is nothing better."

GAGE MADE A LEFT turn on Marine Drive, dodged a chuckhole and coasted down the gravel road to a tidy white cottage. He stopped the truck and scanned the area.

All clear.

He had given Frankie some breathing room that week, to let her get used to the idea of having him around before he planned to get physical again. "Tonight," he said aloud. "I've waited long enough." If all those hungry looks she had been giving him when she thought he wasn't looking were any indication, he obviously had her full attention. Time to kick their relationship up a notch before his balls turned blue and fell off.

He knew she had been alone all week. No Lauren. No George Harvey. No unescorted midnight swims—he had made certain of that. Her days were occupied with outdoor activities; paddling her little canoe around the bay and myriad back sloughs. She even subbed a few games for an injured pitcher on the local softball team.

Gage scratched his chin and blinked.

Frankie's Land Rover, scarred from years of abusive back road exploration, was in its usual parking spot on the concrete slab driveway, her butterscotch-yellow canoe strapped on its hood. Beside the Land Rover was a sleek new Dodge. His hackles rose. Was George there? Lauren?

He sprang out of the truck and walked around to the patio. The sliding glass doors were open, letting a soft breeze filter through the screen. Gage started to knock. His hand was up, wrist cocked, prepared to give a sharp rap on the sturdy door frame when he saw something through the window that sent his blood pressure skyrocketing.

An enormous man was standing in Frankie's kitchen.

Scratch that.

An enormous man was cooking in Frankie's kitchen.

Relaxed. At ease. Making himself right at home.

Gage flung the door open with a menacing growl.

"Who the hell are you?"

The giant turned around and smirked. He was wearing one of Frankie's frilly pink aprons over beige chinos and a white cotton shirt.

"I was going to ask you the same thing," he drawled in a rumbling voice.

Gage's gaze narrowed dangerously as he assessed the stranger. The man had black curly hair, clipped just above the ears and spiced with gray. Mid-forties. Refined. Strong. Wealthy? The interloper was well groomed, perfectly composed and totally pissing Gage off. Whoever the guy was, he wasn't the least bit intimidated. Which could only mean one thing.

He felt he belonged there.

"Once more, asshole," Gage challenged. "Who are you and what the hell are you doing in this house?"

The guy was easily half a foot taller and outweighed him a good fifty pounds. Gage knew he could fell him like a tree if the bastard didn't come up with the right answer in a hurry. The giant dried off on a flowered dishtowel and extended his right hand.

"The name's Max," he introduced. "I'm Andie's husband."

Gage took a hesitant step forward, relaxed a bit and shook his hand.

"You must be Frankie's co-pilot," he spoke behind a genuine smile. The tangy aroma of rosemary and fresh baked bread permeated the house. Max turned to place another savory chicken breast in the pan.

"The ladies took the dogs for a walk on the beach," he volunteered with a smile. "They should be back shortly."

Gage squinted in astonishment. An uncanny stillness of spirit surrounded Max. He began to fuss around the kitchen again, stirring a pan of red sauce.

"The trick to cooking," Max spoke casually, "is making the meal come off all at once. Except for dessert, of course." He opened the stove door and gently eased a loaded pan inside. "Dessert is an entirely different matter. Presentation is everything."

Gage arched an inquisitive eyebrow.

"For the taste buds to appreciate sweets, they have to be made to wait." Max's train of thought appeared to swerve. "Your name is Gage, isn't it?"

"That's right."

"I expected you earlier," his voice calm and deliberate.

Gage curbed the urge to spout something sarcastic. "Why?"

Max turned to give him a meaningful look. "Those are your footprints near the patio," he motioned with his head, "and outside her bedroom window." He pointed with a long forefinger. "You're wearing the same running shoes."

Gage bristled at the accusation.

"Who are you, Sherlock Holmes?"

He answered, "Something like that."

"I've been keeping an eye on her," Gage admitted.

Max nodded. "I'm sure she would appreciate the fact if she knew." No censure in the reply. He simply paused in his culinary chores, reached into the refrigerator and tossed a microbrew in Gage's direction. Gage snatched the beer out of midair without breaking eye contact.

"Sit down," Max gestured to a chair. "Stay for dinner."

"Good idea." Gage settled into the deep cushions of Frankie's favorite recliner and stretched his legs. The evening hadn't exactly turned out as he planned yet it was still early and he had no intention of leaving.

Max stood at the sink while he worked. Silent moments passed between them while he diced tomatoes and grated Parmesan cheese. The latest issue of Victoria's Secret, earmarked with a dozen yellow sticky notes, lay on the coffee table. Gage picked up the catalog and began to thumb through it.

The mailing label was addressed to Andie yet many of the notes were written in Frankie's distinctive scrawl. *"This would look great on you." "I like this color." "WOW! This is hot."*

Then, the one that really got his attention, *"This is the most beautiful thing I've ever seen in my life."* Gage thoroughly scrutinized the picture, committed every detail of the silk negligee to memory.

Max materialized at his side, "What are you looking at?"

Gage grunted an incomprehensible reply. Max joined him. A solemn beauty stared back at them from the slick catalog. Her perfectly coifed hair wrapped around her neck and breasts like a cloak.

"That looks like Andie's writing," Max stated, pointing to a sticky note on the edge of a meritorious burgundy chemise.

"No, it's Frankie's."

Max shook his head negatively. "Here and here," he pointed. "The 's' looks like a sloppy 'f'. That's my wife's writing."

"Maybe so," Gage acquiesced. "This note is in Frankie's loose scribble."

Silence hung between them for a few moments before Max suddenly asked, "Where's your dog?"

"I don't have a dog," Gage answered peevishly.

"No? My mistake," he apologized. "I heard my wife's end of a phone conversation with Frankie the other night and assumed you had a dog named Spotz."

Gage cleared his throat. Spots? Juicy gossip traveled fast. By now, he suspected every woman in the Sisterhood had been thoroughly informed that he was doing his best to get in his captain's pants.

Telephone. Telegraph. Tell-a-nurse.

Sensing Max was probably aware of much more than he let on, Gage kept his posture neutral and his voice unaffected. "No pets," he calmly announced. "I was thinking about getting a little puss—cat, that is."

Max turned. The solid amused expression on his face was one of those classic priceless moments. "Yes," he grinned. "That was the general consensus among the ladies."

Gage swallowed the bait. "I was the subject of a consensus?"

"The Sisterhood often engages in speculation." Max paused long enough to retrieve his drink and remove his stained apron before he joined Gage again in the living room. "They also indulge in the gender specific practice of taking polls."

"Like some meat-of-the-month survey?" Gage asked with a trace of bitterness.

Max smiled. "At one time or another I think all of us have been the subject of their intense scrutiny."

Gage quirked an eyebrow. "So it was my turn?"

Max shook his head.

"The ladies voted between themselves for a man they thought would make a good Chippendale dancer. You won." Max suppressed a grin. "Apparently they consider you a hunk of 'beefcake' and would be happy to pay twenty bucks apiece to watch you dance around in a G-string."

Gage stared straight ahead.

G-string? Beefcake? His face was calm but his thoughts spun like a tornado. Did Frankie really discuss his beefcake with a bunch of her girlfriends?

He couldn't stop the slow smile that crept over his face.

Chapter 8

DINNER IS SERVED

MAX DANIELS INSPECTED GAGE ADAMS OUT OF THE CORNER OF HIS EYE, PROFILING the younger man with his cold, detective's logic. Everything he had seen so far, Max liked. Everything he had heard from his wife, Max liked. The most telltale sign, however, was the one Max witnessed this very moment. He liked that one too.

Gage, a beer to his lips, stopped drinking and stared. Max turned to the source of his paralysis. Frankie, bewitchingly windblown, had appeared at the top of the bluff. Silhouetted like some enchanting fairy-sprite, her angelic features were focused on some unknown place beyond the curve of ocean. A light breeze stirred her curlicue tendrils of thick hair.

Max watched Gage as he sat there. The younger man was transfixed, gazing at Frankie with a longing that Max recognized and understood. He felt for the guy. Love could rip your heart out.

When Andie suddenly appeared, clad in a yellow dress continually whipping up to expose a fair amount of her shapely legs, Max's face took on the same wrenching look. He sauntered through the living room, abandoning his duties in the kitchen and assumed the role of enchanted husband.

Max's deep voice resonated across the porch. "Welcome back." He stood inside the patio door. Both dogs perked up and bounded his way. Max fended them off while his wife strolled over to give him a lingering kiss. He turned her head and whispered affectionately in her ear. "Code yellow. Adams is here." Andie nodded against his cheek. She understood that the situation might be tense and should prepare to defuse. Not that defusing a situation was her style. When it came to matchmaking, Andie was more of an instigator.

Max turned to address their hostess.

"I invited a friend of yours for dinner."

Frankie couldn't help but gawk at Max and Andie, vicariously basking in the warmth of the love they radiated. "Really? Who?"

Max cleared his throat. "I believe the ladies call him Legs."

Her mouth fell open. In the space of a singular heartbeat, a throng of neurotic thoughts soared through her mind. *I need a bath. I've been working in the dirt all day and my nails are filthy. My hair is sticking straight out. I should have washed it last night. I wonder what he and Max have been talking about?*

Frankie steeled herself. She could hear Max's quarterback-huddle instructions to his wife. "Let's have a quick dinner, grab the dogs and get out ASAP. They need some time alone." Andie nodded twice, turned and planted a wet kiss on his lips.

Frankie slipped through the screen door with two enormous Great Danes trying to squeeze in beside her. "Knock it off you two," she protested. They bounded across the floor to the water bowl.

Frankie looked up. Gage was standing alert next to the sofa, watching the commotion, beer in hand. He was all hard, sculpted muscle. She could feel the intensity of his gaze burn over her face, her body.

She froze. A slow smolder began in the pit of her stomach. For a moment her legs refused to move. Palming sweaty hands down her shorts, she took a shaky breath and tried to quell the excitement that bubbled inside.

"Legs. Ah, I mean, Gage. I hear you're staying for dinner?"

"I wouldn't want to leave Max alone in a pink apron with two wild women." Gage gave her a radiant smile that amped up the wattage in the airy room.

"Great. I would love, we would love, to have you stay." Frankie tunneled her fingers through her hair self-consciously. "I wasn't expecting you. I'd have cleaned up. I'm a mess." She picked at the fabric of her shorts.

Gage continued to grin. Frankie continued to ramble. Monica trotted up beside him and pushed a slobbery muzzle under his hand. He gave her an obligatory pat.

"How long have you been here?"

"Long enough." A weird glint lit up his dazzling eyes. Frankie rocketed to new levels of anxiety. She swallowed hard.

"I should go take a shower. I've been working outside all day in the garden with the plants and dirt and stuff." Her shoulders drooped, "I'll be right back," she stammered. "Make yourself at home."

"That's my plan," he answered in the smoothest of tones, turned to watch her rush past and disappear into the bathroom like vapor.

FRANKIE WAS SPASTIC. APPREHENSION and a freakish anxiety ran rampant through every cell of her being. She caught sight of her image in the full-length mirror behind the bathroom door. Her nerves were on red alert. Why? Intuition was the only answer she could come up with, the feeling nagged at her that life was about to change, forever.

A breeze gusted through the room, and cooled the flesh at the nape of her neck. She groped through the medicine cabinet for the bottle of sedatives she knew were in there…somewhere. If nothing else, half a pill might take the edge off her nerves. They had been prescribed back when her sister had been her sickest and Frankie was too anxiety-ridden to sleep.

Gage had been there for her during those bleak times. Quinton and Damon too. They cooked, cleaned and forced her to eat. Occasionally someone gave her a killer backrub that worked out all the kinks and relaxed her to the point that she actually slept for a couple of hours. Jeri's death was something they never talked about. The team picked up the slack until she could shake off despair and return to normal function.

Her fingers latched on the yellowed plastic bottle tucked behind the dental floss. Frankie clawed it forward and gaped at the ancient expiration date.

Where had all those years gone?

"Shit," she hissed and tossed them into the trash.

Frankie peeled off her dirty clothes, took a quick shower, towel-dried her hair then rummaged wildly through her predictable wardrobe in search of something nice to wear. It had been a long time since she felt the yearning to wear a nice dress and look appealing. Jeans and sweatshirts were the predominant items in the closet.

After four years of comfortable, platonic friendship, Gage had transformed himself into someone she seriously desired to fuck.

Yes, it was all his fault.

He stared at her in a way that sent a cyclone of wicked thoughts funneling through her brain. Even his accidental touch sizzled her skin with anticipation. Frankie rubbed her arms, forcing herself to relax. She pulled on a pair of snug jeans and navy blue sweatshirt, took a shaky breath and steeled herself for whatever might come.

DINNER WAS DELICIOUS.

Frankie was surprised at how quickly it was finished. Max was an excellent cook. Andie's eyes sparkled with mischief during the entire meal, occasionally winking at her when nobody was watching. She was waving goodbye when Gage's powerful presence slid up beside her.

Frankie shut the door and turned.

His mouth closed the scarce inches between them and came down hard on hers. Frankie almost shot out of her skin. She put her hands up, trying to get some breathing distance between them and push away. He shackled her wrists with an unbreakable hold and silenced any protest with the tempting slip of his tongue across her teeth. He hauled her up against his hard body and kissed her until she went limp.

"Francesca, open your mouth," he whispered against her warm lips.

Frankie took a gulp of air and Gage was in, his tongue dueling with hers while his fingers splayed in the soft hair at her temples. His mouth was ruthless. Sparks flew behind her closed eyes. She couldn't have said how long the kiss went on.

Minutes?

Days?

Nobody had ever kissed her like that before. Infinitely sweet and soothing one moment and harshly demanding the next, shock-loading her brain cells.

His arm slid around her waist and dragged her tight against his chest. Aware that her feet were no longer in contact with the floor, Frankie wrapped her arms around his neck and let him carry her to the sofa. His hands moved with practiced precision. Through dim eyes, Frankie saw her sweatshirt sail across the room without realizing when and how it was removed.

"This is probably not a good idea," she contended in a breathless voice.

"Wrong." His mouth caressed along her jawline, breath hot and ragged against her ear. "This is an excellent idea."

"I'm not sure," she whispered.

"Cowards are the first to cry foul," he teased.

"Then I must be a coward."

"Wrong again." He nipped her earlobe. "You're just off balance because you're not in control." He captured her mouth before she could answer, sinking his tongue into its depths. Her world pulsed with lightning. Frankie shuddered, sighed softly in his embrace before responding with equal vigor.

His hot mouth slid a sensuous path to her breast. He teased, taunted the sensitized skin, taking her nipple into his mouth and sucked greedily through wet lace.

Frankie heard herself panting. She felt a brief moment of panic, the knowledge that everything between them was about to change. Lust won out and shoved the fear away. She clutched a handful of his hair to pull him closer.

Her bra was expertly coaxed down her arms by his large, skilled hands. Frankie moaned and arched beneath him. Her breasts were sensitive, quick to peak when he latched onto a straining nipple. Rational thought deserted her. She sifted her fingers through the short silky strands of his dark hair, and anchored his head in place. The pull of his hot mouth nearly drove her insane. "Please," she whimpered. His thumb and fingers spanned her stomach, sliding up to trace her ribcage.

Gage paused in his attentions to glance up at her face. Her eyes were closed, her head tipped back to expose the creamy smooth flesh of her neck. Her mouth was soft, and parted as she gave herself up to the pleasure. Pleasure that *he* gave her. Nothing he'd ever seen was more beautiful than that moment. She lost herself in his arms, quivering. Her slender body trembled on the brink of explosion. He felt heat and moistness through the thick fabric of her jeans, heard the shivering hiss of her breath—too shallow and rapid.

"Easy," he murmured, trying to soothe her. "We've got all night."

Her head whipped from side to side. "Gage, NOW!" she panted through gritted teeth, tugging at him with all her strength.

It was a plea he couldn't refuse. He peeled jeans and panties off her lean hips in one smooth tug. Pulling her closer to the edge of the sofa, he opened her wider, using his thumbs to expose her swollen labia.

He bent his head and took her clit with his mouth.

Frankie shrieked and reared up. A strong hand in the middle of her chest pushed her back down and held her there. "Easy." He tasted her with one slow lick. Powerful arms pinned her in place. He sucked and flicked, bathing her clit with his tongue while his broad shoulders kept her quivering legs apart.

Her head thrashed. The pleasure was so sharp it robbed her breath. She was tangled in an overload of sensation. Frankie clenched her teeth, shuddering as she strained against his mouth.

Gage clasped her hips tight.

She'd have fingerprint bruises tomorrow, she knew, but didn't give a damn right now. She couldn't catch her breath, couldn't get her mind to work.

Frankie gasped out, "Gage, please!"

Something incredible was going to happen to her.

Gage sucked a little harder, the barest sharp flick of his tongue. A thick, penetrating finger slowly stretched her vagina. The sensory onslaught was torture. Pure sweet agony. She let out a shrill, helpless cry. A low throb had begun to build deep in her belly, coiled inward like a taut spring. Sharp, staccato breaths moved in and out of her flared nostrils. She gulped for air in the vacuum of space.

A rising numbness replaced the tingling sensation around her lips and mouth. She gripped the sofa cushions, her fingers curled into frozen claws that dug into the palms of her hands.

Air!

She had to have air!

Through the roar in her ears she heard a sound like a steam engine huff and puff up a steep mountain. Fear of the unknown turned to stark panic that reared up suddenly and caught her in its dizzy grasp. Her ineffective breaths doubled, tripled. Fluttering specks began to dart along her field of vision like specters. Frankie watched their frenzied flight with awe. Her last conscious thought was one made in erroneous silence.

"I see spots."

Her eyes rolled backwards.

She fainted.

Chapter 9

SPOTS

FRANKIE WAS BAFFLED TO HEAR THE SOUND OF GAGE'S DEEP VOICE GENTLY URGING HER TO wake up. She moved slowly, her body heavy and strange. For an anxious moment she thought herself blind before her eyes fluttered open to stare blankly at the ceiling.

A pale moon shone through the window, casting the room in a ghostly glow. Light and shadows danced across every surface. Frankie realized with a start that she was on the hard floor, naked, her head in Gage's lap. She struggled to sit up, reaching out for something to cover herself.

Gage held her in place. "Wait," he soothed. "Rest awhile longer."

She let out a held breath and stared at his large hand. His nails and cuticles were immaculate.

"What am I doing down here?"

He tilted his head. Brilliant eyes, the color of Burmese peridot, pinned her in place. A dark shadow of stubble covered his square jaw. "You hyperventilated and fainted." His lips curled in amusement. The look on her face was so serious he couldn't resist teasing her. "Next time I'll bring a paper bag with me."

She blinked. *Was this what Kristen had been excited about when she talked of seeing spots?* Frankie didn't see the fun in it.

"I am so embarrassed." Frankie turned her head and came face to face with the zipper of his jeans. "I need some clothes."

"No, you don't," he answered softly. "I'm not done with you yet."

Frankie closed her eyes and tried to shake out the cobwebs. Her thought processes were scattered and there were a few things that didn't make sense.

"Syncope prior to orgasm," he mused out loud and reached to brush her hair back. "Have you ever done that before?"

"Done what?"

80

"Fainted during sex." He bent down and brushed a kiss across her damp forehead.

"No," she whispered. "I haven't."

Dread clawed at her gut. Her terrible suspicions were right. Something *was* wrong with her! Gage's soothing voice cut through her angst.

"I'll talk you through it next time, sweetheart."

"That wasn't an orgasm?" she stammered.

His hand wavered. "No, that wasn't an orgasm." He maneuvered them both until she rested in his arms and then he bent to kiss her again. "You get two more minutes to recover and then I'll give you a real one," he replied.

"Promise?" She stared at him with a fiery mixture of hope and trust and naked desire.

"Time's up." He lunged to his feet and carried her straight up with him.

"Cheater," she protested. "That wasn't two minutes."

He didn't bother to answer, instead threw her over his broad shoulder and carried her into the cluttered bedroom. Setting her down in the middle of the mattress, he stepped back and swung his arm wide with flourish.

"Let me re-introduce myself," he spoke, melodramatic behind the sweetest of boyish grins. "My name is Gage Parker Adams and I'll be your beefcake entertainment for the evening."

Frankie lifted herself up on her elbows and started to giggle. Even with her limited experience, she knew Gage was well over the top end of the Sisterhood's wicked beefcake scale. He was the sexiest man she'd ever seen. His eyes, sparkling gems on a jeweler's velvet pad, never left her body.

He unbuttoned his shirt. It fell to the floor in a heap. Heavy muscles rippled across his sculpted chest. Frankie's gaze moved down his body in mute appreciation.

She stopped giggling.

"Looks like I've got the best seat in the house."

"You have the only seat in the house," he answered, his voice deep.

"Are you going to dance for me?" she teased.

"Depends."

"On what?"

"If you've got the right kind of music." He flexed a bicep. "And how big a tip you're willing to give for a peek at my unit."

"What if I sang for you?"

"Spare me."

"Whistled?"

81

"No."

"Hummed?"

Gage grinned and took a step towards her. "I'll make you hum."

His pants were next to hit the floor. Frankie's eyes widened. Rooted to the spot, she couldn't look away. Not only did he hang to the left, but he was *hung*, as well. Her hands itched to run the length of him—just one touch of that satin-covered steel cock. Gage moved his hips in a slow, sensual roll. Frankie felt the overwhelming urge to whistle and gave into it.

Loudly.

Laughing, he started across the bed towards her. She scooted backwards and cautiously pressed herself against the headboard.

"It's show time, Frankie. Last chance to change your mind." He grew serious. "What will it be?" Gage moved his face closer. "No or Go?" He let his breath wash over her. His strong hand reached around to massage her back.

The chill of uncertainty began to thaw.

It was a rare time in her life that Frankie made decisions based solely on primitive urges. She reached out to touch his shoulder. "I'm nervous and scared that I'll fail," she replied with quaking honesty.

"I know. That's why we're doing this together. Let me take the controls awhile. I'll get you there safe and sound."

His voice was a husky rumble that did strange things to her willpower.

"Promise?"

"I promise." He held up his hand.

"Gage, I'm not even sure that I can."

"You can."

Frankie took a tortured breath and whispered, "I'm thirty four years old and I've never been able to have an orgasm."

"You will."

"How can you possibly know that? You don't know everything." The pitch of her voice escalated. "What if there's something wrong with me?"

"There isn't."

"What if there is?"

He reached out and pulled her close. She gasped.

"Trust me," he whispered, inhaling deeply. "There is nothing wrong with you that I can't fix."

Frankie trembled in his arms. If there was anyone in the world she trusted, Gage topped that list. If he really thought it was possible, she would try one last time.

Frankie nodded.

Gage caught her lower lip between his teeth and nipped gently. Her eyes fluttered closed. He held her head firm between his hands and devoured her mouth with his tongue; thrust in, backed out, repeating the motion until Frankie moaned with each breath. His lips clung to her, coaxed and nibbled their way across her throat until she sobbed from the pleasure of it.

He muscled her thighs apart and rested his weight against her. "Wrap your legs around my waist," his voice was seductive, as it whispered over her skin. "Higher."

She complied, offering herself completely because there was no other option. She soaked up the feel of his skin. His strong hands reached around to cup and tilt her ass for maximum penetration.

He entered her in one slick thrust.

"Gage?"

"Right here, baby," he rasped. "I'm not going anywhere."

She surrounded every inch of him with tightness bordering on pain. Her body flexed and held him hot, wet captive. She moaned his name over and over in a lover's mantra as he pushed his big cock deeper and deeper until his balls nestled against her ass. He took a nipple in his mouth and sucked as if starved.

"God you taste good," he groaned.

Frankie squeezed her eyelids closed. Pleasure licked flames higher and higher. When he slipped her legs over his shoulders and began a slow rotation of his hips, she screamed and clutched the sheets.

He started slow and almost brutally deep. She was so hot and needy he knew one good fucking wouldn't be nearly enough. He'd make love to her all night if that was what it took. He listened to her body, felt its tension as she writhed beneath him. She moved frantic and unknowing, helped by his large hands as they guided her clumsy rhythm. He kept their pace steady, slowed her down when she tried too hard. Her body knew the place it needed to go. It was up to him to show it how to get there.

Frankie was taking in huge gulps of air, eyes glistening with unshed tears. Her breath came in heavy pants. Gage had been waiting for this moment. His deep voice grabbed and held her attention.

"Francesca, purse your lips."

Frankie shook her head.

"Hold your breath," he coaxed. "Do what I do."

She watched, listened, followed his lead.

"Now blow it out." He exhaled.

She exhaled rapidly.

"Take another deep breath."

He inhaled.

She inhaled.

He thrust, pushing against her cervix.

She ground against him.

"Again," he ordered.

Gage brought her closer with each penetrating glide. He spoke with a soft measured voice and compelled her to mimic his every breath. She was *right there*. Near the edge yet blind to the fact.

"Please," she sobbed.

"Come to me," he crooned, breathless and tortured as she was. He moved up on her body, changed the angle slightly and surged into her again, faster now, and harder. He could feel her answering quivers deep inside. Her head thrashed from side to side. She grabbed at his body, unsure if pulling him close or pushing away was the answer. Gage was relentless. He changed his angle again and gave—

One.

More.

Thrust.

"Come to me, sweetheart," he whispered in her ear.

"Yesssssss!"

Her orgasm surged forth in one momentous tidal wave, swamping them both with its intensity. He took her cry, a high, keening sound of unbearable pleasure, into his open mouth. She screamed long and loud, an agonized sound as every muscle in her body celebrated its first exquisite release.

Gage paused a moment to regain his own control. He stared down at the woman he had known for so long, stunned that he was sharing an intimacy he had never believed possible. She was beautiful. His lips hitched upward in a wry smile. She still rode the edge. He rolled his hips and surged forward, his fingers biting into the flesh of her ass. Her second orgasm came harder, quicker and sharper than the last and with a guttural sound he followed her over the brink.

For several minutes only the hard sound of their breathing, coming in heavy pants, filled the darkness. She stirred, exhaled a soft sigh and brushed a kiss across his lips.

"Thank you," gusted in his ear.

"I'm here to serve," he answered breathlessly.

She gasped in surprise when he flexed inside her. Frankie countered with her own brazen move, a seductive clench that hitched his breath. Her internal muscles held him fast.

"Hmmmm, I think I might be getting the hang of this."

"You're a fast learner," he choked.

Gage tenderly stared into her face. She was radiant in the light of the bedside lamp. He took a shaky breath. Sex with one particular woman had never been so essential. Only one sensible reason explained why it would be that way now.

Quinton was right. This was worth the risk. She was worth any risk. He pulled her closer in his arms and settled them both under the covers.

She sighed and snuggled into his chest. "I don't think I've ever been this exhausted in my life."

"Sleep."

He brought her hand to the warmth of his mouth and kissed each finger. Buried deep in the back of his mind, Gage knew that at some point a long talk with her was necessary. Maybe once she had a nap and the afterglow was gone he could let her know what he expected. Monogamy. Honesty. He was not ready for a disastrous repeat of the last failed relationship, even though the idea of dredging up old emotional garbage made his skin crawl. Lying sprawled across his chest, Frankie was already asleep. Gage brushed her soft hair with the palm of his hand, stared at the ceiling and made plans that only he could see.

IF ANYONE WOULD HAVE dared suggest that one day she would be curled up in her bed, watching Gage Adams sleep after a blistering night of wild, uninhibited sex, she would have suggested they check themselves into the nearest rehab center. Yet there he was, tucked in beside her and it felt absolutely wonderful.

A secret little smile curved her mouth.

Soft morning light filtered through gauzy curtains, suffusing mauve colored walls with its magic and burning his image on her mind for eternity. From the unshaven angle of his jaw, the slope of his strong chin, the rise and fall of his muscled chest; Frankie was mesmerized.

The bells of the harbor buoy clanged through the peaceful haze. She could hear the familiar morning song of her neighbor's canary drifting in through the open window.

They needed to have a long talk and get back on track. They had to remain professional at work, no matter what had happened in their private life. Frankie had no regrets but she'd seen careers destroyed by this sort of indiscretion. Gage had made his point. He did what he set out to do. She'd seen spots, hundreds of them. He didn't need to torment her further at work.

Frankie blushed.

Gage looked so relaxed and sexy lying there. She hadn't realized how much her body could want a man's touch. She chewed on her lip. One last memory wouldn't change the eventual outcome, would it? One more time before he woke up, got dressed and left her?

She took his earlobe in her mouth and gave it a small nibble. She reached around his hip, running her hand over him with a feathery touch. He was hot and hard. Was he awake? She held her breath and waited. He didn't move. She began to slide her hand over him.

His rhythmic breathing hitched.

"Wake up, sleepyhead," she whispered seductively. "I want to have my way with you."

He grunted but didn't move. Her hand ran up and down his length.

"Wake up, I know you feel me."

Gage's full lips peeled back in a lazy, seductive smile. He heaved a dramatic sigh, rolled onto his back and stretched his muscular arms overhead.

"Climb on," he yawned.

He didn't have to tell her twice. Primed and ready to go, Frankie lunged across his lean hips and scrambled to guide him right where she needed him most. She jerked upright and gasped, erotic vibrations skittered over her like pulsating waterfalls. Carnal heat spiraled upwards.

"Gage?"

"Uh huh?" His voice was husky with sleep.

"That feels really good."

"It's supposed to," he drawled.

It took all her will to speak. "No, I mean, really, really good."

He opened one suspicious green eye to peer at her.

"It would feel even better if you'd start moving."

Frankie shook her head negatively. "I can't."

He reached out and grabbed her waist in both hands. "Why not?"

"Because, if I," she stuttered, staring straight ahead with the glazed expression of someone teetering on the brink.

Sensing precisely what the holdup was, Gage gave a long forward thrust. His thumb found her sensitive bud and hurled her into ecstasy. She clutched his forearms and screamed her release.

It took several minutes for her to recover. Instead of the orgasm leaving her limp and pliable, Frankie jumped off him and immediately scrambled about the bedroom. She tugged on a sweatshirt and gathered her hair on top of her head in a loose, wild ponytail. Gage rolled on his side, propped up on an elbow and watched her mad dash. Frankie stepped into a pair of khaki shorts.

"Going somewhere?" he asked.

"For a walk on the beach," she answered from the bathroom while washing her face. Soap bubbles lathered up. She splashed them away.

"If you want more exercise, get back in bed."

Frankie shot him a sanguine glance. "I'm hungry and I need coffee."

He frowned when he answered in a surprisingly edgy voice. "I'll make you coffee when I'm done making love to you."

"When you are done?" she asked. Her pewter gaze raked him from head to toe and zeroed in on his burgeoning erection. She smiled sweetly. "I'm not sure my blood sugar level can wait that long. Get your cute ass out of my bed, buster. I need sustenance. You've got too much stamina for this girl."

"Poor baby," he clucked. "Did all that screaming wear you out?"

"Screaming?" she feigned. "Who me? *You* were the one auditioning for the opera."

Gage chuckled. Frankie bent, grabbed a pillow and lobbed it at him. She had a wicked right hook, a strong, softball-pitching arm. The feather pillow arced straight for his face. Gage shot to his feet, wiggled his outstretched fingers in a wavy pattern that insinuated an old-fashioned tickle was in store for her. She squealed, took off through the open door and into the living room at a dead run, stumbling over the sofa before she regained her balance. Gage, naked, sleek and muscular, was right behind her.

"Still hungry?" He feinted left.

"Famished." She dodged the move and put an extra three feet of distance between them. The idea of being chased down for a good fucking had her so turned on she could barely see straight.

"Stop running and I'll give you something good to eat."

"You gotta catch me first, big guy."

Frankie bolted toward the kitchen table with Gage breathing down her neck all the way. She had uncanny reflexes and moves that rivaled a football running back yet she knew she had to be ultra-tricky to evade Gage for any length of time. He chased her around the house and eventually cornered her by the fireplace, tossing her flat on her back. Frankie struggled while his fingers plied her ribs. Every exhalation was a red-faced scream at the top of her lungs.

"What's the matter?" he tickled. "Huh? Do you give?"

Curled into a protective ball to shield her ribs, she gasped a breath to scream, "Never!" And then she changed tactics.

Frankie started to sob.

Gage stopped, his victorious expression turned to one of curious alarm. He leaned back. It was the break she was waiting for. Kneeing him in the gut, she scrambled off to safety only to find herself tackled to the ground almost immediately.

"Stop fighting me," he murmured lustily. He tossed her on the sofa, pinned her down with his larger body and dragged her shorts off. "You can't win."

"I already have," she gasped and spread her legs wide for him.

GAGE SOMBERLY WATCHED HER over the rim of his coffee mug. He tapped a finger on the edge of his plate. Unease flickered in Frankie's downcast eyes. The death grip she had on the mug she held was classic white-knuckle. When she'd asked him to go for a walk that morning and have breakfast at her favorite café, he was delighted to go. But when they passed George Harvey on the crowded beach and Frankie stopped to socialize, even inviting him to come along, he was pissed and hadn't said two words since that time. Fortunately, George had the good sense to decline the offer.

Gage had not made the effort to seriously communicate with a woman for many years. He and Frankie were accustomed to long spells of comfortable silence, never demanding more than the other was willing to give.

Gage grimaced.

What should he do next? Apologize and start up a heart-to-heart talk about all his past sins in the middle of a coffeehouse? Neither of them would want that!

"Gage?"

Her soft voice snapped him out of his dark thoughts, once again bridging the distance between them.

"Yes?"

She kept her eyes glued to the table while she asked in a voice too low for the others in the coffee shop to hear. "I was wondering if you—" She stopped short, trying to regroup wayward thoughts.

"Wondering what?" he probed.

"Would you like to stay with me today?" She swallowed hard, looking around nervously. "Tonight too, if you don't have anything else planned? I mean, I would understand if you're busy and need to be somewhere else."

Of all the things he expected to hear, that one was not on the list. He scrutinized her closely. She was literally holding her breath, waiting for a positive answer. Gage thought he had been reading her fairly well. The offer blind-sided him.

"Absolutely," he blurted. "I intend to spend the entire week with you. Day *and* night."

Frankie blinked up with open excitement. "Really?"

His gaze narrowed. "Really," he echoed. Then he lowered the boom and dealt with the other issue he'd been stewing over. "Whatever plans you made with Lauren, call her and break them."

"I don't know."

"Do it," he insisted.

She hesitated. "Okay."

Gage had been anticipating more of an argument. When victory came so easily, he couldn't help be suspicious. He made a sweeping motion with his fork. "The same goes for date plans with George Harvey or anyone else Damon has tried to set you up with."

"I haven't made any plans with George yet," she admitted.

"Good," he barked. "Don't bother trying to."

"Have you always been this bossy?"

"Affirmative," he snapped, the hint of a grin crossing his features. "Now eat your breakfast before it gets cold."

"Yes, Daddy."

Gage responded with a cocked eyebrow and set about finishing his meal. "Eat," he ordered. "You'll need your strength for what I have in mind."

Frankie smiled. Calmly, she scooped up a load of scrambled eggs, levered the spoon between her fingers and launched. They catapulted in a perfect yellow arc, splattering right between his eyes. Gage reached up and swiped the mess away with a napkin. "You know you're going to pay for that later, don't you?"

Frankie snickered. "I certainly hope so."

SHE'D BEEN SO CERTAIN that at any moment Gage was going to say "*Adios amiga,* see you at work" and take off for his cabin, agreeing to stay with her came as a total shock. She wrestled with the idea of asking him in the first place. After all, she reminded herself, he had done what he set out to achieve.

What he told her he could do.

Her luscious co-pilot had boldly taken her where no man had gone before, shown his exceptional prowess and didn't need to tie her to the bed to prove it. One look at him as he hovered above her, inside her, stroking slowly, was enough to make her vision blur and Frankie wanted more.

So, she wondered, why was he still browsing the waterfront shops with her? And *why* did he seem to be enjoying himself so much? And *why* was being tied to the bed the predominant thought returning time and again to her mind this beautiful sunny morning?

She wasn't mistaking the enjoyment on his face. Gage was having fun and he was having it while doing what most women enjoyed above all else.

Shopping!

She walked past a freshly washed window and caught the reflection of her satisfied smile, saw the kiss-bruised lips, *aware* of her body in a way she'd never experienced before. She blinked and inhaled a sweet aroma, strolling into a saltwater taffy shop with Gage a few steps behind.

"What flavors do you like?" she asked him.

"Lemon, lime and anything berry."

"I didn't know you liked taffy."

"You don't know a lot of things about me," he smirked.

She bought a mixed pound of the fruitiest and they moved on.

The tourists negotiating the sidewalk had nearly doubled within the last hour. Frankie stepped into the street and kept moving, window-shopping until she wandered past a gardening store, stopped and went inside.

She purchased a new trowel and assorted wildflower seed packets before she noticed that Gage no longer lurked over her shoulder. Frankie wondered when and where she had lost him, backtracked. Fifty feet down the sidewalk, she caught him as he slipped out of a boutique with a small pink bag tucked under his arm.

Gage knew he had been caught. He smiled widely, threw his free arm around her shoulder and gave a squeeze. "Can you fly a kite?" he asked.

"Of course I can."

He laughed in spite of himself.

"Just because you're a pilot doesn't mean you can fly a kite."

"Wanna bet?"

He watched her hands when she spoke. Deceptively delicate fingers articulated each word. Gage remembered their feel as they ran along his spine, clutched and kneaded, pulling him closer while he rammed his cock deep inside her. His gaze fell to her lips while she spoke and conjured images of that same mouth against his ear, pleading him for release. Not a minute went by that he didn't think of touching her, kissing her.

"I'll bet you two tickets to the Bon Jovi concert in Portland next month that I can fly a kite better, longer and do more tricks with it than you can." She paused for a deep breath of salty air while Gage considered her offer. He stopped and turned to stare at a car driving past.

"It's a deal," he answered.

Frankie turned, poised to make the sprint back to the kite store. Gage saw the twinkle of competitiveness in her eyes.

"I'll race you there," she piped up.

"I've been chasing you all morning," he complained. Frankie was already jogging down the sidewalk. Gage let out a curse and pursued.

IT WAS DARK BY THE time they wandered back to the beach house. In the distance, an engine stuttered and backfired. Gage ushered her inside and shut the front door. Turning, he found her on tiptoe, lips seeking his. Her teeth tugged at his bottom lip. With a deep groan and a rush of air, he caught her up in his arms and took long steps to the kitchen counter. Setting her down gently, his hands roved her body while he smothered her face in a blaze of urgent kisses. A heavenly wave of lightheadedness rushed over her.

"I have a present for you," he whispered.

Frankie smiled against his mouth. "I've been wondering when you were going to show me what's in that pretty bag you've been pretending so hard not to have."

"Presentation is everything," he echoed Max's line.

Gage placed the bag in her hand and eased her down off the countertop, letting her leisurely slide the entire distance down his hard thigh. Frankie gasped and shuddered, disappointed when her feet hit the floor

"Put it on," he ordered.

She eyed him suspiciously.

"It's the least you can do after trashing my kite."

Her mouth pulled into a smile. When it became clear that Gage matched her flying ability, she had deliberately plunged her multi-colored, tri-level starcruiser kite into his, hopelessly entangling both their lines and calling the bet a draw.

She snatched the bag from his hand and skidded across the tile into the bathroom. He had bought her a present! Other than a few obligatory apology-flowers, Frankie had never received an unsolicited gift from any man. She dove into the bag and found—

A lace camisole and matching thong?

Not the cheap stuff but expensive silk in an unusual shade of peach. Frankie peered closer, swept by a sense of déjà vu. She'd seen this same outfit somewhere before. Where? She fondled the camisole until an answer popped into her head.

"Andie's catalog," she mumbled.

Frankie closed her eyes on a deep sigh and quickly toed off her sandals. She couldn't get undressed fast enough. Blouse and shorts flew through the air and hit the shower curtain. Her faded bra and underwear made roughly the same arc and fluttered into the bathtub.

She knew the frills had cost Gage a bundle. For months Andie had been trying to convince Frankie to get a complete wardrobe makeover, starting at ground zero. Andie was an aficionada of naughty nighties, gourmet garters and teddies that made you want to go bump in the night. She was eager to impart her knowledge to others.

Frankie looked but never bought. She couldn't justify the expense of paying big bucks for something that would never be seen by anyone but a few inebriated girlfriends.

With extreme reverence, she slid the delicious fabric over her naked flesh. Her nipples tightened as the fabric slithered over her bare skin. Frankie gawked at her reflection in the full-length mirror. A perfect fit. Even the tiny spaghetti straps had been adjusted to accommodate her size.

She turned slowly, inspecting herself from every visible angle. She smiled and shook her head in wonder. From the other room a deep voice called to her.

"Come out here and model it for me."

Frankie took one last look at her fabulous reflection before slinking into the kitchen. She stopped a few steps away from him and spun in a seductive twirl.

Gage stared heatedly. Raw desire burned in his eyes. His gaze settled on the clearly visible mound of soft pale hair between her legs. He held out his hand and crooked a finger.

"Bring your tattoo over here."

"Why would I want to do that?" she responded coyly.

"Come here and I'll show you," he purred.

Frankie shook her head no.

"Do I have to chase you around this house again?"

"Chasing is not what I have in mind," she spoke in a breathy whisper.

There was a new look to her, one that spoke of knowing she was sexy, desirable, and able to use that power to seduce.

Frankie gingerly touched her aching breasts through the translucent cloth, feeling heated skin beneath. Running her hands slowly down her waist, she stopped at the juncture of her thighs and slipped her fingers under the lace. Sharp green eyes followed the gleaming path her hands took. Beneath half-lidded eyes glazed with hot desire, she touched herself and whispered his name on a sigh.

Gage swallowed convulsively and lunged. He was on her before she could blink, throwing her over his shoulder in a perfectly executed fireman's carry.

For Frankie, the rest of the night was a glorious blur.

He gave her no mercy. She asked for none. He took her on the kitchen table and in every room of the house, in every position they could think of. When neither had strength enough to walk a straight line, they crawled into bed and fell asleep in a tangle of satisfied arms and legs.

Chapter 10

A NEW TRICK

SHE WAS MAKING UP FOR THE YEARS THAT ORGASM HAD BEEN DENIED HER and SHE WAS doing it all in the course of one short week. Gage leaned against the back porch wall and inhaled a long, deep breath. The tinkling wood and aluminum wind chimes played a pleasant tune in the cool evening air. Overhead, clouds gathered in shades of pink and blue-gray. He glanced down. On the beach below the bluff a flock of seagulls congregated to rest, facing into the wind to keep their feathers unruffled.

Like any new physical relationship, he and Frankie couldn't get enough of one another when it came to sex. She had a lot to learn. He had been pleasantly surprised by her inexperience and overjoyed at her responsiveness. Mixed in with an intimate shyness she was quickly overcoming, he found a passionate, enthusiastic lover eager to try anything.

From time to time melancholy over the loss of Zena dampened her spirits. She occasionally mentioned the helicopter in conversation and though she bore no guilt, Zena was special, Frankie's first full-fledged assignment as a pilot. Gage also knew the loss of her father's dog tags weighed heavily on her conscience.

He blinked and looked out across the horizon.

The honor of nicknaming the new helicopter had been given to him in a unanimous vote among every New Harmony crew. Gage was stunned. He chose the name *Stella*—after his mother.

He glanced up. The sky was changing again. Mauves and oranges of sunset shimmered across the sky as old ghosts of the past combined with a host of new troubles to bombard him.

He was in great physical shape but Frankie was wearing him out. He needed a rest. If they kept up their current lovemaking pace, they'd never make it into work the next morning. Maybe he should give them both a break

94

and head home for the night.

His mouth quirked in a sly grin.

Was he really complaining about getting too much sex? Had his brain slipped a cog? Frankie had found a manual at the library and was in the midst of doing intensive research—on him.

"I hope you don't mind," she'd announced. "Some of these pictures are downright bizarre. I have a lot of questions and you're my partner of choice when it comes to getting answers."

His eyes squinted into a frown at her remembered words.

Partner of choice?

Did she really think she had a choice? Hadn't his actions made the fact very clear that Frankie belonged to him now? She was his woman. There would be no experimenting with anyone else. If she had a question, he'd gladly answer it for her. If she wanted to try something out of the ordinary realm of acceptable sexual behavior, he could provide that service too. Gage didn't have many taboos. Whatever Frankie wanted was hers for the asking. Except for one thing. She would have no other lover, no partner but himself—period.

Gage sucked in a breath.

Period. *Period?* The word drifted wistfully through his thoughts. When was she due for her next menstrual period? His mind raced across the four years they had worked together. Was it the first or last of each month? She never paid attention and the event usually caught her unawares. It was Quinton who always received the dubious request of running to the store for feminine toiletries while she waited in the bathroom for his return, trying to pretend she wasn't embarrassed. Gage scratched his head, mentally matching calendar to event.

The first of the month.

Noises from the beach below captured his attention. A host of sightseers clogged the shore, strolling across the warm sand not more than fifty feet from where he was leaning against the patio enclosure. He didn't blame anyone for wanting to be near the ocean when the weather was so outrageously fantastic. Migrating to the beach on a beautiful day was popular sport.

However, those same people could also get themselves in hellacious predicaments, oblivious to the danger an incoming tide presented until stranded on a rapidly disappearing island.

The grating of the patio door opening drew his attention from the frolicking tourists. Gage glanced over. His mouth fell open. Blood rushed straight to his groin like fire down a trail of gasoline.

Clad in a flowing skirt and oversized chiffon blouse that all but bared her breasts, Frankie stepped outside. Her hooded eyes made contact with his. She moved toward him. Gage hitched a curious eyebrow.

The woman was going to be the death of him.

A predatory grin twitched at the corners of her generous mouth. If she was trying to seduce him, it was a done deal. She stalked across the patio and stopped directly in front of him, swaying, staring up with smoky eyes.

"I want to taste you," she spoke in a barely audible voice.

Without permission, her hands skimmed under his shirt and down his waist to the shadowy indentation of his navel. Gage felt her work the zipper of his jeans. A thin line of sweat broke across his upper lip. The feel of her hands drove him crazy. Frozen in amazement, he stared down.

Her fingers curled around the pulsing hardness of his erection. She slid to her knees. Silken lips played with the muscular ridges of his abdomen as she pushed his pants below his knees. Her mouth brushed the pear-shaped birthmark on his right hip and returned to give it a little bite.

Gage nearly went airborne.

Frankie drew back and licked her lips. She touched her tongue to the damp tip of his shaft. He bucked as her mouth closed around him. He was too large to take in all the way. She went down as far as she was able and slid back up, adoring the taste, the scent, of his thick cock.

Frankie lazily teased with her lips and tongue. Back and forth. Over and around, in tight little circles. It was impossible not to give up to the pleasure she offered. Gage's eyes drifted shut. She nuzzled him, her hands reaching around to grip and spread his ass. She kissed down the underside of his shaft and licked the soft sac of his balls, swirling her tongue around them, taking first one and then the other gently into her mouth. He almost howled. He gritted his teeth, prepared for her next caress, only to find he wasn't prepared at all. His fists clenched at his sides. Gage was reasonably certain that his heart was going to fibrillate.

"Francesca," he sputtered breathlessly.

Her face was a study in the ecstasy of giving. She murmured something he couldn't hear, circled lightly then plunged the tip of her finger inside his ass as she drew his cock deep into her hot mouth. The moan torn from his lips sent a couple using the beach access path scurrying on their way.

Gage couldn't hold back the explosion. Hot semen poured down her throat. Frankie licked and sucked him, her mouth racing along with his heart.

The center of his universe zeroed in on the singular place where pleasure ruled him completely. His hands wound into her hair as she sucked every precious drop from him.

Blood returned slowly to his brain.

His eyes uncrossed.

His muddled thought processes cleared.

"You swallowed," his vocal cords shuddered the declaration. "Where did you learn to do that?" he demanded.

"Do what?" She smiled and wiped a droplet from the corner of her mouth. He reached down suddenly and yanked her upright. Her eyes bulged at the unexpected roughness. She tried to pull away.

"You swallowed," he repeated.

"Is that a bad thing or a good thing?" she asked. "You seemed to enjoy it."

Gage jerked his pants up and tugged her across the porch. "Inside," he nodded in the direction of the house while he guided her steps. He slid the glass door closed behind them and immediately spun her around to face him. Frankie tried again to wrench herself free of his grasp. Gage held tight.

"Who taught you how to do that?"

"The Sisterhood," she blurted.

"The Sisterhood?" His incredulous look prompted her to keep talking.

"We had a discussion during one of our Margarita Mondays. Kristen had some very interesting theories about performing oral sex. She had us practice on beer bottles until we got it right."

"Practice? You practiced right there in the pub?"

The veins in his temples were bulging, pulsing in time to his heartbeat. Being doused with ice water wouldn't have cleared his head any faster.

"Yes."

"And Edgar didn't throw you out?"

"No, but he did send his wife over to take a few notes."

Gage let out a tortured sigh. "I should've known."

"I'll have to report back to them that Kristen was right on target."

"You won't say a word about this to anyone, ever. And the next time you decide to stick your finger in my ass, could you warn me first?"

Frankie's chin flew up in defiance. "The whole point of it was to be a surprise! Kristin says that if the timing is right, that little fringe benefit in the end will shoot a guy straight to the moon."

"To hell with Kristin! If I'd wanted to go to the moon, I would have become an astronaut," he roared.

"Why is this such a sore subject for you? The Sisterhood says that guys rank a great blow job right up there with one of the eight wonders of the world."

Gage shook his head. Too many secrets existed between them. He would have to tell her. Sooner or later he would have to tell her *everything*, even if it squeaked out a little at a time. She had to know it all, judge for herself. Gage shuddered. Now was as good a time to start as any. He released her and took a step backward.

"Robin."

"Who?"

"My ex-fiance."

Anger burned deep in his stony gaze.

"What did Robin do to you?"

Gage forced his voice to a calmness he wasn't feeling.

"She moved out." He began pacing the confines of her living room. "She left me three days before our wedding."

Frankie clenched her hands spastically. "Why?" she gasped.

"The note said she couldn't handle the long amounts of time I was away. She was tired of being alone."

"Didn't she realize your lifestyle was exactly that from the start? It's not as though you sold vacuum cleaners for a living. Pararescuemen can be called upon to do some cloak and dagger stuff. Was Robin aware of that fact?"

"She underestimated her ability to deal with it," Gage replied evenly.

"She doesn't sound like a very smart woman," Frankie insulted. "I hate her already."

"I was a fool," he spoke quietly, staring at the ashes in the cold fireplace.

"No," Frankie countered. "You were in love and she was an idiot."

Gage shook his head to clear it. "About a week after she left me, I was drowning in a bottle of scotch when an old acquaintance wandered into the bar."

Gage's jaw twitched but he couldn't formulate the words.

"And?" she finally prompted.

"He walked up and congratulated me. Shook my hand, said he was glad to see I had finally wised-up and there might be hope for me yet."

"What?" she blurted. "That rude bastard. I don't like him either." Frankie was shifting from one agitated foot to the other.

Gage kept speaking. "He told me that Robin was infamous for her incredible blow jobs. At one time or another, she had gone down on almost every guy in our unit. I was the only bastard dumb enough to ask her to marry him."

"Did Robin leave you in March?" she asked quietly. Gage nodded yes.

"Is that why you get so moody this time of year?"

He nodded.

"Is Robin the reason you left the PJ's?"

Gage merely looked at her. Stricken. Silent.

"I need to know something Gage," she said softly. "Please tell me."

He squinted as he peered down at her.

"What we did, what we've been doing this week, all the sex. How is it going to affect our relationship at work?"

"It won't." He cut her off short and turned away. Moving slowly at first, he couldn't find the courage to look at her again and see the stark pity he suspected was written all over her face. He wasn't ready to tell her everything. He couldn't. Not yet. Not another word or he would break. He didn't want Frankie to see him like that. A familiar cold sweat beaded his forehead. He needed a long run, some fresh air and he needed it *now*.

Gage grabbed his car keys off the coffee table and headed for the front door.

"I have to leave," he mumbled.

"I know," she whispered.

FRANKIE WATCHED HIM GO without a word, wishing every material possession she owned that she could spend a few moments holding him, offering what little comfort she could give. *Robin*. Frankie knew she'd never be able to hear that name again without wanting to punch somebody's lights out. She took a deep breath and tried to roll the tension out of her shoulders.

Some broken things couldn't be mended. They had to be put together with care, bit by fragile bit like building a pyramid out of toothpicks. She blinked away a single tear and felt sadness at seeing the magical sweetness of their week together scatter like interstellar dust.

Her casual fling was over.

Frankie went from room to room, gathered what he left behind. She placed his belongings in a worn duffel bag by the door. "That must've been one helluva blow job, Moriarty." *Never again,* she promised herself. She'd return the library book first thing in the morning.

99

Chapter 11

BACK TO WORK

CAPTAIN JACK KNIGHT FROWNED AS HE GAVE REPORT TO THE ONCOMING PILOT. Something weird was going on. Moriarty was not paying attention. Edgy, more acerbic than usual, TB stared into space like she'd been lobotomized. *"Must be on the rag,"* he thought with a grunt. Knight snapped his fingers rudely in front of her face.

"Yoo hoo," he whistled. "Anybody home?"

Frankie whirled on him and glared.

"As I was saying," he continued, unable to resist the urge to reach down and scratch his nuts. "There are two separate wildfires raging about twenty miles northeast. We're on standby to assist. The last time I checked there were eighty firefighters deployed and the total combined area covered roughly ten thousand acres."

Ten thousand acres?

Frankie felt a twinge of guilt. She had no idea such a burn was going on. She'd been so absorbed in sex play with Gage all week that neither of them had even bothered to listen to the news. The spring had been unusually dry and lightning had started at least one of the fires. The other was being blamed on careless campers.

"When was that?" she asked.

"When was what?"

"When did you last check on the firefighters' progress?"

"The top of the hour."

Frankie nodded her head. Knight squinted and stared down his hawkish nose at her. He cleared his throat and began officiously, "With the cutbacks the forest service has taken in the last few years, resources are spread thin. The Regional Air Center in Piercy has requested that we provide assistance in case of emergency and HQ has given the go-ahead. Piercy has two helicopters

100

on the fire. One of them is coordinating all of the air to ground efforts," he sniffed. "The other is dropping fire retardant."

Frankie gazed across the ocean at an ominous bank of dark clouds. She felt small, intangible—depressed. A fierce squall formed on the horizon with lightning zigzagging from cloud to cloud. "How many fixed wings are helping drop fire retardant?"

"Four air tankers out of Brewster," he answered.

"The Bureau of Land Management only contracted four planes this season? They have their work cut out for them," Frankie commented. "That won't be nearly enough," she whispered as an afterthought.

Knight paused for a moment and tapped her shoulder lightly.

"Are you okay?"

"Fine," she answered absently. "Yourself?"

It was common knowledge that Jack Knight never missed an opportunity to talk about himself. He was his own best friend and fan club president. Frankie used that knowledge now to cover her own apprehension.

She was transparent!

Anybody who cared to look could see right through her. Flesh and blood, muscles, every vital organ, all the way to the bone. What they would see was a clear violation of her rule number one:

Frankie had shagged Gage.

Repeatedly.

Enjoying every millisecond.

The time she spent with him was undisputedly the most awesome of her life. She knew it must have been a 'pity fuck' on his part but she was grateful, nonetheless. Gage had been generous, caring and compassionate, more doting than either of her previous lovers had been. He went the extra mile to show her a great time.

So, why did she feel like shit?

She arrived fifteen minutes early to work that morning after a night of terrible dreams and scant sleep. She placed the bag with Gage's clothing right inside the laundry room and set about her duties as usual. Quinton came in a few minutes later. He made direct eye contact with her, smiled, winked and walked away.

He knew!

Her heart skipped a nervous beat. Quinton knew about them! Did Gage say something? Could he read her mind? Would he think less of her for what she had done? Waves of humiliation rolled over her. Ten minutes later Damon and

Gage staggered through the front door together. Instead of the warm greeting she normally gave them, Frankie hung her head and took off in the opposite direction, mumbling something arcane about the off-going pilot.

She had found Knight seated in *Stella's* cockpit picking his nose. Frankie pursed her lips and bit back a curse. The second the bastard left the area she was going to scrub *Stella's* cockpit with disinfectant and give the helicopter a thorough rinse down.

Knight was talking again.

"The least of which," he sniffed, "will be the difficulty the hotshots will encounter trying to build an organized fire line."

You've got to be kidding, she thought wryly. The peckerwood was lecturing her on the dynamics of fighting a forest fire? Frankie held her tongue and let him prattle on, deciding not to enlighten him that before her sister got sick, Jeri worked as a hotshot each summer after graduating from high school, eventually pounding her way up to squad leader.

Jeri and her team would hike into a burning area, heavy loads of equipment on their backs, then proceed to clear a path wide enough to stop, or at least slow down, the fire's progress. She had some close calls. One in particular spent hunkered beneath a thin aluminum shelter as the flames roared past. A brown-and-serve-bag, Jeri had called the fire blanket.

Frankie's jaw twitched. She stared at the fluttering orange windsock and out at the choppy ocean swells. To the northwest, almost at the edge of vision, a lone sailboat, pushed south by a stiff northwest breeze on her stern, had reefed its mainsail, preparing for stormy conditions. The weather was changing for the worse. She took a pensive breath. Disinfecting *Stella* would have to wait.

FINGERS OF LIGHT CRAWLED along the exposed beams on the ceiling and down the white walls to the floor. The room held a chill despite the fleeting comfort of the sun's rays. Frankie sat on the edge of her bed and stared at the latest marine weather reports. They confirmed what she already felt in her bones.

The unseasonably dry weather had made a tinderbox out of the inland Pacific Northwest. A low front was moving in off the coast, bringing only wind. Atmospheric conditions were ideal for a real barnburner.

There would be no rain to aid in the firefighters' efforts. Warm, wet air would lift over the mountains of the coast range and condense into clouds, spilling its precious load of water long before it reached the wildfire. By late afternoon, lightning and the threat of more fires erupting would further complicate Forest Service efforts.

She checked the latest fax from Piercy Regional Air Center. The bad news list got longer. The larger blazes were attempting to join together.

A third helicopter was now working the blaze. Two of the helos made water drops and the third acted as Air Attack Coordinator. For a fire of this magnitude, it was a pitiful show of force and dangerously inadequate resources.

Frankie bit her lip. No wonder they'd contacted the Coast Guard. Fighting fires in the northwest was not unlike going to war. One hoped for the best and prepared for the worst.

Frankie did the math. Of the hundred or so firefighters now on the ground, about twenty of them would be actual smokejumpers. The smokejumpers were the initial fire crew, parachuting in and working near the head of the fire to slow it down. The other eighty ground-pounders would be scratching fire lines elsewhere. Their tactics were all about containment. Eventually, if the task went as projected, the entire contingency would meet up and work together.

She hunkered over topographical maps scattered across the bed in a cartographer's nightmare, shooed Stewie off a pile of charts for the millionth time and scowled. The breeze that filtered in from her open window did little to quell the acid of dread rumbling in her stomach.

Theoretically, on level ground with no wind and equally combustible sources of fuel in all directions, fire would spread in a predictable pattern. Frankie knew that in reality, that was never the case. Wind and terrain were the major factors used to determine and predict a fire's movement and they were always present to one degree or another. A plan began to form in her mind. With a full crew onboard and enough fuel in the tanks, *Stella* could carry three to six survivors. Stretching that number would require some modifications.

A tentative knock on the half open door of her quarters drew her attention from the reports spread across the bed. Damon stood at the threshold. Anxiety clouded his roguish good looks.

"What's up?" she broke the silence.

"I just heard about our standby status," he replied. "I wanted you to know that my old smokejumping team is working this wildfire. Would you let me know if you hear anything?"

Frankie blinked.

"I didn't know you were a smokejumper," she set down the report.

"Only for a couple of seasons before I got into the Coast Guard."

Frankie nodded.

"I'll let you know if I hear anything."

Damon too had seen the weather change, watched the winds whip up the ocean. Those same winds would fan the flames of fire with equal gusto. Frankie wanted to give him the reassurance she wasn't feeling herself.

"We'll be airborne in seconds if they need us. Give me a few more minutes to get the data together and I'll brief everyone."

"Thanks, boss."

"Oh, and if you're looking for something productive to do in the meantime." She tucked a curl behind her ear. "How about putting some extra supplies in the helo?"

"Medical supplies?"

"Yes, just in case."

"Already done."

"Well then, pack a few granola bars for them to eat. I've heard that smokejumpers are always skirting the edge of starvation."

"Check."

"Damon," Frankie spoke quietly. "There's not much else for us to do but watch and wait."

"Always waiting," he replied with a frown and trace of bitterness in his voice. "We're always waiting for something bad to happen to someone."

"*Semper paratus,*" she answered in quiet reminder.

"Always ready," Damon echoed.

GAGE COULDN'T BELIEVE IT. Frankie had snubbed him, gave him the brush-off like she didn't want to remember going at it like a crazed mink the entire week before. It wasn't as though he expected one of her voracious, good-morning kisses. The least she could have done was made a little eye contact and let him know she remembered begging for mercy when he had her pinned against the mattress, stroking her into the double-digit orgasm of the night.

Gage sneered at his duffel bag.

Maybe there was more to Frankie's actions than his bad behavior warranted. Had she decided to ignore his warning about taking other partners now that she knew all her inner parts were in working order? Was she prepared to move on already? Hadn't he made his expectations perfectly clear?

He had been places inside her she didn't even know she had.

Rage, sharp and sudden, flared, before his years of training crushed the fury into a controllable planned burn. He would deal with this later when the two of them were alone and she'd be unable to pull rank.

He looked up to see Frankie exiting her quarters. Tight-lipped and focused, she twirled a pen between her thumb and index finger. Stewie made a fast dash between her legs. Quinton and Damon glanced up from their seats at the table.

FOR THE FIRST TIME that morning Frankie looked directly at him. His expression was cool. His aura, dangerous. Eyes hot with fury, his green orbs met hers without their usual mockery. He was pissed, and a pissed Gage was not a nice thing. She steadied her shoulders, cleared her throat and spoke.

"Okay." Her voice was a bit shaky. "Here's the latest rundown."

Frankie recited the facts and figures she'd collected over the last hour. Initially, both fires had been slow to develop, building during the day and then backing off at night. The first fire to be spotted had been driven southeast across the mountain range by the wind. A team of smokejumpers had dug a line all the way down to noncombustible mineral soil, stopping the fire's forward progress. They thought their work was finished and were climbing out of a steep canyon when another fire, less than a mile from their location, was located and called in. The team was diverted to deal with it.

The Air Attack Coordinator now reported that the second fire had taken off and was rapidly gobbling up the acreage. Spot fires flared up everywhere, stretching like crooked fingers across the landscape. More smokejumpers were being flown in to assist. In the meantime, those on the ground were doing their best to contain a blaze leap-frogging its way to a small farming community.

The situation was critical.

Frankie fully expected the Regional Air Center to request they bail firefighters on the ground out of a tough situation. *When* that call would come was anyone's guess. She had spoken with Station New Harbor and apprised its commander of their situation.

"Captain," Quinton spoke up. "I've trimmed down the equipment in the back of the helicopter to bare bones. If we get a water call, we'll be scrambling to reassemble."

Frankie nodded. That tidbit of information told them all that they were officially housebound. No quick trips into town while on pager or lengthy runs on the beach. They had to be ready to go at a split second's notice.

"Any other questions?"

Silence.

"Comments?"

Nothing.

"Advice?" she asked.

Damon raised his hand. "Have you heard who their crew supervisor is?"

"Someone named Robinson," she replied.

"Spanky Robinson?"

"I believe that was the name they gave me," she answered.

Damon shook his head in acceptance. "He's good. One of the best old-timers in the service. They nicknamed him Obiwan. He's an exceptional fire boss."

"Spanky? Obiwan?" Quinton asked in disbelief. "One nickname wasn't enough for this guy?"

Frankie smiled at the Aussie's wry wit, glanced from Damon to Gage to Quinton and back to Gage. His jaw was set tight.

"Is there anything else we need to discuss?"

"A word in private, Captain?" The words snapped out.

"Of course," Frankie replied and motioned to her quarters. She moved in sync behind him and edged the door shut with her hip.

In the blink of an eye, Gage whirled on her. He moved so fast she couldn't distinguish a single individual motion. Frankie blinked up at him and took an evasive step backward. The motion pinned her against the door.

"What the hell is going on with you?"

His resonant voice flooded her senses.

"What do you mean?" she asked.

He pointed a finger in front of her face. His eyes narrowed into shards. "Your bad attitude."

"What?" Her jaw shot up defiantly.

"You heard me." The breath exploded out of his lungs, which doubled the volume of his voice. "You're not deaf."

"There's nothing wrong with my attitude or my hearing," she defended. "So, if you're looking for bad attitude, mister, I suggest you check your mirror."

The comparison was out of his mouth before Gage could stop it. "You sound just like Robin."

Frankie thrust her chin out. A series of satisfying, extremely vulgar replies rose to the tip of her tongue. Oh, how she wanted to use at least one. She bit them down.

"You did your duty, Gage. You got me off. Now get out of my way. I've got a job to do."

"Who said it was my fucking duty?" he yelled.

"It was exactly that, wasn't it? Just fucking?"

"What are you talking about?"

"It's done, Gage. Over! That's what I'm talking about," her voice trailed off.

"Done?" He hovered, glaring down at her. "Done?" he repeated. "What the hell do you mean, *done?*"

Frankie glared back, refused to budge an inch or speak in the face of the anger that shadowed them both.

"Well?" he demanded.

A knock on the door, Quinton interrupted them.

"Captain, there's a call for you."

She pushed her way past Gage and stomped into the main room. Damon anxiously handed her the phone.

"Moriarty here," she snapped.

All three men crowded close while she scribbled coordinates on the corner of a thick yellow notepad. She raised her right hand to Damon and made a circular motion with her forefinger in the air.

"It's a go."

Quinton and Damon sprang into action.

"Affirmative, Harmony Bay is en route."

Frankie disconnected. She pulled her flight jacket and helmet off the wall pegs and met Gage's curious look. She wasn't sure how it was possible but he looked ready to strangle and jump her bones at the same time.

"Eight smokejumpers. At least one injured. They're making a run for it but the fire is gaining on their position. The Air Attack Coordinator predicts they'll be cut-off with no way out." Frankie moved toward the door while she spoke. Gage grabbed his own jacket and helmet and followed.

"No," she shook her head firmly when she saw his intent. "Damon's in the back. You and Quinton stay here and monitor our progress on the scanner."

His expression moved from anticipation to rage.

"What?" He caught her arm and forcefully swung her around. "You need my help in the cockpit."

"I need you to obey my orders," she answered.

"It's different in the ravines with all those trees and current updraft. Combine that with no discernible horizon, no landmarks and nothing to give you a point of reference in the middle of all that smoke? You need an extra hand up front." He backed her against a metal filing cabinet, getting right up in her face. "Leave Damon and take me instead," he hissed.

"No," she blinked and dragged her eyes away. "There are injuries. I need a medic, not another pilot."

"I can use scissors as good as the next guy and you know it," he snapped.

Frankie leered up at him and then glanced out the big windows.

"I've made my decision," she spat.

She saw that Damon had strapped himself into the flight mechanic's seat. Frankie pulled on her gloves. No time left to argue. "You controlled me in the bedroom, Gage, not here. It's my decision and it stands." She ducked under his outstretched arm and sprinted to the helipad.

WHEN THE DEDICATION OF aviation pioneers succeeded in revolutionizing search and rescue with the introduction of Sikorsky's helicopter, little did they anticipate that one day a tattooed woman with sweat-plastered hair under a heavy helmet, would share that same vision with a passion bordering on the suicidal. One look at her face was proof enough.

"It's gonna get hot up here," Damon warned needlessly.

They were forty miles northwest and heading inland over the coastal mountain range. Her hand pulled back, adding power to the climb. Ahead of them, black smoke filled the sky like the mushroom plume from an atomic bomb. Farther north she could see the formidable Beaumont Dam with its riveted iron penstock leading down to the hydroelectric generating plant.

Frankie triggered the intercom switch. "Did you bring any marshmallows?"

"No," he grumbled. "I forgot the wieners too."

"That's why we're here," she joked and then grew serious. "Just make sure you keep your buns and weenie out of that barbecue."

"Roger that."

The smokejumpers working the southwest ridge containing the valley had planned their best escape route. They were almost out of harm's way when the wind made a freaky change, trapping them in a ravine between steep vertical cliffs. One of the eight jumpers fell and fractured his ankle, which slowed them down even further. They radioed for help. An air tanker was diverted to drop fire retardant ahead of the group, trying to buy them a little time but the flames skirted the perimeter, picked up speed and advanced once again. Hampered by their injured firefighter, the smokejumpers were running out of time.

"Coast Guard helo, this is Air Attack Two-Twenty."

"Go ahead Two-Twenty," Frankie answered.

A deep voice came back over the radio with updated coordinates and urged her to "proceed with haste."

Frankie dropped down the lee side of a ridge into a deep, narrow canyon. A meandering, brackish river wrapped around granite boulders the size of a truck. The helicopter caught a sudden circular downdraft, bucked and bounced all over the sky. Frankie fought to break them free, found calmer air seconds before hostile head winds slammed into them. Her gloved hands plied the controls. Her boots caressed the pedals at her feet.

Acting.

Reacting.

Anticipating.

They were three hundred yards from the western edge, close enough to feel extreme heat and see flames licking up two hundred feet and more. Much of the sky was a putrid yellow-gray with poor visibility due to the hazy smoke. The world had turned into a cauldron. Tears streamed down her face. She tried to blink them clear. *Stella* was slammed down hard and jolted to the right in the swirling air currents.

"Good thing I skipped breakfast," Damon joked.

Frankie was too busy to answer. They hit another stomach-wrenching gust of turbulence. She pulled them up and away.

The fire had crowned out, jumped from ground to high in the canopy of fir and pine trees, exploding in enormous balls of flame. Flames were spreading fast, leaving large unburned areas beneath. Frankie could see the vertical development as the fire pulled trees out of the ground and sucked them into a vortex of destruction. Coils of layered black smoke rolled up from the flame front. Frankie glanced at her GPS. They were right on target.

"Okay, kids, where are you? Help has arrived. Come out, come out, wherever you are," she sang softly and circled *Stella*, waiting.

As if in answer, eight soot-stained yellow jumpsuits popped into sight below. She angled in their direction and nudged the controls for more speed. The group cleared the ravine and headed toward an open field about fifty yards to the south. They had discarded their heavy gear in a last ditch race for survival.

"Looks like they've got more problems than a fractured ankle," Damon announced.

One jumper limped along, assisted by another. Two jumpers at the rear of the group staggered under the weight of a third they were carrying. Hearing the sound of a helicopter, they looked up and waved frantically. The fire skipped from tree to tree and spread across the thick canopy, gaining rapidly on them. Frankie watched in horror as the greedy flames sought them out, seeking the fuel needed to feed itself.

The smokejumpers got a renewed blast of adrenaline with the prospect of impending rescue. They moved faster, spread out in a thin line. She over flew them and hovered, searched for a suitable spot to land before she angled in a steep descent.

"Ready for hot-load," Damon's voice came over the intercom.

Dust and debris flew up around them. With the fire so close, they both knew she would not risk turning off the engines. The main rotor would continue to spin and she would stay at the controls. In the back of her mind, Frankie gave silent thanks to whoever watched after her that Gage was nowhere near this hellish maelstrom.

"Roger that," she replied.

They touched ground.

"Go."

Through her peripheral vision, Frankie could see Damon streak across the meadow at a full-out run toward the jumpers. She turned and peered through her shaded helmet visor at the flames descending upon the group from all sides. The sight was hideously fascinating, Mother Nature in her most furious glory.

Sparks flew everywhere, starting spot fires that sprang up like measles across the forest. The thunderous roar of conflagration could be heard above the helicopter rotor noise, even with the ear protection her padded helmet afforded. Sweat rolled down her cheeks and dripped into her lap. Frankie craned her head forward. She watched, mesmerized, and waited. A malignant black cloud rolled out of a stand of birch to her right, propelled by forty-foot flames.

A fire-breathing dragon.

"Sis, you told me it was impossible to describe," Frankie whispered. "I understand now." Instinctively, she reached up for the reassuring touch of her lucky charm and found nothing. Frankie grimaced. "I hope you're watching after me Dad, Jeri and anyone else who might be out there. We could really use some help right now to save these kids." As an afterthought she added, "Sorry about losing your dog tags, Dad. I was kind of busy at the time."

Reverberating thumps, felt through the hull, signaled an arrival. Frankie glanced behind her and was rewarded with the exuberant "thanks" of a freckled boy not much older than twenty. Next to him, a similarly ash-covered youngster gave her a crisp, mock salute. She smiled in return, but felt faintly sick to her stomach.

A deafening crash sounded from outside the helicopter. Frankie spun to the source. A huge ball of fire rose high above the trees at the edge of the field and sent flying coals hundreds of yards in all directions. Looking around, Frankie searched for Damon and found him at the rear of the scattered line. He and the squad leader were half-dragging the injured jumper. Sparks and flames licked at their heels. She keyed her radio and reported to the Attack Coordinator that the smokejumpers had been found and evacuation was in progress.

"Two apparent injuries," she informed him. "Will update you on their condition once my medic has fully assessed them."

"Copy that, Coast Guard. Appreciate your help. Two-Twenty clear."

Thump.

Another smokejumper found sanctuary in Stella's belly.

Thump.

The fourth tumbled in.

"Come on, come on. Move it, Damon," she urged aloud, not realizing her microphone was still keyed open. "Come on, kid, run. The fire is right behind you." Her fingers were damp and itched at the controls.

"Faster, Damon!"

Thump.

A fifth jumper arrived.

Frankie keyed the intercom. "This is your captain speaking," she announced. "Welcome aboard. Please keep the aisles clear. Your flight attendant will be coming through the cabin with the meal service shortly. Remember, this is a non-smoking flight. All of our lavatories are equipped with smoke detection devices. If you are caught lighting up, stiff penalties will be assessed; up to and including physical ejection from the aircraft."

Frankie could hear a few chuckles. She palmed the sweat from her eyes and glanced around. All eyes were on the men who were running for their lives.

Frankie reached over and keyed the public address system. "Move your ass, guys. This bird isn't leaving without you."

Damon was thirty yards away and moving steadily towards the helicopter. His grueling physical training was paying off. Frankie could tell that he was doing most of the work. Damon had shifted position, not only carrying the injured smokejumper but dragging the team leader along as well.

Glowing red embers, kicked up by the rotor wash, flew by the cockpit window. Frankie looked through her side window. A pillar of smoke lofted hundreds of feet overhead. She heard the rumble and roar of the approaching fire. She took a deep breath and stilled her trembling hands.

"Hurry up, kid," she whispered. "My heart can't take much more."

A loud, shuffling disturbance sounded from the back, followed by a shout. Frankie turned her head to look. Damon's breathless voice clipped an order.

"Get us out of here."

"Gladly."

She plied the controls. *Stella* rose slowly, straining to clear the ground, hampered by the extra weight and thin, superheated air. Frankie coaxed every ounce of power. Whoops of joy filtered into the cockpit.

"Take us to the closest trauma center," Damon requested in a tone that was really a demand. "I've got an unstable patient with internal crush injuries."

"Affirmative," Frankie answered and angled towards Fairhaven.

GAGE REACHED OUT, THUMBED the volume on the scanner down a notch and eased back in the creaking chair. He sat in stunned silence. In disbelief. Scared shitless. Impotent, while Frankie and Damon risked their lives. He hadn't dared twitch a muscle in over an hour. His chest hurt, he was drenched in sweat. His mangled nerves were zinging. Quinton tapped him lightly on the shoulder. Gage jumped, startled.

"You can let your breath out, mate."

He looked up into the Aussie's troubled blue eyes.

"What?"

"Relax," Quinton spoke softly. "It's over."

"No," he shook his head in a burst of insight. "It's only begun."

Quinton's long fingers held his arm in a loose grip. "Do you want to tell me what happened between you and Frankie?"

Gage stared absently into space. He wasn't entirely certain what had gone wrong between them or how to answer for it, so he started at the beginning and glossed over the details. "We spent the week together. Now she's pretending it never happened."

"Have you talked to her?"

"I tried."

Quinton shook his head. "You were arguing, mate, not talking."

Gage looked at him quizzically.

"The walls are thin," Quinton said slowly. "We heard every word."

Gage rose from the chair onto wobbly legs. He took a shaky breath and stuffed his hands deep into his pockets. "Are you telling me I blew it?"

Quinton released his hold on Gage's arm and gave him a brotherly pat on the back. "I'm saying that you need to talk to her. Put your temper on hold and tell her how you feel. It's as simple as that."

Gage stared.

Simple? Nothing in his life had been simple.

Chapter 12

AN UNEXPECTED APPEARANCE

STRETCHED OUT IN *STELLA'S* COCKPIT, FRANKIE WAS HALF-ASLEEP. SHE DRIFTED ALONG in a relaxing *A*-wave state and soaked up some vitamin D. Every so often her ear would pick up the low voices of Gage and Quinton. She calculated them to be somewhere near the northeast edge of the helipad. What they were discussing was anyone's guess. At the moment, she had no desire to know.

Gage had pounced on her the moment she returned from delivering the smokejumpers to safety. They had argued heatedly about her decision to take Damon instead of him. Accusations swung back and forth like a tennis ball until they finally gave up, called it a stalemate and stayed as far away from one another as humanly possible for the remainder of the day.

She was tired of fighting, fed up with the need to justify her actions. Exhausted, all she wanted to do was take a nap. Gage had left her alone and that was good enough for now. Why were their conversations deteriorating into argument lately? Every single time! Ever since they'd started having sex!

Damon was even referring to the Air Station as Disharmony Bay. If the kid's optimistic disposition was being affected, she knew the situation was bad.

"This is what happens when you shag your coworkers," she whispered to herself. "You ruin everything."

Yet, she craved Gage's touch so sharply that her body was nearly humming whenever he came near. Even while he yelled she could scarcely focus, unable to adequately defend her actions when all her desperate lips wanted to do was mesh with his. Instead, she yelled back and wondered how long the terrible longing was going to last.

When the signature rumble of a Harley Davidson motorcycle cut through the stillness of the afternoon, she didn't bother to raise her head. *"Probably one of Damon's buddies."* With the forest fire still raging, the crew was stuck at the Air Station indefinitely. If his friends wanted to visit, they had to come calling and a steady stream of callers had besieged the station.

Frankie kept her eyes shut and daydreamed she was on a secluded beach in Nice doing some topless sunbathing while an agile Frenchman smoothed her in sunscreen from head to toe.

GAGE PAUSED IN HIS conversation with Quinton.

"Looks like we have another visitor."

Quinton squinted against the sun. A darkly tanned jock in bulky leather chaps and black muscle-shirt was throttling his enormous motorcycle around the concrete sidewalk bordering the northern edge of the station. He stopped the bike a few feet from the garage door and used his booted feet to balance it upright. The shiny thoroughbred cycle gleamed in the sun.

Damon bounded out of the house.

The man on the cycle reached up and removed his black helmet. Extending a hand, he greeted Damon in a deep and distinctive voice.

"I'll be nicked," Quinton exclaimed. "I think that's Vin Diesel."

They watched in disgust as Damon crowded the bike, a stupid grin on his face.

"Isn't that just great," Gage muttered. "Now we've got two Diesel groupies on the team."

"Let's go pay our respects," Quinton answered.

It wasn't often that a celebrity came calling and it wouldn't take long for word of the visit to spread, especially with Damon's connections. By evening, half the phone directory would know.

"Good afternoon," Vin greeted the two Guardsmen.

Quick introductions were made. Vin held out his massive hand and gave Quinton's a firm shake. Gage crossed his arms over his chest and kept them there. Vin paused a moment and cleared his throat. His mellow voice boomed across the air space between the house and helipad.

"A friend told me what you did for him and his wife."

"Bergmann," Damon affirmed.

"That's right."

"A nice old couple," Quinton responded. "They were shaken up pretty badly."

Diesel arched a prominent brow. "They were terrified. You saved their lives. Ira was so impressed he's decided to become a co-producer on a new

115

boat wreck survival reality show."

Diesel stopped talking and grinned. Quinton let out a little chuckle.

"Seriously though, Ira told me it was a comfort having the Coast Guard there to talk them through it."

Gage started to say something and stopped himself. From the corner of his eye, he caught an incredible sight. Frankie was on her haunches, contorted at a bizarre angle in order to catch her reflection in the glass of the control panel. She finger-brushed her hair, licked her lips, and swiped a grease smudge from her cheek.

Gage felt his blood pressure spike.

"Ira said your lady pilot had a fondness for me. Uh, my movies, that is. I thought I'd drop by since I was in the area and thank her personally, thank all of you, for being there when he and Lonnie needed your help."

"Are you on a road trip?"

Diesel's bald head turned toward Damon and nodded. "Bought it last week. I've got some free time before my next project starts. Thought I'd go on a test run up the coast."

"Where are you headed?"

Damon's whiskey colored eyes roved over each nuance of the special-edition motorcycle.

"Victoria," Diesel answered.

Frankie emerged from the helicopter. Behind her, *Stella* glinted in the afternoon light. Good thing he was wearing sunglasses, Gage scolded himself. It wouldn't do to have everyone see his eyes pop out of his head.

With her flight suit unzipped to the waist and thick hair in curly disarray, she gave the appearance she'd just crawled out of bed after a vigorous romp.

Gage swallowed hard.

His blood pressure eked up another ten points when she walked straight up to their guest and extended her slender hand.

"Hello, I'm Captain Moriarty. Welcome to Air Station Harmony Bay."

Her voice smacked of drowsy seduction. Diesel's eyes never wavered from her. He took the offered hand and pressed her knuckles to his lips.

"Pleased to meet you. I'm Vin Diesel."

Gage felt every muscle in his body go tense.

Damon coughed.

Quinton saw trouble brewing and took action. He cleared his throat and asked in a booming voice, "When did you lay your bike down?" He pointed to a small scrape on the back fender.

Diesel jerked like he'd been struck. He twisted his head down and around, dark eyes narrowed. Frankie's hand slid out of his grasp.

"I didn't lay it down."

"No?" Quinton replied distractedly. "Hmmmmm. A real shame, mate."

Diesel's rough hand smoothed over a nearly invisible scratch before he turned back to Frankie. She gave him a wily grin and shook her head. He glanced from Frankie to Gage and back to Frankie. A big smile spread across his face. "Wanna go for a ride?" he asked her.

Gage almost bit his tongue in half. "We're on fire alert," he reminded, the veins in his forehead protruded to the point of rupture. His anger was a tsunami, gathering force.

"Just around the block," Diesel spoke up. "I won't keep her more than five minutes."

Everyone turned to stare at Frankie.

She sidestepped and swung her leg up and over the bike in one graceful swoop. "The fire has laid down considerably," she turned to stare up at Gage. "I'll be back momentarily."

She settled into position behind Diesel, wrapped her bare arms around his sturdy waist and leaned her breasts against his back. The actor kicked the engine over, revved it a few times for effect, and gently eased out onto the street.

"Take care of her, you son-of-a-bitch," Gage cursed under his breath and stormed inside.

TEN MINUTES LATER FRANKIE found all three of her crew gathered in the garage. By the solemn looks on their handsome faces, a funeral was in order. She hoped it wasn't hers. Right now she was filled with excitement that was impossible to contain. She wasn't about to let their grimness spoil her buzz.

Looking around at her team, she asked in a practiced, smart-assed voice, "So, who died?"

Quinton, nearer to her than the others, bent down and whispered low in her ear, "Tone it down, sister. He's about to go ballistic."

Frankie puckered her lips. Her flushed cheeks reddened even more.

"No problem."

She swept past the three pretty boys in a jazzed rush. Moments later, from somewhere deep within the bowels of the house, they could hear her celebratory whoops of joy.

Damon scratched his head. "She sure is giddy," he said. "I wonder if they compared tattoos?"

"Damon?"

"Yeah, LC?"

"Go clean the head in the workout shed."

"What?"

"You heard me," Gage barked.

"It's not my day to clean that stinking bathroom."

"It is now."

Damon opened his mouth to protest again.

"That's an order. Go!"

IT WAS NIGHT. HE'D run the beach for hours while his anger simmered. Despite fatigue, sleep was not on the menu for Lieutenant Commander Gage Adams. He had a raging, painful erection. He hadn't touched Frankie for what seemed like months and according to Quinton, if he ever expected to do so again, he had some serious work to do on his communication techniques. If her infatuation with Vin Diesel was any indication, the big Aussie was right. Memories of abandonment flew up to plague him. He pushed them back down. Gage bit back a snarl and jumped from his disheveled bed. He slipped from his room and moved without a sound, down the dark corridor and wide stairs.

The door to her quarters was open, the room cool and quiet, with curtains pulled tight. A pulsing green light from the computer cast an eerie glow along the walls. Frankie was on her side, curled into a crescent.

He listened to her soft, rhythmic breathing for a moment before he moved forward. Without a sound he lay down behind her, molding her body with his own. He covered her mouth with his hand.

She awoke on a startled gasp. He held her still, bound by his powerful arms and legs. Gage whispered, "It's me."

She relaxed slightly. He kept his hand over her mouth and began to ease up her shirt. He bared her breast and cupped it with his hand. His fingers ran over her nipple, circling with a light, insistent touch. Her breath hitched. He felt her heart speed up.

"Make a sound and I stop."

Frankie nodded her head.

"Do you want me?"

She nodded again.

Gage ground his pelvis against her sweet, soft bottom. She stiffened. Hot moisture pooled between her thighs. He lightly pinched her taut nipple. Frankie arched, shuddered a moan. Gage pulled away.

"I told you," he silkily murmured. "No noise."

Frankie tensed. A wicked smile came to his lips. His hand moved across her abdomen, circling her belly button. He draped a leg over her torso and nibbled her earlobe. His tongue slid across her shoulder and found the exact spot on her neck that drove her wild. He bit.

Frankie gasped.

"Sshhh. Do you want me to stop?"

She shook her head no.

His hand moved lower, tracing the juncture of her thighs. Frankie pushed against it in urgency. He could feel her entire body trembling.

"Be still."

Her curls were wet. His fingertips grazed her hot center. Using a leg to wedge her thighs apart, he splayed her wide.

"Not a sound," was all the warning he gave.

His finger sank home deep inside her, stretched, claimed her. Frankie convulsed around him, head thrashing from side to side.

"Too easy, I'm not done with you yet. Spread your legs wider."

Frankie exhaled a pleading mewl. Gage clamped his hand down hard over her mouth and pulled away.

"I told you, make a sound and I stop."

His teeth found her neck and nibbled. She shook her head in frustration.

"Do you want me?"

She nodded.

"You don't come until I tell you to come."

His voice was raw. Gage slid his moist finger across her lips.

"Open your mouth," he ordered. "Suck my finger."

Her hot mouth pulled his finger deep into her throat.

"Do you want my cock?"

She nodded desperately. Holding her legs open wide, he swiftly buried himself, pounding into her in a savage rhythm. Frankie writhed against and with him as he continued without restraint, each hard stroke driven by the force of his lower body. His fingers coiled in her hair. Hot and fast, Frankie climaxed violently, her body shaking, inner muscles clenched and clasped as she suckled his finger. He hammered into her with an aggression she met equally and exploded into her womb.

"Mine," he growled. "Only mine."

His hands gentled on her as sanity returned. Gage kissed the nape of her neck. She was damp with sweat, barely moving. Gage sat up and looked around. The linens beneath them were drenched. He quietly rose from the bed, tugged on discarded sweatpants and walked back to his own quarters.

Chapter 13

DISHARMONY BAY

"MY GRANDFATHER TOLD ME TO NEVER WASTE AN ERECTION."
Damon and Frankie stood side by side, doing the breakfast dishes that wouldn't fit in the dishwasher. She washed while he dried. Up to her elbows in lemon-scented detergent bubbles, she scrubbed furiously on a blackened frying pan. As was the custom, he was steering their conversation in his favorite direction.

S-E-X.

"Do I dare ask what other pearls of wisdom your grandfather imparted?"

"He said that I'd better use it as much as I can while I'm young, because in a few years it would stop working the way nature designed it."

"Really?"

Damon nodded his head. "Scary, huh?"

"Almost as frightening as the public bathroom in the fourth avenue Mini-Mart," she replied in all seriousness.

"Yep, I second that one. Grandpa also says that the older I get, the worse it will be. By the time I'm sixty, instead of getting a semiannual hard-on," he paused for a better grip on the slippery plate he was drying, "my sex life will deteriorate to an annual, semi hard-on. Nowadays, gramps is a happy camper if he can seduce some woman into fixing him a sandwich."

"What a grim legacy," she replied. "You don't think the malfunction was triggered by overuse, do you?"

"No way. It's not a malfunction, it's a genetic thing, some hereditary form of planned depreciation."

"No more jollies after age sixty, huh?" Frankie made a pained face. "Maybe you should put the gun to your head right now."

Damon missed the mockery in her voice and kept right on talking about what a ladies man his beloved grandpa had been in his prime. Frankie looked up. Across the room she met Gage's wicked smirk, directed at her. A clear reminder of just how hard he had been when he snuck into her bed the night before. Was he trying to drive her crazy? Surely he knew how much she craved his touch? How terribly she wanted him. Looking into his cool green eyes, Frankie was certain he knew exactly what she was thinking. She glanced away.

"So," she interrupted Damon. "I heard a rumor that your buddies at Station New Harbor have a new pair of night vision optics that they've been using to spy on the patrons of the Oceanview Bed and Breakfast."

Damon grinned, showing brilliant white teeth.

"It's not a rumor," he confirmed. "They're the most righteous binoculars on the market. Real quality optics made in Germany. Impressive."

"And the B and B guests?"

"Oh, the guests, yeah. Well, every night some of the guys take the inflatable out to check the channel marker buoys."

Frankie handed him a dripping pan.

"Any chance to get some practice navigating is a good one," she said nonchalantly.

"Did you know there's a hot tub on the deck of each suite? The place just screams extramarital sex. Fireplaces, champagne, foam mattresses that don't squeak. The nightly rates are orbital because every businessman on the coast wants to take his mistress there. I did some checking and found out there's a reservation waiting list almost two months long."

Frankie tried not to take the bait. "How long have you been spying on the guests at the B and B?"

"Spying is a strong word," Damon corrected.

"What description do you prefer?"

"Audience participation."

"Audience participation?" she echoed.

"You know what I'm talking about. Voyeurism. They perform and we watch. We are providing a highly valuable service to the residents of this community. The guests have sex on the balcony all the time and they do it because they know we're out there. It turns them on to know that we're watching them."

"You need counseling."

"I've got a better grip on reality than most people twice my age," he answered.

"You're too young to be so perverted."

Damon shrugged his broad shoulders and smiled. "I started early."

Frankie changed subjects.

"How are you coming along on our little bet?"

"You'll find out soon enough," he answered.

"Really?"

"I shagged Claire last weekend."

Frankie dropped a plastic bowl into the sink. It bounced twice before she caught it.

"Call her if you want a preview," he said defensively. "But she'll probably tell you all about it at your next alcoholics-un-anonymous gathering. I know how you girls love to talk."

"What?" she recovered quickly. "Your think the Sisterhood compares notes about your family jewels and prowess in a public setting? That would be extremely bad form, don't you think? Sort of like spying on the hotel guests of the local B and B. And for your information, we are not alcoholics."

"Oh no?" Damon laughed out loud. "You and your girlfriends have a gravitational pull towards tequila stronger than anything I've ever seen. It's almost cosmic."

"You're only twenty-four years old," she countered. "You haven't earned the right to make that kind of brash generalization."

"I may be young, but I've seen more than my fair share of drunk, rowdy women and your Sisterhood ranks right up there."

Frankie closed her eyes and prayed Sophia would be stronger than she had been. Her body clenched and ached at the thought of Gage's caresses. She longed for more. Whatever point he was trying to make, he'd done it. The man was in her blood. She was at her wit's end.

Frankie took a steadying breath and shook her head to clear it. She missed the good old days, the amiable banter, the teasing and laughter. She floated back on the memory of all that had passed between them. More than anything, she wanted her friend back.

Lately he had managed to find a way out of getting cornered. Every time she worked up the nerve to seek him out, she found him unapproachable. Exercising with Damon, helping Quinton or running the beach.

Gage was forever running the stupid beach.

Busy. Busy. Busy.

Had he started training for a friggin' triathlon or something? For a man who normally had tons of spare time, Gage Adams seemed to be keeping himself overly occupied lately. If she didn't know better, Frankie would have thought he was ignoring her.

The VHS radio crackled and Seaman George Harvey hailed them. Gage glared at the radio and grabbed the microphone.

"Go ahead, New Harbor," he spoke succinctly.

"Harmony Bay, we just received a medical distress call from the charter vessel *Mathilda May*."

Frankie and Damon looked at one another and shrugged. The scanner had been silent for hours. They hadn't overhead a distress call.

Quinton poked his head in from the garage to listen.

Seaman George continued, "Their skipper land-lined us to report one of his passengers complaining of severe abdominal pain. He has requested immediate assistance and possible medical evacuation."

Quinton's sun-bleached eyebrows lifted skyward. Damon stuck his finger in his mouth and crudely mimicked the act of vomiting. Frankie gave him an elbow in the ribs.

Gage scowled at them.

The *Mathilda May* was known within the boating community as a "puker". The streamlined motorboat was part of a small fleet working the tourist population. Frankie immediately understood why their skipper had used his cellular phone to place the call for help.

Competition was stiff amongst the tourist boats and reputation was everything. Gray whales migrated north up the coast to feed all summer before they returned to the Baja Peninsula in winter to mate and give birth. Landlubbers paid exorbitant prices to ply the waters alongside them and snap a few pictures.

It was early March, the whale-watching season had just begun and the fleet had a standing policy, a money-back guarantee to all of its clients. A whale *would* be sighted or their fees refunded. The result was a three-hour high speed, zigzag chase across the waves in search of the appropriate mammal. By the time a whale was spotted, most of the customers onboard were too seasick to hold their cameras steady.

Gage remained aloof while he scribbled coordinates.

"It figures," Damon groused as he suited up. "It wouldn't be March without a flight to a puker."

Quinton snapped the chinstrap of his helmet.

"Look at it this way, mate. At least we're getting it over early in the season."

Frankie grabbed her helmet. "Let's go guys. Maybe we can make this call the fastest of our careers."

Damon's head bobbed as he walked. "Get in, get the patient, get out."

Frankie redlined *Stella* to the boat. Quinton lowered Damon on the hoist in record time while she and Gage steadied them above thirty dismal sightseers below.

"Looks like a bunch of Martians down there," Quinton exclaimed.

"I bet next time they'll rent a wildlife video and stay home."

A six-foot swell combined with choppy waters to pitch and toss the boat about in constant, disorganized motion. Even some of the *Mathilda's* crew had also turned a putrid shade of green.

"I've never seen Damon work so fast," Gage piped up.

"Forward three. Prepare to hoist," Quinton instructed.

"Damn!" Frankie looked out her side window. "I don't see much movement in the litter. Is it possible to barf yourself into a coma?"

"Why don't you ask the Sisterhood next time you're powering down those pitchers of margaritas?" Gage teased.

"I'll do that."

Frankie felt a thud in back of the helo.

"Boom stowed. Ready for flight," Quinton calmly announced.

She worked the controls. They landed at the hospital while Damon was still giving a radio report to the ER personnel.

THE CALL TO STAND down from the inland wildfire came later that afternoon. Damon answered the phone and took the good news. "Awesome! Glad to hear it," he spewed to the fire boss on the other end of the line. "You're welcome. Anytime you need us, we're here for you, man." He disconnected and whooped for joy.

"The blaze is under control," he announced. The others gathered round to find out the cause of all the hoopla. "They don't need us anymore. Both the injured smokejumpers are going to be okay."

Frankie cheered and gave him a big hug.

"Excellent." Quinton high-fived Gage.

Damon paused in the celebration to launch an idea. "Hey, there's a new Greek restaurant in town that just opened this week. Why don't we drive into New Harbor for dinner?"

Quinton rubbed the grit out of his eyes. "Sounds good to me, mate. I don't think I can take another night of your cooking."

"Count me in," Frankie spoke. "I've got a bad case of cabin fever."

Gage gave her a strange look.

"How about you, LC?"

"Sure."

Within seconds, all four had piled into their official white van and headed south with Quinton behind the wheel and Damon riding shotgun. Frankie rolled down her window and enjoyed the crisp air. Beside her, Gage stared out the opposite window, his thoughts concealed behind reflective sunglasses.

New Harbor was bustling.

They hit the town limits and listened to Damon's running narration.

"Make a left on Monroe and follow it to the end of the street and turn into the first parking lot on the right," he said and glanced at his watch. "I hope we miss the dinner crowd."

"No worries, mate. We'll miss them."

Quinton turned and punched the accelerator. Damon's head snapped back. Up ahead, an orange and gold marquee marked their destination. They raced into the gravel parking lot and skidded to a halt. Damon was out of the van, scurrying to reserve a table before the dust had settled.

Frankie shook her head.

"I wonder what percentage of his monthly income is devoted to groceries?" she mused aloud.

Quinton grinned in the rearview mirror. He set the parking brake and got out.

"If you really want to know, I'll bet he has an entire computer file devoted to it," Gage answered and slammed the van door shut. "It should be easy enough to find. It'll be the only one with more megabytes of information than his sexual conquest list."

Quinton started chuckling.

"Conquest list?" Frankie asked in awe. "He keeps track of all the women he has, um," she struggled to find the right words, "had liaisons with?"

Quinton's laughter turned into guffaws that doubled him over.

"Liaisons?" Gage eyed her incredulously. "This isn't Elizabethan England, Frankie. What Damon has are called 'one-night-stands'."

"Are you telling me he keeps a running tally of them on the computer?"

"Of course he does."

Her face wrinkled into a frown. "What about the potential one-night-stands?"

Gage nodded. "And all the ones who got away."

Quinton turned heads with his laughter.

"Damon considers all information useful and saves it for later dissection and deliberation."

"You're kidding."

Gage gave her an over-the-glasses look. "I'm not kidding. He's a meticulous record keeper. Everything he's ever done is in a file on his laptop."

"I can't believe this! Why didn't I ever know about this?"

Their boots crunched gravel as they walked.

"Haven't you ever wondered about all those hours he's on the computer each day?"

"Well, I just figured he was doing a continuing education project."

Gage stifled his own laughter.

"He's farming, Frankie. The kid has a network of contacts that would put the CIA to shame."

Frankie trudged across the parking lot and did what she often did when she didn't know what else to do.

She kept her mouth shut.

MEDITERRANEAN SPICES AND SULTRY perfume permeated the restaurant. From concealed speakers came the subdued sound of Middle Eastern folk music.

They were hustled to a C-shaped booth by a thin man with ink-black eyes that never wavered from Frankie. She scooted in, sandwiched between Gage and Quinton. Damon handed her a menu.

"I want one of everything," she stated without looking.

"That's called a sampler platter," Damon spoke.

"That's exactly what I want, along with a small order of spanakopita."

"Span who?" Quinton asked.

"It's a spinach and feta cheese pie," Gage answered.

Quinton wrinkled his nose. "I'm not eating anything I can't pronounce the name of."

Damon spoke above the noise of musicians warming up. "Hey, it sounds like we've got live entertainment tonight." He thumbed a leaflet on the table. "Belly dancers too."

Frankie watched Quinton's face as he perused the menu.

"Do you want me to order for you?" Frankie asked.

"Abso-bloody-lutely. Get me something with red meat in it." Quinton scratched his head. "Why isn't this menu in English?" he complained.

"Because we're in a Greek restaurant," Gage interjected.

Frankie was giggling when the waiter came back to take their order. She had to raise her voice to be heard above the music and tinkle of cymbals.

"Whoa!" Damon exclaimed. "Check it out!"

She glanced up to see two sequin-covered mammaries jiggling in time to a drum solo. She widened her field of vision and found that attached to those impressive breasts was an exotic beauty methodically whirling her way through the crowded tables directly towards them.

Large, almond eyes, heavy with black kohl, peered out from behind a veil. Waist-length coils of black hair twinkled with jewels that caught the light in a prism of colors.

"Look at her," Damon groveled. "Now that is one hot babe."

"Down, boy," Frankie warned.

It was impossible not to look at her. Dressed in flowing layers of chiffon and embroidered silk, the woman's serpentine movements were outrageously sensual. Frankie was caught in the same spell as everyone else in the restaurant. They all stopped to gawk as the exquisite dancer shimmied across the glossy parquet floor.

Heading right to their table.

Drawn like a moth to flame.

Frankie held her breath.

"Here we go again," she whispered and shook her head.

The dancer halted directly in front of Gage and glided into a series of carnal undulations that had every male heart in the restaurant working double-time. Sliding her talented pelvis in circles, the dancer's hips looped into a mesmerizing figure-eight pattern. Sinuous arms, adorned with snaky copper bangles, plied the air in time to the music.

Frankie glanced at Gage, swallowed hard and gave herself over to the first harsh waves of resentment.

The dancer's rounded belly rolled in a subtle wave that brought an uncontrolled squeal from Damon. She fought the urge to haul off and smack him. Quinton started to chuckle. Frankie wanted to smack him too.

The tempo of the music sped up. Attuned to the beat, the dancer paused briefly, smiled at Gage and began to shimmy her hips in a wild blur of motion that brought cat-calls from the crowd around them. Triangular rows of tinkling coins and fringe flipped riotously through the air.

Frankie flashed Gage a surreptitious glance. His attention was riveted on the dancer. A lecherous smile brushed the corners of his mouth. Frankie's gaze dropped to the napkin in his lap. She squinted in the darkness of the corner booth.

The napkin was tented!

Frankie jerked her head away and immediately lost her appetite.

SHE WAS STILL FUMING about the belly dancer incident when she found Gage alone in the laundry room later that night. Quietly, she shut the door behind them and took a heavy breath. The smell of fabric softener permeated the air. Liquid detergent and chlorine bleach tickled her nose. Having methodically sorted through all available options, she settled on the one that had the most marginal chance of success.

Everything hinged on Gage's willingness.

"Okay, here's the deal," she said suddenly.

He glanced over from stuffing wet shirts into the dryer. "Deal?" His curiosity kicked into turbo drive.

Frankie cleared her throat. "Tit for tat. You take care of me and I'll grant you something in return."

"Take care of you?" he asked dumbly, his head halfway inside the dryer.

Her foot tapped, "I'm talking about sex without any emotional complications."

Gage's mouth fell open in surprise.

"What?"

"You heard me. Don't play dumb."

Gage blinked. Frankie took a shaky breath.

"There's nothing wrong with your hearing," she barked. "I won't say it again."

"I'm thinking," he stalled.

"Make it quick," she snapped. "This is a one-time offer. Take it or leave it."

Gage stood up and hovered over her, pinning her with a heated stare.

"If I refuse, will you take your generous transaction elsewhere?"

"Absolutely," she sneered.

That was the biggest, fattest lie she had told since she was eight years old and had blamed the family dog for breaking her mother's favorite vase. Her body knew what it needed and there could be no substitute. It was Gage or nobody. If she pulled this one off, she should get a damned academy award!

"What do I get in return for being your whore?"

Frankie's jaw quivered, then tensed. "What do you want?"

His voice lowered an octave and took on a calm quality. "I've never seen you this desperate."

"I'm serious, not desperate," she reassured. "I need you to take the edge off whatever this hormonal thing is that's driving me crazy. I can't sleep. My stomach hurts all the time. I think I'm getting an ulcer." Frankie clenched her fists at her side. "I need your help."

"Do I have to carry a beeper?"

There was a dark undercurrent to his voice that threatened to pull her under. Frankie shot him a scathing look. Gage threw his hands up in mock surrender.

"Sorry," he grinned.

"What do you want from me in return?" she repeated.

Gage took a moment to consider.

"Teach me how to waltz," he blurted.

"I don't know how to waltz and you know it."

"Then we'll learn together. Parks and Recreation offers a class twice a year. I'll sign us up for the next one."

Frankie's wary gaze narrowed. His eyes were gleaming.

"Is that too much to ask for being your sex slave?"

"No, I guess not."

"Good. Then I'll ask for one thing more."

Frankie held her breath. She should have known that a dance class was too easy a trade. What was coming now?

He took a step forward and loomed over her. "I don't believe in sharing. If I accept this arrangement of yours, I want exclusivity." He pointed to his chest and then hers. "You don't sleep with anyone but me. Understood?"

Frankie started to protest. Gage moved closer and boxed her in. "You only sleep with me," he repeated. "Or it's not going to happen."

"Okay."

"Then you have a deal," he agreed with a grin. "When do we start?"

Her hungry gray eyes roamed his body without restraint. He was hard and powerful, a perfectly proportioned treasure trove of sexual delight. Frankie gnawed her lower lip. She had been smoldering for days. She needed him, wanted him. In a trembling voice she managed to answer, "I'm not sure I can wait much longer."

Gage arched a triumphant dark eyebrow, reached around her and thumbed the lock on the door.

Chapter 14

ADVICE FROM THE SISTERHOOD

A STEADY FLOW OF CUSTOMERS DRIFTED IN AND OUT OF THE PIONEER BREWPUB. IN the background, a dozen conversations blended into white noise. Frankie sifted through the cacophony and honed in on the most bizarre. No surprise, it came from her table.

"He had what stuck where?"

Before anyone could blurt an answer, Frankie cupped her ears with both hands and tried to visualize a kinder, gentler world.

Sophia's face contorted in a rictus of horror.

Frankie whistled to drown out the voices. By the time it was safe to remove her fingers, the girls had moved on to another sizzling topic. She topped off her margarita glass from the pitcher and gave thanks to the God of Short Attention Span.

"We've tried," Claire tried to explain. "I swear that woman is coated with Teflon. Nothing ever sticks to her."

There were nods and shouts of agreement all around.

A few of the Sisterhood complained about the latest in a string of incompetent nursing managers. From the general insults being volleyed about the table, it was a hot subject. Experienced nurses were difficult to come by and even harder to control. Managing them was like herding cats. Frankie grinned at the thought.

"We need to find an alternative for her," Sophia encouraged.

"Like what?" Claire spat. "A fragmentation hand grenade?" She gesticulated wildly, her wrinkled cotton shirt billowing in her own tumultuous wind.

"Calm down," Sophia soothed.

"Claire is right. That woman is a complete waste of egg and sperm," Kristin chimed in.

Frankie wrinkled her nose. She reached over, refilled an empty glass and pressed it to Sophia's lips.

"Is that a hint?"

"You're falling behind," Frankie replied. "Drink up or you'll never hold your own in an argument with them."

Frankie glanced up just in time to see Lauren emerge from the dim hallway to the public bathrooms. A fluttering length of toilet paper dangled off the heel of her shoe. Andie was a few steps behind, kangaroo-hopping, trying to dislodge the white streamer. Frankie smiled and held her breath, hoping that Lauren would be spared the humiliation of knowing what was going on behind her. The rest of the Sisterhood continued their discussion, oblivious.

"All humans make mistakes and all leaders are human," Sophia patronized, ending the statement with a loud hiccup.

"That's my point," Claire said stubbornly. "She's not a leader and I'm not even certain she's human. The staff is in turmoil because of the situations she's mishandled. In the best interests of the unit, she has a moral obligation to resign."

"Morals?" Sophia spoke in a stern voice. "Since when has that word ever been in your vocabulary?"

Claire shot her a look that embodied every four-letter word she could think of.

"Time out!" Andie stood before the table. She put her forefingers up to form a wide X. "We need to move along to a new topic. I've listened to this one for months. It's overcooked." She plopped down in a chair and took a deep draw from her glass. "Incompetent managers should never interfere with the Sisterhood and their drinking habits."

"Okaaaay," Claire drawled and popped a handful of popcorn into her mouth. "What do you want to talk about?"

"Let's talk about dicks," Kristin blurted.

Lauren gave her an imperious glare. "Real men named Dick? Or real dicks who also happen to be men?" she asked.

Kristin smiled. "Remember the paramedic with the beautiful body and eyes to die for that I was telling you about last week?"

The other women leaned closer.

"Last weekend I finally got into his pants." Kristin paused in her confession to take a sip.

"What took you so long?"

"Give me a break! I was off my game, recuperating from the flu."

"Hey! I want to hear about his dick," Sophia said loudly.

The crowded pub grew silent.

"His penis makes a forty-degree turn to the right in mid-shaft," Kristin said and giggled. "Nature must've designed it for those hard to reach places."

Lauren choked on her margarita.

"There's a medical term for that condition," Andie sniffed.

"Yeah, it's called being in high demand with the ladies," Claire burped.

"Was there anything else odd about it?" Sophia asked.

"Isn't that enough?"

Andie drained her glass. "It's always a good idea to take a close look at a man's unit before proceeding," she advised the group. "Preferably in a well-lit room. You never know what he might be hiding in the dark."

"No, honestly," Kristin continued, "It was so strange looking, that I lost track of what I meant to do."

"Which was?"

"Okay," Lauren interrupted. "I know I'm in the minority here, but I can't take anymore penis-talk," she shuddered.

Frankie signaled for another round of drinks. "I concur with Lauren. No more penis stories, please. Isn't there some other body part that interests you?"

Andie squinted and pointed directly at Frankie.

"Legs."

Frankie let out a grunt and quickly launched a diversion. "I thought you were more interested in my gritty details about Vin Diesel's visit. After all, you spent the first hour of Margarita Monday grilling me about him."

Andie refused to be derailed. "You've already made it clear that until he calls and the two of you can spend more than a few minutes riding his Harley, you don't actually have any gritty details to discuss," Andie said loudly. "Until that happens, let's deal in realities."

Frankie swallowed a lump in her throat.

Andie continued, "I have a hunch about what occurred after Max and I left your house the other evening. Are you willing to confirm or deny my suspicions?"

Frankie closed her eyes and exhaled a sigh.

"I thought so."

"Confirm what?" Kristen shouted.

Lauren leaned over and asked, "What happened between your legs?" Red-faced, Lauren corrected herself quickly. "What I meant was, between you and Legs."

There was a moment of absolute silence and then Claire squealed with sudden insight. "Did Legs get between your legs?"

All heads in the bar swiveled their way. On a gasp, the Sisterhood leaned forward simultaneously, hunkered over the littered table, and pinned Frankie with earnest stares.

"Come on," Claire needled. "We're going to find out sooner or later, Frankie."

"Give it up, girlfriend," Andie urged.

Sophia's brown eyes were huge. "Please Frankie, tell us all about Legs. He's got a dangerous look to him. Were you scared?"

Frankie looked down. Her stomach was in knots. "It was a pity-fuck," she whispered.

Sophia didn't get it. "You pity him, what?"

Lauren rolled her eyes and leaned over to whisper in the younger woman's pink tipped ear. Sophia let out a gasp.

"No," Andie shook her head.

"It's true," Frankie confirmed. "Not that he doesn't care for me as a friend, of course."

Andie gestured with open hands. "What are you saying?"

"That he was obligated to show me a good time."

Andie was still shaking her head, flinging long tendrils of chestnut hair into Lauren's face. "I don't believe that. You are way off! It goes against everything I saw in his eyes."

"A good time?" Sophia asked. "What sort of good time?"

Lauren looked at her and barked, "You really need to get out more often."

"What do you mean? I get out all the time. I'm very athletic. I hike and ski."

Frankie interrupted, eager to get her troubles off her chest. "A good time means that he found out I was incapable of having an orgasm and he fixed the problem." She paused to let her words sink in.

Claire's drink slipped out of numb fingers and crashed to the table in an explosion of white froth. The bar grew eerily quiet. Lauren, Sophia and Kristen sat paralyzed, staring at her with looks of shock and revulsion. Andie cradled her head between both hands and moaned.

Edgar scurried over to clean up the mess.

"Gage was your first orgasm?" Claire asked.

"Yes," Frankie nodded, indifferent of who might overhear. "He was kind enough to spend the entire week with me, let me experiment and stuff. Now we have an arrangement."

"Kind enough?" Sophia parroted. "Arrangement?"

Frankie blushed. "We made a deal to take care of one another's sexual needs."

Kristin's accent was strong and slurred. "Are you telling us that Legs is now your fuck-buddy?"

"I prefer the term *friends with privileges.*"

"That's terrible," Sophia wailed.

"That's ridiculous." Andie shook her head wildly. "Wait a minute. Let's find some clarity amidst this profound confusion." She took a slurp from her glass. "Max and I were there for dinner, remember? It's no hallucination on my part. We both saw it. Gage really cares for you."

"Of course he cares. He's one of my most trusted friends," Frankie replied calmly.

Frankie looked at each woman in turn. "Really," she stressed. "He wanted nothing more than to prove I was able to get off." A hint of sadness tugged at the corners of her mouth. "He got his wish. I even saw spots—before I fainted."

A chorus of, "You fainted?" arose from the Sisterhood.

"Hyperventilated first, then fainted. I was naked, with his head, uh, you know, between my..."

"Bloody hell," Claire exclaimed.

"Jesus, Mary and Joseph!" Kristin shouted and mumbled something in *Gaelic.*

"I'm so sorry for you," Sophia apologized. "How horrifying."

Frankie shrugged as she distanced herself emotionally. "Let's just say it would have been a whole lot easier to take if it had happened to someone else."

Lauren, always business-minded, wanted specific facts about the deal. She spoke up quickly. "You said you made a bargain with him. What terms are involved besides sex? Did you sign a contract? What happens if he defaults?"

Frankie shook her head. "He won't. That's not his style. Besides, he wants to learn how to waltz."

Lauren's bushy blonde eyebrows rose skyward. Andie rolled her eyes again and slugged down the rest of her drink. Frankie thought she heard her say "bullshit".

"He signed us up for a class next month. We're going to learn together."

"Anything else?" Lauren urged.

"I'm not allowed to sleep with anybody else during the duration of our deal."

Kristin and Claire simultaneously cursed and gave each other a knowing look. Andie clutched her stomach. "This is such utter crap I think I'm going to be sick."

GAGE EASED FORWARD IN his chair and rubbed his stubbly chin. He could barely hear her low voice above the background noise of chitchat and laughter. From the regulars at the bar who recognized both he and Frankie, Gage received a mixed review of *atta-boy* looks and *what-the-hell-are-you-thinking?* From a booth beside the glassed-in room that housed Pioneer's stainless steel brewery vats, he glanced up to acknowledge pity on Edgar's solemn face.

Gage shook his head in exasperation.

With the stealth of a culprit, he had slipped into the bar an hour before the scheduled Sisterhood gathering with the sole intent of spying on Frankie during their monthly drunk-fest. He hoped she might confide in her girlfriends, since he'd been left out of the information loop, and had spinelessly resorted to using covert methods. He was hearing a lot more than he ever expected. He was confused and stunned by the bargain she had struck with him. He had been trying to lay low and give Frankie the opportunity to sort things out when she blindsided him with her offer of sex. And now, listening to her ramble, he was clueless why she felt the heat between them was merely some hormonal thing.

Frankie was spilling her guts.

She'd actually convinced herself she meant nothing more to him than an occasional one-night-stand to vent the hormone overload. What the hell had he ever said to make her think that? Only Andie had the vague notion there might be more to it and at the moment she was vastly outnumbered.

How was he supposed to fix this mess?

Women! He never professed to understand more than their physical needs. He eased back in the booth, rubbed his aching head.

At least, she wasn't as enamored of her favorite actor as he first suspected. She downplayed the entire visit. Even when the Sisterhood called her on it, accusing her of holding out on them, Frankie seemed almost indifferent.

As Gage contemplated her odd behavior, two inebriated loggers approached the Sisterhood's table in an attempt to strike up conversation. They were quintessential 'mean drunks'. Burly and rude, emboldened by alcohol to act on the nastiness that always lurked in the back of their minds.

Gage watched intently. Edgar never allowed his customers to be hassled, but the big man might need a hand. He was relieved when Edgar sent them on their way with a few quiet words.

A familiar voice, pitched low, sounded behind him.

"Hey, LC. Scoot over."

Dressed in black jeans and a ratty Foo Fighters shirt, Damon slithered onto the hard bench and peered around the corner.

Gage groaned. "Let me guess," he spoke quietly. "Your visit has something to do with Sophia."

"Right on target, as always." Damon took a swig of beer from Gage's bottle and immediately zeroed his attention on the gregarious table of females.

"Nice place."

"It was until you got here."

Damon glanced around at memorabilia collected from over three decades of commercial fishing and logging.

"Hey, LC. I recognize that blue fender. It came off a catamaran that capsized last year."

Gage looked up and nodded. "The *Egret.*"

"That's the one. Didn't the owner get slapped with some heavy maritime fines?"

"No."

"Why not?"

"The courts claimed *Egret* wasn't the burdened vessel."

Damon frowned. "That's not how I remember it."

"The *Egret* was owned by the Governor's son."

Damon shook his head. "LC, you remember everything, don't you? Like, total recall or something."

Gage gave him a look.

The smell of grease wafted out from the kitchen as a waitress swept by hefting a tray of burgers. Damon's attention diverted to her backside.

"Did I miss any good gossip at the Sisterhood's table?"

"Not much," Gage said casually. "Sophia commented on how much she's looking forward to riding you like a pony."

"Really?"

"Says she can hardly wait for her turn in the saddle and after Claire's testimonial on your abilities, even Lauren is thinking about making the switch."

Damon's boyish face brightened at the suggestion.

"Lauren? You're kidding. Do you think I could convert her?"

Gage threw his hands up in disgust.

"I'll take that as *no.*" Damon scratched his day-old growth of beard. "I came here hoping to get a handle on Sophia," he continued. "You know, try to get closer to her and find out what makes her tick. Something about the girl has me stumped."

"How about 'good taste'?"

"What about you," Damon continued, ignoring the insult. "Frankie still got you tied in knots?"

"Go to hell, kid."

He craned his neck, "You know, if you ever want to talk about women and what it takes to make them happy, I'm here for ya, dude. I was trained by the best."

Gage stared incredulously. He could think of only two things he'd rather do less. "Thanks for the offer. I'll pass."

"Seriously, LC. I'm a chick-magnet. I might even be able to help *you.*"

"I don't need anyone's help. Especially yours."

Damon looked offended but didn't back off. "You're not exactly scoring big points on the home front. Somebody needs to lend you a hand and I happen to know a lot about women. They're my specialty."

"Don't get me started, kid. I'll just get pissed off all over again."

"Okay, okay. But don't say I never offered. If you change your mind, you know where I'll be." Damon grinned widely and launched into another tirade. "So, I was talking to some of my bros yesterday and we came up with a great idea."

Gage braced himself.

"How about you and I go diving on Zena this week?"

Let's go diving on Zena.

Damon made it sound so simple. Just strap on a tank and start paddling. Gage arched a dark eyebrow. The truth was, exactly that thought had crossed his mind several times since the accident. Somehow, Gage found it irksome that the kid was first to openly make the suggestion. He glanced at Frankie across the room. Her petulant lower lip jutted out while she stirred her margarita with a finger.

"You know how much sentimental value TB puts on those dog tags," Damon continued. "Why don't we grab our scuba gear, take your boat and go get them for her? I got the coordinates from Sakajawea's logs. It'll be a quick grab-and-go."

Gage clutched his beer. Plenty of chores waited at home. He hadn't swept the floors or dusted since Christmas. The grass in the back pasture was high enough to hide a velociraptor and he was still having plumbing problems, this time the kitchen.

He heaved a deep sigh.

Who was he kidding? He hadn't done a thing since thoughts of seducing Frankie started filling his brain. She consumed him. House chores were on indefinite hold. He had to straighten this mess out with her first.

Let's go diving on Zena.

Gage smiled inwardly and pondered how it might play out. He could show up on her doorstep, the precious dog tags wrapped in a velvet box. She would be speechless with shock and grateful. After she writhed in ecstasy underneath him, her defenses down, maybe he could hammer some sense into her postorgasmic head and flush all those other crazy misconceptions down the toilet. Gage considered all the possibilities while Damon yammered on about the dive, oblivious to the furor of emotions seated beside him.

"Zena's on stable ocean floor at about a hundred and thirty feet. The helmsman on Sakajawea did a sonar sounding and plotted her exact location after she went down."

Gage quietly sipped his beer.

"It's a straightforward dive. We can make it on one tank of air."

Gage thought a few moments longer then nodded. "Meet me at the marina on Thursday morning with the coordinates."

"Outstanding." Damon high-fived him. "I've got a new BC vest I want to try out."

A battle of wooden chair legs versus tile floor reverberated across the bar. Both men looked up in time to see Frankie bolt to her feet in a feculent huff. They dipped low in the booth, stayed in the shadows. Her spotting them now would ruin everything.

"Sssh," Damon whispered. "Here she comes."

Edgar suddenly moved to block her line of sight, keeping his considerable bulk in front of the small booth. Frankie stumbled past him on her way to the bathroom, dodging a barstool and dart throwers. She muttered loudly, "I'm just a pity-fuck to him," she groused. "That's all I am to him. Nothing more. Damned pretty boy."

Edgar turned and placed drinks on the table. He laid a heavy hand on Gage's shoulder. "You look like a desperate man on a hopeless mission, son."

139

"You don't know the half of it, Edgar," Gage replied.

"Sounds like you've got your work cut out for you, Lieutenant," he commiserated. "Can't say I envy you the prospect. That's one tough little lady and she's got some mighty strange ideas in that pretty head of hers." Edgar stared at him. "Wonder why she'd have her wires so crossed?"

"Because he's such a gnarly electrician," Damon interjected with a wicked grin.

Gage grumbled an unintelligible response and threw his wallet on the table. Damon grabbed it and thumbed out a hundred.

"Thanks for the beer, LC."

"I sure hope you can work things out with her." Edgar took the bill and made change from a wad of smaller notes in his vest pocket. "You know," he began, his heavy jowls quivering. "I've been watching women, looking out for them, listening to them laugh and cry for most of my life. I still ain't figured them out. They don't think the way we do. Not that I mean that in a disrespectful way. It's just a fact."

"Absolutely," Damon concurred.

"They're a challenge," Edgar spoke. "But our lives sure would be dull without them."

"Amen," Damon cheered.

Edgar gave Damon a disdainful look and turned back to Gage. "You're not someone who backs down from a challenge, Lieutenant. Everyone here wants to see you find some happiness. We're all pulling for you to make a go of it with the little redhead."

"I wouldn't bet any money on me if I were you," Gage said softly.

"Don't give up, son. My wife thinks you've got a lot of love to give. I agree with her."

Gage glanced away as Edgar wandered off to serve another customer. He stared straight ahead, running frustrated hands through his hair. How the hell did things go so bad between him and Frankie? What did he say wrong? Why was it so damned difficult for him to have what normal guys had?

A wife?

Kids?

Loving family to rush home to after a long week at work?

He glanced over at Damon. The kid's mouth had slowed to a steady stream of one-way conversation as he scrutinized Sophia from across the room. Gage cocked an eyebrow at him. Did he ever stop? Would he still be yapping a hundred feet beneath the ocean with a scuba regulator in his mouth? He envisioned a cauldron of bubbles boiling up around him. Gage shook his head to clear it and scanned the other occupants of the Brewpub.

The licentious brunette was there, wearing roughly the same button-popping blouse she was in the month before. She gave him a blatantly sexual look. Gage held her gaze a moment before moving on. She was not what he needed. Damon prattled on about the joys of group sex. Gage tuned him out. He was too preoccupied. He couldn't shake the sinking feeling that the situation between he and Frankie was going to get worse before it got better, no matter what he tried to say. He upended another pint of ale and scratched his head.

THE LOCAL BAND WAS warming up when Frankie stumbled back to her table. She had a raging pre-hangover headache and her stomach was growling so loudly she could hear it over the noise in the bar. She stood behind her vacant chair and swayed side to side like a reed in a stiff breeze. The Sisterhood was now venting its animosity on the hospital's new surgeon.

"Physician and sperm," Claire compared, "I think they both have a one-in-a-million chance of becoming a human being."

Frankie winced, slanted a quick glance at Andie and staggered off in the direction of the stage as a microphone-enhanced voice boomed across the bar.

"Good evening, ladies and gentlemen," the guitar-playing singer announced. "Our first tune tonight is dedicated to all the single ladies in the audience."

The grubby bandleader winked at Frankie.

Screeching metallic noise flooded the room from enormous freestanding speakers. Frankie was blown an involuntary step backwards. Half a dozen anorexic girls dressed in Goth black and spiked dog collars materialized out of nowhere. Edgar's youngest daughter Mia was among them. Frankie blinked. Where had all these funky kids come from? "Now I know I'm getting old," she mumbled.

She felt, rather than saw, someone sidle up next to her.

Andie bent down to her ear and spoke above the jarring din. "One of my brothers had a garage band when he was a teenager. He told me that his secret to success was making enough noise with his guitar that nobody could tell how awful his voice really was."

Andie gave the bandleader a sly smile.

"What does your brother do now?"

"He owns a record company."

Both women laughed.

"You know," Andie said, "For years I was a veritable queen at bullshitting myself. You've heard the lines—*I'm happy being single. I don't need a man to make me whole. I'm much too busy for a relationship. I can't get over the last asshole that did me wrong.* You get the idea." She stopped to clear her throat. "I was so good at fooling myself that when the real thing finally came along I didn't even recognize its worth." Andie grimaced. "I was so certain that love would never happen to me, I kept pushing it away. Being stubborn isn't always a virtue, Frankie. I was such an ass that it nearly cost me the love of my life."

Frankie blinked. She could feel Andie's hot breath in her ear.

"There's no reason for you to give in to the Sisterhood's curiosity. You don't owe us a damned thing. It's none of our business. We're all a well-meaning bunch of gossip-hounds." She paused. "At least be honest with yourself, girlfriend. You owe yourself that much."

"I can't hang onto something that's not there," Frankie answered. "Gage has never given me any reason to believe that I'm anything other than some needy friend he's obligated to take care of."

Andie cringed. "Frankie, I love you. But I still think you're full of shit."

Frankie shrugged.

"Gage doesn't strike me as the type to make sex an obligation."

"Are you implying our agreement is foolish?"

"Not foolish, perplexing. You and Gage need to have a long talk and get on the same page. I think there's more to your relationship than you're letting yourself comprehend."

Frankie stared at her friend for a moment then gazed back to the band. A few seconds of blaring music passed while neither woman attempted to speak.

Andie bent close again. "The girls are ready to leave. We've consumed all the tequila in the bar and Edgar has officially cut us off."

"All the tequila?" Frankie squealed. "Again? No wonder my head is swirling. Let's get out of here before I embarrass myself."

GAGE AND DAMON WATCHED as the Sisterhood left a generous tip on the table and staggered, single-file, to the rippled sidewalk outside the pub. Last in line was Sophia. Trailing behind the others, her wavy dark hair swayed with each step. She was almost out the front entrance when she stopped abruptly, turned and made a frantic dash for the bathroom, bowling over chairs and dancers in a clumsy sprint. The other women continued up the street unaware of her fate.

"Whaddya think, LC? Is she going to make it there in time?"

"I think you need to go check on her."

Damon was already on his feet, more than happy for any excuse to enter the hallowed porcelain domain of the women's bathroom. So much the better, Gage thought. He could use a few moments alone to figure things out.

"What did I say to make her think she's only my plaything?" he whispered to himself.

He chewed his lip and tried to remember every argument. There were plenty of them to consider. Hurtful words had been flung back and forth for what seemed an eternity yet nothing specific came to mind.

Couldn't she tell by the way he treated her when they were together that she was more than a fuck-buddy?

He was brooding when Andie came stomping back into the pub looking for Sophia. She gave a cursory, no-nonsense glance at the patrons of the cramped establishment and proceeded directly to where Sophia and her high-octane tummy had gone.

"Damn it," he whispered.

Gage glanced over and met Edgar's amused smirk.

"Swordsman!"

Damon spun to face the voice calling him by nickname, ready to defend his actions. "Andie?" Damon quickly lowered his defensive stance and went immediately to the offense. "Hey lady, how are ya doing? It's been a long time. You're looking great. Are you still married?"

Andie surged forward through the heavily perfumed lavatory, dodging unidentifiable wet spots puddling the floor.

"What are you doing in here?" she demanded.

"Me? Oh, I'm helping Sophia get cleaned up," he answered sheepishly and pointed toward an open stall. "She had a little accident."

Sophia swayed precariously. Damon was there in a flash to catch her before she fell. Andie scurried over. Sophia's eyes were wide with the blatant look of surprise coming from sudden, uncontrollable regurgitation. She let out a violent belch.

Andie met Damon's wary look.

"I'm sure she's finished," he said. "There can't be much left in her stomach."

Andie nodded. "She's never had much tolerance for alcohol. Let's get her washed up and I'll take her home."

Together they dragged her from the bathroom stall.

"After all these years of drinking, she still can't hold her liquor? Why does she go out drinking with you girls?"

Andie glanced at him impatiently. "I assume she enjoys our company."

Sophia let out another burp and blurted, "Why don't you just ask me? I'm standing right here?"

Damon veered them toward the sink. "You hang out with a pretty rowdy bunch, Sophia. What's the attraction?"

The faucet cranked on with a gush.

"Admiration," Sophia stuttered.

"Really? Why's that?"

Damon rinsed her hands. There was a long pause while Sophia's murky thoughts coalesced into something verbal.

"Because they're everything I'm not."

"And what would that be?" he asked with a bit too much interest.

"Naughty."

Andie coughed.

"Sexy," Sophia continued. "Confident."

The pulse in Damon's neck raced like a greyhound after a rabbit. Sophia looked up into his face. "You have the most beautiful eyes," she mumbled. "It is true that they change color and sparkle like sapphires before you come?"

"Well, I've never watched myself come. I could try next time and let you know how it turns out."

"So, Damon," Andie interrupted, "Why are you here?"

"Here? Right here?" His eyes narrowed. It was time for some creative half-truths. "Gage and I were in town for dinner and stopped by to have a drink. I happened to notice Sophia making a run for the lavatory. She was looking distressed so I thought I'd see if I could help out."

Andie splashed cool water over Sophia's face. "Gage is here?" she asked.

Damon mumbled something intelligible, suddenly realizing that not only was he caught, but he'd handed over Gage as well. Sophia stared at him with a dreamy look that signaled she either wanted to be kissed or was on the verge of passing out. The odds were fifty-fifty.

"How long have you and Gage been here?"

"Oh, about—"

Sophia interrupted by pulling on his sleeve. "Did you need antibiotics for those scratch marks Claire says are on your back?"

Andie groaned. Damon grinned, grabbed a paper towel and dabbed at the corners of Sophia's damp mouth. "Better?" He thought it best to ignore her question.

"A little," she nodded. "Is it really true that your unit can make women see spots?"

"I think it's time to go," he hedged. "I've gotten myself in enough trouble for one night."

With Sophia wedged tight between them, they squeezed down the musty hall. The three zigzagged their way to the front door. Unbelievably, the bar was even more crowded.

"Damon, you never answered how long you and Gage have been here?" Andie reminded.

Damon saw the wheels of her mind spinning. "Oh, not too long."

"Where are you sitting?" she asked.

"Near the fermentation vats."

Andie craned her neck and honed her vision in on the corner booth. Gage sat at a table littered with the empty bottles. "Not too long, huh?" With humor sparkling behind the warmth of her eyes, she raised a hand and waved. Gage grimaced and slunk down in the booth.

"Thank you, Damon," she spoke loudly and winked. "I think I can handle Sophia from here. Have yourself a wonderful night. Tell Gage that I wish him the best of luck. He's going to need it."

The band geared up for another spine-jarring number. Andie caught Sophia gawking at Damon's crotch. "I'm sure I'll be hearing about you soon." With that, she clutched Sophia's arm tightly and the two of them weaved off down the street.

EDGAR WATCHED ANDIE AND Sophia leave before wandering over to Gage. "They cleaned me out of tequila again. I sure hope they make it home okay."

Gage was beat, depressed, dejected. The women were on their own tonight. He wasn't up for another welfare check.

"Sorry to hear it, Edgar. Maybe you should talk to your tequila distributor about placing a larger order next month."

A sea of bodies converged on the dance floor. Gage was relieved to see the amorous brunette had changed tactics and quarry. She had secured Damon by the wrist and was leading him to center stage for a dance.

Gage stood up and stretched. He was exhausted. It was time for bed. Catching Damon's gleaming eye, he waved him over. The kid frowned and headed his way.

"This better be good. She's hot."

"Go check on the Sisterhood," he ordered.

"Why me? I haven't been laid for almost twenty-four hours." He pointed to the brunette. "She's a sure thing!"

"Stop sniveling. The brunette will still be here when you get back. I need you to make sure nobody bleeds to death from one of Andie's IV starts. She's been around since leeching was in vogue. Be sure you tell her I said that."

"How do you know the brunette will still be here when I'm done checking on the Sisterhood?"

"Because she's Edgar's oldest daughter. She always closes the place down."

Damon's eyes grew wide with worry.

"Relax. I'm only kidding," Gage confessed.

Damon gave a nervous laugh. "Don't scare me like that, LC!"

"Flip the brunette a twenty on your way out. She's a working girl out of Portland. She'll probably wait for you."

Damon looked horrified. "I never pay for sex!"

Gage rolled his eyes.

"Okay, okay. I'll go check on the girls. Maybe I can get more scoop on Sophia."

Damon headed off for the nearest exit yelling something about Andie and payback. All Gage could clearly hear was, "See you Thursday morning."

Gage stood up and left the way he came in.

Chapter 15

BENT

FLUORESCENT LIGHTS FLICKERED INSIDE THE HYPERBARIC OXYGEN CHAMBER AND WENT dark. Andie Daniels stood in the anteroom and made a brief notation in the daily log. She scooped up a few outdated magazines, threw them in the trash and reached for her wrinkled lab coat.

She promised to meet Max for dinner. A message, written with a bar of soap on the bathroom mirror, had ordered her to 'come straight home after work.' She had a hunch there was a surprise waiting. Andie had seen remnants of colorful wrapping paper in his wastebasket during a frantic search for her car keys that morning. It was too early for her birthday and their anniversary was months away.

Since their marriage, nursing had become a part-time undertaking done for personal satisfaction. Today had been no exception. For six hours, she entertained a friendly group of diabetics suffering from wound ulcers, while they sniffed higher than average oxygen levels under pressure and listened to classical music.

"Andie?"

"I'm in here."

The chamber's office manager rumbled into the anteroom a few seconds after her perfume. Yards of rayon skirt whipped pink roses violently around her chunky ankles. Air flowed in and out of her nostrils in a harsh sound.

"What's up, Priscilla? You look stressed."

"We've got a problem. I know your shift is over and I've notified the on-call nurse but there are two patients being flown in from the coast with an ETA of five minutes. It will take Nicole thirty minutes to get here. Can you stay until she arrives?"

"You bet I can," Andie replied without a second thought. "What's the story on them?"

"Two males with serious decompression sickness who'd been diving on a wreck."

Andie geared up. She shed her lab coat and flipped the switch operating the interior lights and power. Priscilla grabbed two blank charts and started the admission paperwork, following behind Andie while she talked.

"Word from the emergency department is they were trapped inside, overshot their decompression time and had to make an emergency ascent to the surface."

Andie felt a shiver of intuition crawl down her spine.

"Any concurrent injuries?" she asked with trepidation.

"Unknown. The report I got was a heads-up. A Coast Guard helicopter is bringing them in."

Andie nodded. "Please let me know as soon as you've identified them."

Priscilla reached into her pocket and produced a scrap of paper. "Here," she handed it to Andie. "I scribbled their names down. I was in quite a hurry, my writing's barely legible."

Andie read the names, inhaled sharply.

"Priscilla, do me a big favor."

"Anything."

"Call my husband and let him know I won't be home till late."

PAIN.

An explosion of excruciating pain.

Agony wracked every joint in his body, contorting him at violent angles.

"Damon?" he called out. "Damon!"

"Relax," came soothing words. "Let us help you."

It was the voice of morphine. The same voice that had answered the same question innumerable times, knowing he could not remember the answer and would not be able to for quite some time.

Through the haze of drugs, he recalled paddling down and down, deep into murky black water that swallowed all light. Without their headlamps, visibility was zero. He glanced at his compass and GPS coordinates. They were right on track. Ahead of him, a steady trickle of bubbles rising to the surface belied his diving partner's position.

A few moments later Zena, shining bright and broken, came into view. He had glanced at his depth meter and then at his watch, calculated the safety margin at one hundred thirty-seven feet.

Eight minutes and counting.

Memories floated by as he swam into the torn belly of the helicopter and paused to take a look around. A multitude of fish had already claimed the twisted wreck as their home. They stared at him with disdain. Jagged bits of glass and metal protruded everywhere, eerily illumined by the light of their lamps. He made an open-fisted hand signal to Damon and turned to the cockpit. In single file, they cautiously swam through the helo. Spiny red rockfish scurried out of the way.

It took him three precious minutes to locate the dog tags and another two minutes to dig them free with his knife. The chain on which they were attached had wedged beneath the broken pilot seat. He felt Damon tapping on his ankle.

Hurry up.

Gage stuffed the tags into his vest pocket and scanned his watch again. Two minutes remained. He checked the air gauge. Fifty psi left in his tank. They were cutting it short. He motioned to Damon and floated into the back of the mangled helicopter with a minimum of movement.

Only their lights cut through the desolate blackness of inner space. Damon turned and gave a light scissor-kick of his fins. A bevy of curious fish scattered.

What happened next Gage witnessed in the classic slow-motion of disaster.

The pressure hose from Damon's scuba tank brushed against Zena's inflatable life raft and hooked the emergency inflation pull-cord. With his next sharp stroke toward open water, the hose yanked the cord from its bindings.

On the Richter scale of vibration, it felt like an eight. The raft explosively inflated, rupturing their eardrums and filling the limited space they occupied. Damon was pinned against the hull. Blood flooded the water around him.

Gage thrashed on the gurney and called out again.

"Damon? Damon!"

The voice of morphine returned.

"You're safe. Everything will be all right. Relax."

THE BENDS.

Another name for the physiological disorder caused by a rapid decrease in atmospheric pressure. Liquid nitrogen, always present in the bloodstream, is released as bubbles into bodily tissues. Bubbles cut off the oxygen supply. Lack of oxygen causes nausea, pain in the joints and abdomen. In severe cases there is shock, paralysis and death.

There is only one cure.

Andie secured the main entry door, toggled the controls and rapidly brought the chamber's depth down to six atmospheres, forcing nitrogen bubbles back into a liquid state. Her ears popped wildly while she chewed on cherry bubble gum.

She glanced over at her two patients. Both men rested quietly, their vital signs monitored continuously with the results displayed on a large control panel screen. Over the next several hours she would bring them slowly back to the pressure at sea level.

Damon sported a three-inch gash on his right thigh. It was not a life threatening condition and a tight bandage had been applied to stop the bleeding. Once out of the chamber, the laceration could be properly sutured.

First things first.

Despite receiving small, frequent doses of morphine, the narcotic effects were short lived. Both men would awaken suddenly, thrashing, call out in confusion and pain. With the liberal protocols of the chamber's medical director, Andie generously supplemented the morphine with an anti-anxiety medicine having the added benefit of amnesia. If all went as she planned, the two men wouldn't remember a thing. She engaged the wireless communication system between the chamber and outer room.

"Priscilla? Are you out there?"

"I'm here."

"This cut on Damon's thigh is really deep. He's going to need some antibiotics and a tetanus booster. Is Nicole here yet?"

"She just arrived," Priscilla replied. "I'll have her bring them in when she pressurizes."

"Any word from Frankie?"

"I just got off the phone with her. I broke the news gently like you asked me to but she's pretty shaken up."

"All right," Andie sighed. "Thanks."

A flashing yellow light on the temperature panel caught her attention. She made a few adjustments and jotted some notes on a chart.

A cheery voice greeted her a few minutes later.

"Hey girl, I've got the drugs you wanted, along with two big chocolate bars for us."

Andie chuckled. "Fabulous! Take your time pressurizing. Max isn't expecting me until later this evening and I want to make sure these guys are alright before I go home."

"Sounds good to me. I still have some paperwork I need to do from yesterday. Anything else you want while I'm out here?"

"I don't think so," Andie replied. "Hey, Nic! I can hear the outer office phone ringing almost constantly. How's Priscilla holding up?"

"The media's got the story and they're going nuts. The place is locked down tight and a security guard is posted at every entrance."

"I take it that Priscilla is responsible for that?"

"She's in her element," Nicole answered. "Rambo in a muumuu."

"Just make sure the guards let Frankie through when she arrives. She's really freaked out. If they try to delay her, she might pull a Terminator and drive her car through the front office."

"Priscilla has already spoken with them about Frankie."

Andie laughed. "Of course she has."

Nicole approached the inner chamber window. "So, how is your darling husband?" She drawled the question suggestively. It was no secret that the couple enjoyed a very healthy sex life.

"Whatever do you mean?" Andie toyed with her.

"Oh please, you get laid more than anyone I know."

Andie turned to the window and gave her a toothy smile. "You're not jealous, are you?"

"Just satisfying my highly curious nature."

"If you're really that curious, you should take us up on that offer to join the Sisterhood. You'd learn all sorts of things."

Nicole cocked an eyebrow. "That's exactly what my husband is afraid of."

Andie glanced over at the screen displaying vital signs. "Let me give these boys a little more Versed and I'll tell you about the new outfit Max bought me last week."

"Deal."

Nicole gazed around the chamber while she waited for Andie. The Fairhaven Hyperbaric Center was large and well designed, boasting a floor width that allowed patients to recline on gurneys against both walls while the staff maneuvered down the center of the aisle. A small bathroom had also been installed. The seven-foot ceiling, covered with jokes and funny pictures, reduced the claustrophobia patients often experienced. There was also a television and stereo system to combat the boredom of hours spent in *the tube*.

"So Andie," Nicole whispered. "Lauren told me the younger guy is nicknamed Swordsman. She also said that he's sleeping his way through the Sisterhood and doing it very well, if you get my meaning."

Priscilla chose that moment to hustle up to the outer window and peer inside. Her plump cheeks were flushed with excitement.

"Damon is a legend in his own mind," Andie answered. She jotted his respiratory rate and blood pressure on a clipboard then turned her attention to the expansive control panel displaying the breathing mixture of gases and chamber contaminants. Monitoring the panel was as important as tending to the patients.

"The word among the girls is that he's quite a stud," Andie continued. "In fact, Claire still breaks out in a sweat just talking about him. His unit is supposedly perfect, according to all reports."

"Really?" Nicole made a whistling sound. "Perfect in what way?"

Andie cleared her throat.

"Dimensions, I believe. Along with appearance and firmness."

Nicole blew out a wistful sigh. "Hmmmm. Andie, don't you think it's time to check that leg dressing and make sure it's secure?"

"Past time, I think," she replied officiously.

Both Priscilla and Nicole had their noses pressed against main chamber viewing windows, leaving oily smudges on the reinforced glass, while Andie gently eased the blanket away and exposed Damon from the waist down.

Priscilla gasped.

Nicole shrieked. "That's impressive even at half-mast."

"They call him Swordsman?" Priscilla squealed. "Why, he's more like Eleven-and-Change. I bet he's popular with the ladies."

"You have no idea," Andie drawled blithely.

Nicole started to laugh.

Damon's eyelashes fluttered. He yawned and mumbled, "I'm not a sword, I'm a bayonet." Just as quickly, he was asleep again.

Gage began thrashing on the cot. "Frankie? You're not a pity-fuck," he raged in delirium. "Listen to me! Frankie, where are you?"

Andie grabbed a syringe from her vest pocket and rushed to his side.

FRANKIE WAS SICK WITH fear. Worry had churned her stomach into a queasy knot despite the solid reassurance Quinton did his best to give her. She had called him in stark panic, driving with one hand on the wheel and the other with the cellular telephone stuck in her ear; treating red lights and stop signs as mere suggestions. She hadn't felt so helpless in years. Quinton and his family were on their way. Frankie had a head start on them and lived only an hour from Fairhaven.

Cylindrical hay bales and miles of farmland flew by her window. Her mind barely registered the slope-roofed red barns and acres of dense corn stalks and rye grass swaying in the morning breeze. Ordinarily the trip would have been a lovely drive with the sultry voice of some jazz diva to keep her company. Right now she would have given anything for her own personal helicopter.

Frankie swerved the Land Rover into the hospital parking lot, jumped out and sprinted across the pavement like an antelope. At the main entrance she flashed her Coast Guard identification to a nervous security guard, barged into a vacant outer office and ran headlong into a robust lady identifying herself as Priscilla. Frankie blinked twice, trying to simultaneously digest the woman's rapid speech and read the nametag verifying who she claimed to be.

Coffee? Donuts?

No, she didn't want either.

Tea? Water?

No thanks.

Yes, she knew it could be hours before Gage and Damon would be out of the chamber.

Yes, she knew they were in the best of hands.

No, she didn't need to sit down.

Yes, someone else was coming to be with her.

Yes, she realized both men would be admitted to the hospital overnight for observation, perhaps longer if there were complications.

No, she really didn't need to sit down. What she needed was to see them. See Andie. See for herself that the men were alive and well.

Priscilla escorted Frankie into the cavernous room housing the huge hyperbaric chamber and scurried off to answer the telephone just as Andie's tense voice reverberated over the intercom.

"Nicole, pressurize fast and get in here."

A little blonde rushed past her in a blur of motion. An alarm sounded from somewhere deep inside the chamber. Frankie stood still, brittle and silent, trying to keep out of the way. Bile rose in her throat.

Frankie listened to their voices for a few moments before easing up to the observation window. Through a cloud of anxiety, she peered inside. Andie held firm pressure on Damon's thigh. He was bleeding profusely around her hand. Each time she readjusted her grip, dark red blood gushed from the wound. Frankie was so startled it barely registered that he was naked.

Damon moaned and tried to roll over. Nicole's gentle hand forced him to his back. "Close your eyes," she encouraged in an angelic voice. "Go back to sleep. Everything is fine."

Frankie shuddered from the top of her head down to her toes. Trembling, she searched further into the chamber. What had they been doing when they were injured? They were both exceedingly cautious, expert divers. They didn't take needless chances. What had happened down there?

Once, during her rookie year as a pilot, she had helped carry the litter of a navy diver to an awaiting hyperbaric chamber. That chamber was a scaled-down, less forbidding version of the monstrosity now housing half her crew. The navy diver had not survived.

Frankie wrapped her arms tightly around herself. She couldn't stop shaking.

There was a line of three stretchers against the far wall. Frankie swallowed hard and forced herself to look again. She could see Gage's dark mop of hair and the curve of his angular, unshaved chin jutting out from under a blanket. He was pale, sweating. His brow was knitted in a damp frown. Her knees almost buckled. She looked back to Damon and the nurses hovering above him.

"He started bleeding the moment we got to four ATA," Andie's voice carried eerily through the big room. "He severed a big one."

"Arterial?" asked Nicole.

Andie shook her head no. "Venous."

Nicole gently eased a specialized tourniquet strategically above the wound and inflated the device over the ragged laceration. The pinpoint pressure stopped the bleeding immediately. "These guys look strong and fit," Nicole talked while she worked. "Do you know what they were doing when this happened?"

"Nope." With the tourniquet securely in place, Andie bent down to check the pulses in Damon's foot to ensure adequate blood flow remained.

"Do you want me to hang another bag of saline or a unit of O-negative this time?" Nicole asked.

Andie looked at the blood soaked sheet. "O-neg. He needs the extra blood."

From the corner of the chamber, a sudden cry jolted them to a new problem.

"Greg, look out." Gage screamed. "Cutaway! Cutaway!"

He thrashed on the cot like a trapped wildebeest, heaving blankets across the chamber. He tore off his monitoring equipment, nearly ripped the IV from his forearm while he fought some unseen enemy. Gage half sat up, his unfocused eyes turbulent with confusion. Nicole dashed over but kept a measured distance between herself and his powerful, flailing limbs. "Gage, wake up. It's a dream," she tried to calm his delirium with words first. "You're safe."

"No! Where's Greg? Where's Damon?" He flung himself partially off the gurney, still too out of it to know what was happening yet strong enough to do serious damage if he kept struggling.

"Gage, wake up, you're dreaming."

"No!"

Nicole produced a syringe from her jacket and found an open port on the IV tubing trailing down to his forearm.

"Okay, wild-child, it's time for a nap." She swiftly administered the medication while dodging the plastic oxy-sat monitor he sent soaring across the chamber. Gage swayed for a moment and collapsed backward, mumbling something about a woman leaving him. Nicole shook her head and heaved his legs back on the gurney.

"What's with these two guys?" She spoke while replacing the equipment he'd dismantled. "They both go nuts at the same time." She added mischievously, "Have you checked him for other injuries?"

Frankie's face was pressed to the window.

"No," Andie waved to her. "Maybe later."

FRANKIE WAS GLUED TO the outer chamber.

The last words she heard Gage utter as he went under the effects of a strong sedative reverberated in her head and lodged deeply, painfully, within her heart, "Robin, why did you leave me?" His face contorted in a look of shattered despair that almost dropped Frankie to the floor. She clung to the window ledge as realization slammed into her. *Gage was still in love with Robin.* Waves of suffocating nausea rolled over her. She took a numb step backward, straightened her slumped shoulders and reassessed the situation.

Damon's bleeding had stopped.

Gage was sleeping.

Her presence wasn't necessary. Quinton would arrive any moment and take care of notifying Damon's parents. He might even know how to get in contact with Robin. Gage told him things he never confessed to anyone else. Things he never told her. She fumbled in her pocket for the car keys, dropped them, picked them up, and dropped them again.

"Pretty boys." Her stomach coiled into a knot. "They are always wanting someone else." She turned and sprinted from the room.

When the situation in the hyperbaric chamber was under control, Andie looked up to find Priscilla where Frankie had been.

"Where's Frankie?"

"She just left," Priscilla answered. "She told me that Quinton would know what to do."

Andie frowned.

"Did she say where she was going?"

"No."

Chapter 16

THE MORNING AFTER

HE AWOKE TO A BRIGHT LIGHT SHINING PAINFULLY IN HIS EYES. ROUGH FINGERS HELD his eyelids open wide. The stench of antiseptic and sweat stung his nostrils. He had every intention of saying something vulgar when a loud voice called out, "Hello? Is anybody in there? This is Doctor Dorset. Can you hear me, Mister Adams? If you can, hold up two fingers."

A long middle finger flew up to jab the unfortunate doctor in the solar plexus.

Gage Adams was awake.

"What the hell is going on?"

"You had a diving emergency," Dorset coughed, retreating to the foot of the bed to nervously rub himself. Gage peered out with one blurry eye and tried to connect the dots. His befuddled brain didn't recognize the bullnecked, thick-waisted, rounded shoulders as belonging to anyone identifying himself as a doctor.

Used car salesman, maybe. A physician? No way.

"Where's Damon?" his voice rasped.

It was Quinton who answered, "Good morning, sunshine. Damon is asleep in the next room. Glad to have you back with us, mate."

A bad taste hung in Gage's dry mouth. He moved his jaw, trying to work up some saliva.

"How is he doing?"

"Weak and tired," Quinton said. "He's got some point A to point B memory deficits. They're keeping him here an extra night for IV antibiotics."

"IV antibiotics? What for?"

"He had a deep cut on his leg. They're worried about infection."

Gage nodded. Details of the accident rapidly clicked into place. He remembered the blood, their race to the surface and Damon's calmness, his trust in Gage to save him.

"What about his parents?"

"Already been and gone." Quinton shook his head in humorous disbelief. "His mother knows how to work a crowd. The woman left twenty pounds of Almond Roca at the nursing station. With that much chocolate and McGoldrick charm, he'll get the best of care."

Gage's voice was a ragged whisper. "Who's his nurse?"

"A lovely little bird by the name of Sophia. She's on loan from the ICU." Quinton's baby-blue eyes twinkled. They both knew what he was thinking. "Sophia hasn't left his side since they brought him in. Claims she'll be more than happy to drive him home tomorrow after he's discharged."

"Sophiaaaa," Gage let the name trail off musically.

"Mister Adams," Dorset suddenly rallied, aware they'd forgotten he was there. "I would like to give you a complete physical examination. The secondary effects of decompression sickness—"

"I know all about secondary effects," Gage interrupted rudely. He struggled to sit up. His head felt two sizes too big and throbbed with pain. "Where's Frankie?"

"Who?"

Once again it was Quinton who answered. "According to the office manager of the hyperbaric chamber, Frankie left about twenty minutes before I got there."

The expression on Gage's face was thoughtful, yet unreadable. He asked evenly, "Was there a problem?"

Quinton quirked his eyebrows and gave a look that said there was much more to the story that was better left for a private moment. Gage winced and asked a safer question.

"Did you come here alone?"

Quinton shook his head. "Isabelle and the girls are with me."

"Where are they?"

"In the cafeteria getting something to eat. They should be back to torment you shortly, mate. It was all I could do to keep Grace from painting your toenails peony pink."

In spite of the aches and pains, Gage had to smile. "Pink, huh? That's *not* my color."

"Mister Adams," the doctor blurted, "May I proceed? The sooner you let me examine you, the sooner I can write your discharge orders and release you from the hospital."

"You just stumbled on the right combination of words to get my attention. By all means, Doctor, proceed."

HE WAS QUICK AND thorough, well aware that Gage wouldn't tolerate a lengthy exam. Both of them wanted out of there as soon as possible. After a brief neuro check Dorset was out the door, heading for the golf course. The moment he left, Gage turned to Quinton.

"Now, where the hell is Frankie and what happened?"

Quinton leaned forward and rested his forearms on his muscular thighs. A wisp of blonde hair peeked out from his open shirt. "Nobody seems to know. I haven't been able to get in touch with her."

Dread rolled over Gage in sickening waves. He rubbed his bloodshot eyes and mumbled, "Tell me everything."

"According to Andie, the shit hit the fan. Damon was doing his best to bleed to death. You were delirious and generally trying to tear the place apart."

Disquieting images swirled in his mind. The headache Gage was sporting blossomed into a full-blown migraine.

Quinton lowered his voice. "Andie said that once the medical situation was under control, Frankie left. No one has heard from her since."

"I don't understand," Gage spoke softly. "Why would she leave like that?"

Quinton threw his hands in the air. "Face it, mate. You were out of control. Andie and Nicole had to restrain you just to keep themselves safe. My guess is Frankie couldn't take it so she fled the scene."

Gage hesitated. "Did you try her cell phone?"

"Yes."

"Her home phone? E-mail?"

"Abso-bloody-lutely."

"How about her neighbors? A retired couple live south of her. They watch her house while she's at work. They might know. They would have seen her. Blakemore is their last name, I think. Can you give them a call?"

Quinton was nodding. "Already done. Isabelle spoke with the missus about an hour ago. She said that Frankie asked her to look after the place for a couple of weeks, loaded her bags into the back of the Land Rover and took off."

"Did they say where she was going?" Gage could feel anger starting to rise, replacing the dread. How could Frankie run off and leave him alone and hurting?

"Frankie didn't tell where she was headed, only that she'd call to check in with them later in the week."

Gage blinked over at the big Aussie. Quinton was sprawled in a recliner, looked relaxed and ready-to-spring at the same time.

"She didn't leave an emergency number? A way to get in touch with her?" Gage tore the hospital identification bracelet off his wrist and flung his long legs over the edge of the bed. He instantly regretted it. The room swirled like a gyro. Every joint and muscle in his body reminded him of the insult it had experienced. He glanced down. Both of his wrists bore the blackish-blue circular bruises of leather restraints. He looked up at Quinton.

"I didn't hurt anybody, did I?"

"Quite the opposite," Quinton smirked. "They rather enjoyed tying you up."

Gage scowled and tried to stand.

"Whoa there, mate. Slow down," Quinton pushed him back down on the bed. "No use getting your feathers in a tangle. You took a big hit. The docs were worried you might even be deaf. Ease back."

"I wasn't deaf. I even heard the nurses fawning over the size of Damon's dick."

"Yes, Damon does the male gender proud."

Gage managed a weak smile and tried to stand again.

"I've got to find Frankie."

Quinton was shaking his head. "You need to take it easy. She'll turn up when she's ready."

"I have to see her."

Quinton cleared his throat and lowered the boom.

"I don't think she sees it that way right now."

Gage's head jerked up so quickly his eyes crossed. "What do you mean by that?"

Quinton took a weighty breath. "Apparently you were quite vocal during your attempt to destroy the hyperbaric chamber."

"Oh shit," Gage groaned out loud. "What did I say?"

"You were crying out for your old fiance', begging her to tell you why she left. Andie said it was a spectacular, heart-wrenching performance and Frankie heard every word."

Gage held his aching head between his hands.

"Do you see where this is headed?" Quinton wanted to be sure there were no further communication screw-ups.

Gage nodded.

"She thinks I'm still in love with Robin."

"Bingo."

"I need to talk to her."

"I've been saying that for weeks," Quinton huffed. "If you'd stop shagging her every chance you get and think with your other head for awhile," Quinton pointed to his temple, "you'd realize that too, mate."

Gage looked down at his bare feet.

"Did you bring me any clothes?"

"And spoil the nursing staff's hopes that you'll be forced to display your assets in that flimsy hospital gown?" Quinton answered gleefully then quickly added, "Isabelle made me bring you something." He reached behind the recliner and withdrew a bag.

More questions roared in Gage's troubled mind.

"What about my scuba gear? We dove to retrieve her dad's dog tags. They're the last real connection she's got with him."

"I thought that might be the case."

"I remember putting them in my vest pocket."

Quinton stretched his long legs and yawned. "All your gear is in the back of my van. I've got Damon's stuff too."

"What about *Spare Change?* Was there any damage?"

Quinton knew that Gage took better care of his single-mast sailboat than any other possession he owned.

"She was towed into the marina by one of the local fishing vessels. It appears you were able to get Damon back to the sailboat and tie a towel around his leg to stop the bleeding. You must have passed out right after you made the mayday call."

"I don't remember any of that."

"Mild concussion," Quinton responded. "Maybe it will knock some sense into you. The skipper of the *Buffy Marie* heard you hail New Harbor. He detoured and got there first, saw you and Damon folded up like origami and radioed for the helicopter. I think you owe him a beer."

This time Gage made it upright on his wobbly legs. Quinton was immediately at his side to lend an arm.

Gage allowed himself a moment of self-pity.

"What a fucking mess."

"It can be fixed," Quinton stared at him intensely, knowing Gage was still thinking about Frankie. "You have to talk to her. She has to know the truth and she has to hear it from you."

Gage broke out in a sweat.

"She's your friend, mate. She's your lover. She'll understand. You have to tell her everything."

"I don't want her pity."

"No?" Quinton's stubborn streak made a rare, abrupt appearance. "Well, how about her love? Do you want that? Pity seems like a small price to pay." He shook his head in disgust and added, "The doctors were wrong, mate. You're not deaf, you're blind." Quinton took a quick breath and continued berating, "And then there's Frankie," he muttered an exasperated oath. "She's in love with you and doesn't even realize it. How are you going to fix that, mate and when are you going to start?"

Quinton pinned him with a fiery blue gaze. Gage's vision blurred. For a moment he thought he might throw up.

"I think I need to sit down."

THE TRIP TO NEW Harbor was made in strained silence. In the front seat, Isabelle kept turning around to give Gage worried looks. Quinton kept a close eye on him through the rearview mirror. Sarah and Grace, in brightly colored jumpers and matching sneakers, clung to him like festive barnacles. They took turns patting his arms reassuringly, tag-teaming him with adoration.

It gentled Gage being near them.

One look at the little girls left no doubt about their parentage or that someday they would grow into hauntingly beautiful women. Their long black hair was a baby-soft version of Isabelle's but their eyes were large and Quinton-blue. Grace already had the husky bedroom-voice inherited from her father.

Gage shook his head at the irony of it. Quinton Herriman, legendary womanizer of the Australian Outback, was raising two future heartbreakers. He was going to have his hands full when they discovered boys. He might as well dig a moat and throw up some concertina wire while he was remodeling the house. One day it would come in damned handy.

Gage sighed deeply.

He'd give anything to have those kinds of problems.

THE FIRST THING HE did, once Quinton dropped him at home, was leave messages. "I'm at the cabin. Call me," he spoke gruffly to the automated voice of Frankie's answering machine.

He moved slowly across the cabin floor and fired up his computer, sent her an e-mail with roughly the same demand. He was too exhausted to make it up the stairs to the loft, so he threw an extra log in the fireplace and curled up on the sofa under a thick blanket.

He slept for thirteen hours straight.

The following morning there was still no word from her. He pounded a furious fist into the opposite palm and began to pace. The old fir floor creaked with every step.

"Damn it, Frankie! Where did you run off to?" he mumbled out loud.

He paced awhile longer, contemplated the wretched unfairness of life and made a pact with his own impatience.

He would give Frankie until the end of the day to make contact. Then the hunt to find her would be on. Gage would call in every favor owed him. Shaking his head in disgust, he wandered into the bathroom for a shower.

The warm water did little to change his temperament. His appetite had returned so he cooked up some scrambled eggs and toast. He skimmed the newspaper reporter's version of the accident. The story was peppered with conjecture and facts Gage couldn't remember.

He blinked and stared across the kitchen table at an empty chair. He'd never noticed how eerily quiet his house was. He took a bite of toast. It tasted metallic. He spooned a bite of scrambled egg into his mouth and found the same aftertaste. Gage pushed the plate away and scowled. He tossed the dishes into the sink and stared out the kitchen window, brooding.

THE CEDAR SHINGLED CABIN his grandfather built in the early nineteen hundreds was unchanged except for a dark green metal roof and full bathroom added after Gage claimed his inheritance. Open and enormous inside, the one-room cabin was decorated in hardwoods and shades of green and brown.

Outside, mixed pine and broadleaf trees cradled the cabin in a fond embrace. Situated on forty acres of fertile land, a creek wound its way across the entire length of the property. New trees and old fencing surrounded land that had once been a working farm. Tall grass blanketed the horse pasture. Feral cats roamed the dilapidated red barn unmolested.

The ghosts of his childhood were warm and friendly. He had fond memories of biking through town almost every day to help his grandfather with farm chores, listening to the old man's lively banter while they worked.

Gage never knew his father. The drifter abandoned his wife and son shortly after the birth and was never heard from again. His mother had done what most women in that situation were forced to do—she carried on. To support herself and young son, she taught first graders at the elementary school in New Harbor. It was a good job and she was brilliant at creating a fun learning environment. In her spare time, she steeped her son in love.

He had grown up strong and healthy.

He had grown up self-sufficient.

He had grown up with a deep admiration for women.

Like the best of friends, he and his mother did everything together. Played, laughed, and sang. When he started through the rigors of puberty, she reluctantly gave him the freedom he needed while maintaining a stable, secure home to fall back on when peer-pressure precipitated poor decisions.

Two days before her thirty-ninth birthday, Stella Adams stepped into the deadly path of an oncoming school bus. One week after her funeral, Gage joined the military. Two months after enlistment, his beloved grandfather died of a heart attack. Life as Gage had known it disappeared in a cloud of crematorium dust.

The sweet ghosts of his past.

Gage rubbed his chilly arms. Outside was a sunny morning with the promise of turning into another spectacular spring day. He needed to get away, *now*, and surround himself with the noise of the living.

THE ROYAL BLUE SAIL covers of *Spare Change* weren't hard to spot as he drove into the marina parking lot. She was easily the prettiest boat in the harbor. "Great lines," the old salts liked to say.

Gage was astounded to find her halyards tied off properly, ensuring ropes wouldn't flap loudly against the mast. Extra fenders had been placed between the boat and dock to prevent excessive grinding. She was even plugged into the electrical outlet to recharge her batteries! There was nothing left for him to do but clean up the bloodstains in the cockpit and on the transom where he had dragged Damon into the back of the boat.

When he finished, Gage wandered down the street to the Pioneer Brewpub and found Edgar sitting on a barstool, tallying the previous night's receipts.

"Ahoy there, Edgar," he called out.

"Good morning, Lieutenant!" Edgar clasped his hand in a firm shake. "I heard you and the boy got into some trouble the other day."

Word traveled fast. Undoubtedly, with Edgar's connections, the man knew more details about the accident than Gage was able to remember.

"We were lucky," he shrugged.

"So I hear." His face was warm with compassion. "Have a seat and let me treat you to a beer."

"Thanks." Gage scooted onto the barstool next to him. The bartender, listening to their exchange, pulled a tap and filled a glass. He set it in front of Gage.

"The crew of the *Buffy Marie* spent most of last night patting themselves on the back," Edgar said casually.

Gage smiled.

"Speaking of them, could you do me a favor?"

"Name it."

"Would you send a keg of your best microbrew and a couple of extra-large pizzas to them when she gets back from fishing this afternoon? Put it on my tab."

"All of my microbrew is the best," Edgar joked.

Gage took a long draw off his beer, and closed his eyes in appreciation. "You won't get an argument from me on that one," he answered. "With the exception of this brew, everything I've tried to eat or drink today tastes like a rusty nail wrapped in aluminum foil."

Edgar let out a loud belly laugh. "Then you better have some more of it and reset those faulty taste buds."

Gage downed the brew in one big gulp and leaned closer. "You haven't seen Frankie today, have you?"

"No," he replied. "Not since Monday."

Gage's dejected look told the story.

"Everything okay between you and the little captain?"

"I'll let you know in a couple of weeks," Gage responded quietly. "Right now, it's looking pretty grim."

Edgar nodded in understanding.

"I'm sorry to hear that. You're not so good at talking with women, are you, son?"

Gage shook his head.

"You're the second person to tell me that in the last twenty-four hours. I'm starting to get a complex."

"My wife used to say the same thing about me," Edgar confessed. "All it takes is practice and some research."

The bartender set another beer down in front of Gage.

"I would wait until my wife left for work," Edgar continued. "Then I would sneak upstairs to the attic where she kept her old romance novels. There were so many boxes of them up there it was a fire hazard. Good thing we got insurance."

"You read your wife's bodice-rippers?"

"Every last one of them. I gained a lot of insight into the female psyche reading those books."

Gage was stunned by Edgar's candid revelation.

"What did your wife say when she caught you?"

"Who said she caught me?" Edgar paused to take a long look at the younger man. "What's the matter, son? You look a little pale around the gills."

"I think I need to go back to the hospital for a CT scan," he mumbled. "My concussion must be worse than I thought."

Chapter 17

TEMPORARY DUTY

TWO LUCRATIVE WEEKS OF DOUBLE TIME PAY. A SPRAWLING ATLANTIC COAST STATION urgently needed a qualified pilot when one of their own collapsed with chest pain. Frankie snatched up the offer. The temporary assignment would keep her busy and if Damon should, by some obscene stretch of the imagination, score with Sophia, she was going to need the extra cash.

The voice of her new co-pilot sounded in her ear.

"Engines at full power. Ready for take-off."

Frankie glanced over at him. His pointed chin jutted out from beneath his helmet. She blinked against the morning sun, thumbed the controls and lifted them smoothly into the air. They headed east over the water and then veered south.

The station had received a distress call from the skipper of a fishing trawler after its propane water heater exploded and consumed the boat in flames. With the fire burning out of control, the skipper placed the mayday call and abandoned ship.

A myriad of thoughts ran through her brain, competing with the rescue call for attention. For the millionth time that morning, deep sadness swamped over her. Her mind filled with the echo of someone she left behind in her haste to get away.

Gage.

How was he doing? Did he remember the accident? Was he safe at home? Frankie had called the hospital to find out if Damon was okay. He explained the reason for their disastrous dive. She blinked back a tear. Damon also told her that Gage had been discharged from the hospital and was angry to find her gone. When Frankie called Quinton, he told her succinctly to, "phone Gage" and left it at that.

Frankie heaved a deep breath.

If she hadn't crashed Zena into the ocean, Damon and Gage would never have been injured. It was *her* fault they'd gone after the dog tags. She'd almost killed them twice in less than a week.

Frankie started to feel sick again. She bit down hard on her lip. What was happening to her lately? She'd cried more these last few days than in her entire life. She felt terrible for running out of the hyperbaric chamber yet hadn't been able to work up the nerve to call Gage. She knew he was pissed and couldn't face him just yet.

Frankie swiped a gloved hand across her eyes. The voice of her co-pilot forced her to pull it together.

"I have smoke in sight."

She spotted a thin black column and angled the helo towards it.

"I count three in the water," he announced.

"Affirmative."

In the back, procedures were underway by the rescue swimmer and crew chief. Frankie gnawed on her lip. In her judgment, this new team was technically proficient but lacked camaraderie.

"Ready for hoist power," the crew chief spoke.

"Power to hoist engaged. Awaiting instructions."

"Forward five. Hold."

They hovered above the life-jacketed survivors.

"Swimmer away."

Frankie glanced down at the white-capped Atlantic. In a few hours, trade winds would whip the ocean into an inhospitable state. Frankie stared straight ahead and suddenly realized she could not remember the names of her present crew. She glanced down. Carl, or was it Russell, coaxed a fisherman into the rescue basket and signaled the crew chief.

"Hoist in progress."

One at a time, the fishermen were pulled to safety. She kept her gaze on the horizon, watched the blazing trawler with an odd detachment as it burned itself out and sunk.

"Basket is in the helicopter. Boom stored. Ready for forward flight."

A crisp thumbs-up signal from the co-pilot and Frankie angled them back to the base.

As usual, the moment the mission adrenaline began to ebb, wrenching sadness returned. She went through the ritual of congratulating the crew for a job well done, then wrote the official report before politely excusing herself.

She wandered into her temporary duty quarters, eager for solitude. A light blinked on the answering machine. "Quinton must be calling to chew me out again," she whispered. Frankie shrugged off her flight suit and gave the machine a curious frown. She hit the 'play' key.

Gage's familiar voice filtered angrily across the room.

"I know you're in North Carolina. If I don't hear from you today, I'm flying out there to find out why you're ignoring me."

Frankie's legs dissolved. She collapsed on the narrow bed as her tears flowed freely.

"SKIES CLEAR WITH TEMPERATURES in the high seventies today. Get out the sunscreen, folks, it's going to be a beautiful day."

Gage reached over and clicked off the radio.

"Beautiful, my ass," he grumbled. There was nothing beautiful about the weather report. In fact, the day had all the indicators of being down right shitty. A tight band of stress encircled his cynical skull and squeezed without mercy. Gage stood up, the bed creaked under the weight shift, and he tugged on his jeans in one fierce yank.

He'd set the deadline. She had blown it off. Not only had Frankie ignored his demand but she refused the strong advice of Quinton, as well. In the four years he knew her, that was a first. She always listened when the big man spoke and almost always took his advice. Gage's good intentions had turned into the longest two weeks of his life.

He climbed downstairs from the loft and stalked into the kitchen. A cricket stopped its chirping at his approach. Sunlight warmed the spacious walls and infused the room in a woodsy scent of cedar. Gage glanced around and scowled. The home that had once been a sanctuary now seemed cold and empty.

Precious little in the way of artwork adorned the cabin. Only a framed photograph of the Harmony Bay crew standing in front of Zena remained. The picture hung from a peg by the front door. He stared at it for a few moments. Frankie's cheesy grin smiled back at him.

"Damn it!"

He grabbed a cereal box off the kitchen counter and shoveled a handful of flakes into his mouth. Gage chewed for a moment and swallowed the tasteless lump.

"What in the hell is going on with you, Frankie?" Gage shouted to the photograph. "Why won't you call me?"

He strode over to his darkened computer and powered it up. A few moments of beeps and blips before the screen began to glow and a familiar "You Have Mail" voice greeted his pessimism.

He muttered a curse and opened his e-mail inbox folder. Gage scrolled down the screen impatiently deleting junk mail. At the bottom of the page was a message from Frankie. He opened it and stared, dumbfounded. She had written one simple question. Gage frowned and spoke the words out loud.

"Are you still in love with Robin?"

Gage flew off the chair like he'd been shot out of a rocket. He picked up the phone and dialed her number. No answer except for the automated machine, again.

"Damn it!" He slammed the phone down and stormed out of the cabin.

Chapter 18

CALL ME

SHE DREAMED OF SEASHELLS AND BANANA SPLITS. WHEN THE NOISE OF A TRUCK ENGINE pierced her colorful sleep, Frankie awoke in a cheerful mood for the first time in two weeks. Morning light slipped through the thin cotton curtains. She dragged the alarm clock into view.

"Seven o'clock?"

Reaching across the nightstand to her pager, she pressed the status key and saw the empty screen with its silent green face glowing back at her.

"Sweet," she grinned at the white-speckled ceiling. She had slept for nearly ten hours without interruption.

Frankie yawned and stretched her stiff limbs. She shook her head and knuckled the sleep from her eyes. Her stomach grumbled.

Tomorrow she was going home and her temporary life in North Carolina would end. One more shift with Matthew, Curt and David. Or was it Brian, Keith and Daniel? Nice guys and conscientious, hard workers.

All in all, she was feeling better about herself and the sweeping decision she made the night before. After days of soul-searching and generalized moping around, Frankie concluded it was time to take control of her own destiny. Gage had opened a new door to her sexuality that was too late to close. After much contemplation, Frankie decided to start dating again.

She enjoyed male companionship. She thrived on romance and had more than enough passion to share. It was time to get over the angst of coveting a man who didn't belong to her and get on with her life. Her body clenched suddenly at the remembrance of the one who taught it about passion. Frankie let out a deep sigh and rubbed the chill from her arms. She remembered sending Gage an email during a moment of profound weakness. If she was lucky, the silly message would disappear into cyberspace and he'd never see it. The fact he hadn't responded was a good sign.

"Living in a fantasy world accomplishes nothing," she whispered. There were plenty of available men. If George Harvey was interested in taking her out for dinner and a movie, then she was game for it. The Sisterhood always had a spare brother or two to choose from. Why not broaden her horizons and take on several at once?

Frankie rolled out of bed and extended her arms above her head. Sweeping her hair into a ponytail, she tiptoed to the shower. The warm water felt marvelous on her skin so she lingered under the spray.

The flight line was alive with activity by the time she finished and wandered out of the officer's quarters. Vehicles rumbled and maintenance crews scurried around aircraft, gearing up to meet the day. The rumble of propellers pierced the air as she crossed the tarmac. Across the highway, in an open field used for training, a dozen men and women were in the midst of a grueling exercise regimen.

Halfway to the mess hall, a Fed-Ex truck shot past her and screeched to a halt in front of the administrative office. The driver jumped out, sprinted inside to make a delivery and sped off to his next destination.

Frankie scurried along. She had learned through the grapevine that Monday was waffle day at the cafeteria. Everybody loved waffles and the food line was already forming.

Inside the mess hall, two harried cooks rushed to feed a hungry mob of Guardsmen. A buffet line of sausage, bacon, fluffy scrambled eggs and fresh, delicious waffles stretched ahead of her. Frankie grabbed a brown plastic tray, plate and silverware and started to pile on the food.

"Captain?"

A voice from across the cafeteria caused her to look that way. Keith, or was it Daniel, or Travis, motioned her to join him at one of six metal tables that had seen a lot of wear and tear over the years. Frankie smiled, picked up a container of maple syrup and started his way.

"Ahoy and good morning," a cherubic warrant officer addressed her. Frankie took a seat opposite his two companions. Their uniform insignia announced them as ensigns. Reflective badges put names with faces. Frankie held out a hand to shake.

"Hello, I'm Frankie."

An ensign named O'Keefe began the small talk.

"Glad to meet you. We heard you're here on TDY."

"That's right." Frankie picked up a knife, then spread enough butter on the top of her double stack of waffles to make a cardiologist cringe.

"Where are you from?"

"West coast of Oregon."

"Are you enjoying it here?"

"At double time pay? You bet," she answered.

Frankie grinned and dove into her meal like a ravenous bird. She hoped they would get the hint and let her do a bit of feeding before socializing.

They didn't.

Warrant Officer Hobbs immediately lobbed another question. "Where are you stationed?"

"Harmony Bay." Frankie consumed an entire strip of bacon in one voracious gulp and turned her sights to a greasy link of sausage.

"What's the matter, Frankie? Don't they feed you out there?"

The three men started snickering. Frankie took a swipe at her mouth with a napkin and smiled.

"It's a small air station. We don't have the staffing luxury of dedicated cooks."

Hobbs still laughing, "If you're looking to transfer, we'll probably have an opening soon. The man you're covering for had to take an early retirement because of his heart condition."

"I'm sorry to hear that," Frankie shoved another slice of bacon in her mouth. "How long have you worked with him?"

"About fifteen years. He's an excellent pilot, almost as savvy as you," Hobbs said with a smile.

Frankie grinned and let his flattery roll over her without comment. There was silence for a moment while the men watched her eat. Hobbs took a bite of waffle and squinted.

"Harmony Bay, you said? I think I might know someone stationed there," he stated.

"Really?"

Hobbs thought on it a moment longer. "I think he's still there. It's been a long time since I saw him last." Hobbs scratched his chin.

"Rescue piloting is a small world, especially on the west coast. Everybody knows everybody else. What's his name?" she asked through a mouthful of syrupy waffle.

"Adams."

Frankie schooled her face to remain indifferent. It wasn't easy. Only years of practice made it believable. She chose her next words carefully.

"I know Gage. He's one of our best co-pilots."

"How is he?" Hobbs asked.

"An asset to the Coast Guard," Frankie hedged. "We were lucky to get him."

Hobbs nodded in agreement.

"How did you come to know him?" she asked.

"We were both in the Persian Gulf when the conflict broke out. My flight squadron did a lot of work with his pararescue unit." Hobbs paused to take eat a link of sausage. "It's a shame but I sorta lost track of the man. Life gets busy like that, you know. But I always wondered how Adams was getting along after his friend was killed."

Frankie kept her head lowered and asked, "What friend?"

"I don't recall his name. Some buddy from his old PJ days, I think. A lot of mean stuff was going on back then."

Frankie cleared her throat. "Do you remember what happened to his friend?"

Hobbs frowned, trying to recall details. "Some skydiving accident is all I remember. Adams blamed himself for his friend's death."

"He's good at that," Frankie whispered.

"At what?"

"Putting all the blame on himself."

There was a moment of awkward silence before Hobbs added, "I really felt sorry for Gage. The accident happened a couple of days before his wedding."

The food on her plate suddenly lost its appeal.

"He quit the PJ's shortly after and took a flight position with the Coast Guard." Hobbs paused, eyeing her curiously. "Hey, are you okay? You don't look so good."

Frankie stared at her plate, appetite gone.

SHE WAS STILL REELING from Hobbs' information when she checked in at the flight center an hour later. A couple of training missions were scheduled for the day but nothing slated for her team. Frankie checked the weather reports and then meandered over to the mail bin reserved for temporary personnel. She blinked. There was a small package waiting for her. Frankie bent down and dug it out of the bin. She turned it in her hand. Her breath hitched.

It couldn't be.

Frankie sucked in a deep breath and tried to slow her thumping heart. The writing on the address label belonged to Gage! Her hands started to tremble. She quickly stepped outside into the glare of daylight.

"Open it up," she whispered. "Just do it, you big wimp and get it over with."

She eased the tip of her pocketknife under an edge and carefully pried the tape and wrapping paper away from a sturdy wooden box. She braced herself.

There was a note on top, the printed copy of her last e-mail to him. Her shaky hands unfolded it. Her eyes opened wide.

I am not in love with Robin. Call me!

He had written the words in bold red ink. Under the note, something silver shined in the sun. Frankie slowly extracted it from a protective nest of bubble-wrap and pulled it free. A set of dog tags dangled from her fingertips.

Chapter 19

WELCOME HOME

*G*AGE SCRAMBLED OFF THE RIDING LAWNMOWER, LOCKED THE SHED BEHIND HIM AND glanced at his watch. He had been frantically cleaning up, trying to make the place presentable in case Frankie wanted to come home with him after their next stretch at work. His home was peaceful, tranquil in a way that women had always appreciated. Not only that, but the cabin was secluded enough she could scream at the top of her lungs while he fucked her senseless. God, he loved to make her scream!

Tomorrow would start another week at Harmony Bay. She would have to return home sometime that evening. He wanted to be there when she arrived. He also wanted to check up on Damon and assure himself that the kid's health was sound.

Gage had it all planned. There was so much to straighten out between them that he'd needed to make a list. He had phoned for advice and Quinton suggested the idea. Gage concurred. Tonight was the night and he didn't want to get thrown off track if Frankie needed to talk about something not on his agenda.

He sprinted across the freshly mowed field, thinking positive thoughts. The situation wasn't hopeless. There was plenty of time to salvage their relationship. At least the dog tags made it safely to North Carolina. Frankie thanked him profusely by e-mail.

He hoped she would call.

He needed to hear her voice.

Gage drew in a cautious breath and took one last, long look around the cabin. Satisfied, he grabbed a freshly laundered uniform and headed out to New Harbor.

DAMON WAS NAKED, SUNNING himself on the back patio of his ultra-luxurious condo. Through the open curtains Gage could see everything. The kid was a meticulous housekeeper with excellent, albeit expensive, tastes. The portrait hanging above his fireplace immediately caught and held his attention, eclipsing all else in the room.

Almost.

A bra was draped over one of the matching leather sofas. A frilly pair of pink panties littered the floor. He rolled his eyes. He didn't plan on staying long. Gage knocked once, twice, heard a loud, "Come on in, it's open". He walked through the main room and stepped out onto the patio, somewhat surprised to find the kid alone.

Damon watched his expression, read his thoughts. "She's in the bathroom, soaking in the tub," he stated.

Gage wasn't about to ask who *she* was or what made her decide to take a bath in the middle of the afternoon.

"So, LC, are you ready to start the grind tomorrow?"

"Um hmmm," he answered, distracted by the collection of gels beside Damon's lounge chair.

"You wanna beer?"

"No thanks, I stopped by to see how you're doing."

Damon's upper thigh sported a faint yellow bruising around a jagged red scar. Gage moved in for a closer inspection.

"Amazing, isn't it? The wound is completely healed." Damon nodded over his shoulder at the panties. "Nothing helps the healing process like a little loving."

Gage was speechless.

"How about you, LC?" Damon paused to take a gulp of water. "Has Frankie called you?"

The look on Gage's face was an easy read.

"I didn't think so." Damon's voice dropped an octave. "Don't worry, LC. You've got plenty of time to have a sit-down with her this week and try to straighten things out."

"You sound like Quinton."

"She's just scared," Damon continued. "Strong women don't like to cry."

"It wasn't my plan to make her cry."

Damon gave him an exasperated look over the top edge of wraparound Italian sunglasses. "You don't get it, do you?"

"You're not the first person to tell me that this week."

"Women always cry when a man opens up and lays his feelings out for her inspection. Frankie's a woman, she's gonna start crying."

Gage opened his mouth to speak. A beseeching female voice interrupted before he could respond.

"Damon? Yoo-hoo? Honey, could you come up here and wash my back?"

The kid jumped to his feet.

"I'll be right there," he answered and gave Gage a weak smile. "Sorry, boss. Duty calls."

"Let me guess," Gage pointed. "Sophia?"

Damon gave him a conspiratorial grin. "You better keep this a secret from Frankie for awhile, LC. She's got plenty enough to cry about as it is." Damon took off through the house, vaulting the stairs three at a time.

IT WAS LATE AFTERNOON when Gage pulled into Frankie's driveway. He set the parking brake, retrieved the hide-a-key from under the planter box and let himself in.

He took a deep breath.

The house had a closed-up smell after two weeks left vacant. He opened every window. A light ocean breeze cooled his face. Noise from the beach drifted up to him as he searched the cabinets for a vase. Gage wanted the night to be a memorable one for them both. He'd bought a dozen yellow roses and an expensive bottle of champagne.

The phone rang and Gage automatically reached to answer it.

"Adams here."

There was a long pause before a deep voice asked, "Is Frankie there?"

Gage recognized him immediately.

Vin Diesel.

"She's not here."

There was another pause.

"Can you give her a message for me?"

"Yeah, sure."

"Tell her that Vin called and I'll call her tomorrow."

"Yeah, sure."

Gage hung the phone up and sank into a chair.

"Damn it."

FRANKIE YAWNED, TURNED THE corner and coasted down the street in front of her house. She was drained. Shortly after four that morning, the North Carolina base received their first rescue call and the missions had never let up. She'd flown for hours, searching the waters off the coast for survivors before making a mad dash to the airport just in time for a series of lengthy flight delays and layovers. Hungry and bone-tired, she wasn't prepared for the sudden impact of sensation, a punch in the stomach, when she saw the black Ford pickup in her driveway.

Excitement and nervousness sang along her nerves, then dread. Gage was in the house, no doubt mad and ready to yell. She pulled in next to his truck and held her breath, tried to psych herself up for a fight. Her heart raced. Her stomach churned. She was frozen to the seat. She leaned her head against the steering wheel and tried to slow her breathing.

"Francesca? Are you going to sit out here all night?"

Frankie jumped and let out a yelp. His face was the most beautiful thing she had ever beheld. Then he smiled and she was certain of it. "I just got here," she stammered.

"You got here five minutes ago. I've been waiting."

Gage opened the door and pulled her into an embrace, inhaling a deep breath of her hair. Her scent assailed his nostrils, nearly knocking him down with memories. She slid her arms around his waist.

"I missed you," she said and offered her mouth.

"You've got a strange way of showing it." He covered her lips with his. She returned the kiss with equal force. He pulled back to look at her. "Don't ever leave like that again."

Her eyes were tightly closed around tears. When she didn't respond, he asked, "Francesca?"

She cleared her throat twice. "I am so sorry."

Gage could feel her trembling.

"Thank you for finding my dog tags," she whispered.

Gage kissed the tip of her ear. "Let's go inside and talk." He gently guided her into the house, pushed the door closed behind them and tilted her face up to meet his.

"You look tired."

"It's been a long week. I'm running on fumes."

"Are you hungry?"

"No."

Gage sat down on the edge of the sofa and pulled her to his lap. He reached around, groped to find the list in his back pocket.

"There are some things we need to discuss."

Frankie gave a startled sob. "Gage, I'm sorry I left the way I did. I couldn't take it. Damon was bleeding everywhere and you were going crazy with delirium. Andie and Nicole had things under control and Quinton was on his way."

"I heard I made a real ass of myself." He rubbed his wrists. "Look at my bruises," he held his arms out for inspection. "I think Andie enjoyed tying me up."

"I'm sure she did," Frankie pecked his unshaven cheek with a quick kiss. "And I'm also sure we'll hear about it at the next Margarita Monday."

Gage unfolded the paper. "We need to talk."

"I'm beat right now, Gage. Can it wait?"

Her eyes were rimmed with dark circles.

"You need sleep," he said matter-of-factly.

Frankie shook her head. "I need you." Her hands ran across his chest and paused to rest on his hips.

He brushed the hair from her face, massaging her scalp with his fingertips. "We really need to talk," he reminded her.

"I know," she answered. "And we will." She nuzzled her face against him. "Later."

"Are you trying to seduce me?"

"Yes," she mouthed.

Gage folded the paper and shoved it back in his pocket. "Did you have something particular in mind?" he asked.

There was calmness in her voice when she answered, "Tie me up and make me see spots."

He let out a little chuckle. "I thought you were exhausted."

"I'm never too tired for sex with you."

Without another word, he led her into the bedroom. The candles he had lit earlier flickered on the bedside table. The room smelled of roses and fresh linen. Her skin was cool against his hands. She didn't resist as he used her own shirt to tie her wrists to the headboard. He stripped her slowly, kissing every inch of her bared flesh right down to her toes. He secured her ankles to the bedposts with a pair of socks and spread her wide for his inspection.

Gage sat back on his haunches and looked at her. Candlelight played across her taut belly, accentuated by the shifting tension of her muscles.

Five minutes passed.

He said nothing.

He made no move to touch her.

"God, you're beautiful," his voice was husky with emotion. Frankie opened her eyes just as he slid his tongue up her thigh and licked her like a giant cat. He paused and stared deep into her eyes.

"Is this what you want from me?"

"Yes," she whimpered.

"Are you sure?"

He slid a hand down her ribcage. She murmured content.

"I'll give you what you want," he whispered, "but I want something in return."

"What?"

"A promise that you will never leave me again."

Frankie blinked. Her eyes gleamed. A rhythmic throbbing beat in her chest, spread a heated flush across her skin. His fingers went further down and dipped briefly inside her before he withdrew. Moist and squirming, her hips bowed up to find him. She pleaded with her eyes.

"No," he laughed softly, exultantly. "Not yet." He reached up and ran his hand lightly across her breasts. He pulled a bright red bandana from his back pocket and whisked it past her face. Frankie sucked in a tortured breath.

"Gage!"

His response was the slightest tweak of a taut nipple captured between his thumb and forefinger. His voice never wavered as he asked, "Do you trust me?"

"I'm not sure I trust myself right now," she admitted.

"Giving up control is frightening," he paused to run his mouth along her jaw line. "But the pleasure of the release is worth it." His finger traced a path around her breasts, circling, waiting for a decision. "Let yourself go, Francesca. I'll give you a safe word. Say it and I'll stop immediately."

Frankie's vision blurred with desire.

"Trust me," he whispered.

Swamped by lust, the idea of giving her safety up to him felt so damned good she couldn't help twitching. Gage bent to her mouth and fluttered kisses across her lips. Frankie arched up to meet him and let go.

Chapter 20

NO GOOD DEED GOES UNPUNISHED

"**Y**OU SON-OF-A-BITCH!" SHE SPAT THE WORDS SO FORCEFULLY THAT GAGE TOOK A physical step backward. The beautiful, sunny morning promptly went straight to hell.

"I heard you talking to Quinton about Vin's phone call. Why didn't you tell me he called? His message was for me!" Her fists clenched. "How dare you intercept my phone call! You don't see me screening your messages. Why do you think that is? Huh? I'll tell you why." She took a step closer and jabbed her finger in his chest. "YOU are too controlling and stubborn to have any woman hang around for more than a short-term fling."

Gage met her outrage with his own.

"Do you know how much I hate it when you yell at me?"

"Back at you, buster. If you would pass along my messages like you're supposed to, I wouldn't have to yell at you."

Gage towered over her, seething.

"I don't want you seeing him."

"It's none of your business who I sleep with. Get it?" Frankie punctuated the words with a muffled curse and spun to walk away.

Gage caught her hand and whirled her around to face him. Frankie shoved at his chest with all her strength, sent him stumbling back two steps. His hand darted out to yank her jacket roughly. The rip of material sent her over the edge. Enraged, she began to rain blows on him. Gage grabbed both her wrists and took the kicks stoically, blocking the well-placed ones with his thigh. She tried to pull away. He held fast.

"Damn you, Gage! Let me go, or I'll—"

"Or you'll what?" his fury reverberated through the air. She kept kicking. He spun her around and locked her arms against him, held her tight while she fought.

182

In the garage, Quinton and Damon dropped what they were doing and rushed out to intervene. Damon chanted, "Whoa, Whoa" as if trying to slow a runaway horse.

Frankie's body stilled in Gage's arms, tensed, and then her chin flew up in defiance. Hostility blew out in one great exhalation. "Fuck off!"

Quinton snaked his way between them and gave each a push with his open palms.

"Both of you need to cool down, right now."

Gage snarled once, released her and backed away, content for the moment to pace the helipad like a caged lion.

Quinton turned to Frankie.

"Go to your quarters. I'll be there in a moment."

"Don't speak to me like I'm one of your daughters," she hissed. "I'm the boss. I can go wherever the hell I want and right now it's not my room!"

Quinton pointed a decisive finger towards the house. His voice was pitched low and soothing. "Go inside, Frankie. Wait for me."

Damon crept up behind her and put his hands on her shoulders. He pushed gently.

Gage stopped pacing and turned to her, "Do what he says and stop acting like a spoiled brat."

She lunged at him.

Damon caught her in mid-leap. He held her up, feet dangling off the ground, while she squirmed and kicked and tried to elbow him.

"Put me down!"

"Calm down, boss."

Frankie continued to claw and fight.

"I could use some help here," Damon addressed the other men.

Quinton walked towards her, slow and deliberate. She went dead still and swallowed hard.

"You may put me down, Seaman McGoldrick," she spoke in an authoritative voice. "I'm going to my quarters."

With a nod from Quinton, Damon released her.

"Come on boss," Damon soothed and reached out to guide her towards the house. "I taught Stewie a new trick you really need to see."

Frankie took a reluctant step. "I don't care what you taught that friggin' cat to lick," she shrugged away.

"I know, I know," he coaxed. "Come on, humor me."

Step by step, Damon angled her away.

ONCE SHE WAS OUT of earshot, Quinton turned his attention to Gage.

"You haven't talked to her, have you?" he growled.

"There wasn't time. She got home too late."

"Did you find the time to bed her?" Quinton pinned him with a reproachful ice-blue stare. When Gage said nothing, Quinton shook his head. "I thought so."

Gage whirled angrily, pointed a sharp finger at his chest.

"What the hell would you have done?"

Quinton closed his eyes and exhaled deeply, "Exactly what you did," he spoke through clenched teeth. "I was hoping you were smarter than that."

"Sorry to disappoint," Gage growled.

Quinton held his hands up, "Look, mate, if you want to get inside a woman's head, you have to stop thinking like a dick."

"I don't need your insults," Gage spat. "I've got enough shit to deal with as it is."

"I fully agree."

Gage blinked up at the larger man.

"Do you want my help or not?" Quinton said.

Time slowed as comprehension filtered through Gage's anger.

"Yes."

Quinton nodded. "Alright then, I want you to wait a few hours until she cools off," he spoke quietly. "I've never seen her this volatile. She's acting like Isabelle when she became—" he stopped in mid-sentence and squinted at some distant memory. "When Frankie calms down, go to her. No more arguments, no stalling. Understood?"

Gage stared at his boots like a chastised child.

Quinton pressed the advantage. "Every day is a gift, Adams. Start playing offense. Put a check on your pride and stop reacting to every blow life deals you or you're going to lose her."

Gage's head snapped up.

"It's time to unload." Quinton's tone softened to a more brotherly timbre. "You have to tell her everything. You love her. She loves you. Nothing else is important. Tell her and it'll all work itself out."

Gage shook his head and sighed. The heat in his green eyes cooled to remorse. "How did I slide so far down the rabbit hole?"

"It's a slow process, mate. Bit by bit, year after year, you keep burying your feelings until one day you look around and realize that you've buried yourself alive."

Gage ran his hands through his hair.

"A good woman can save you," Quinton said softly. "You have to trust Frankie enough to be her best friend."

Gage nodded.

"Now that we have an understanding," Quinton concluded, "I'm going to go in there and try to do some damage control."

"Good luck," Gage sighed.

As Quinton walked away, he turned back and smiled wickedly. "Next time you hold her that tight, make sure she sees spots, mate."

As he approached the house, Quinton saw Frankie through the window. She was pacing the small confines of the pilot's quarters. Damon stood guard outside her door. He shook his head at Quinton in a grim, *are-you-really-sure-you-want-to-do-this* gesture. The latch scraped noisily when he turned the smooth knob.

Frankie looked up, eyes dagger-sharp and blazing with rage. "Don't you dare start in on me," she warned. "I don't want to hear it. And tell Damon to get the hell away from my door. I'm not a prisoner. I run this outfit, remember? I'm going for a swim so stay out of my way."

Quinton moved her wetsuit aside and sat down on the edge of the mattress. He kept mute while she vented.

"What is up with you guys? None of you respect my personal space anymore!"

Quinton bit back a grin. Frankie had the typical redhead's temper, flaring hot and fast then dying out just as quickly.

"I don't understand Gage. Why does he keep seeking me out? Can't he find someone else's life to meddle in?" A long tendril of hair fell across her eyes. She whisked it back from her face.

Quinton cleared his throat and hoped he wouldn't be sorry for reminding her, "I believe it was you who made the sex deal with him, wasn't it?"

Frankie stared with marked horror. "He told you about that? That was a private conversation. I can't believe it! Nothing is sacred around here. Everybody knows everything but me! I suppose he also told you that I like it on top and give an awesome blowjob?"

Quinton pursed his lips and made another supreme effort not to grin.

"Actually, until now I've only had my imagination."

Frankie shot him a nasty look.

"I've always thought the walls around this station needed another layer of insulation," he added and glanced up in time to catch Damon snickering.

"Well, that deal is off," she bellowed. "Finished. New rules. My rules." She took a deep breath and clenched her hands at her sides. "I hate this, Quint. Everything about that man is confusing. Half the time I don't know what to think. Or what he's thinking! I'm so tired of second-guessing and failing." She looked down at her feet. "Last night he woke up screaming in the middle of a horrible nightmare. Someone was hurting him, torturing him. I tried to get him to talk about it. He clammed up. All I could do was hold him." Tears welled in her eyes. "He won't let me in, won't let me help him."

Quinton looked down at his feet and whispered, "You're already helping him. Gage cares for you."

"I know that," she sighed. "But the man's got more baggage than an airport carousel. I can't get close enough to really help him unload."

She stopped pacing to stare directly at him.

Quinton met her gaze. "You're closer than you realize," he said.

"Stop feeding my words back to me. That's not what I mean and you know it." She started pacing again. "Gage is eating himself alive and I can't bear to watch it."

Long silence passed between them before she spoke again. "I had a lot of time to think while I was doing temporary duty in North Carolina. I've made a few decisions."

Quinton's eyes narrowed. "What kind of decisions?"

"I'm going to start dating other men, maybe even sleep with a few of them to expand my horizons a bit. Try to get Gage Adams out of my system."

Quinton's pale eyebrows rose at the strange detour her thoughts had taken. "I thought you enjoyed being with Gage."

"Of course I do but I need more experience. I'm not very worldly when it comes to some things," she blurted. "The library has some great books and I've learned a lot."

"You're learning from sex books you checked out of the library?" Quinton asked incredulously.

She nodded and said, "There are times, like when we're playing naked truth poker, that I don't have a clue what you guys are talking about. I just fake it."

"I know," Quinton answered quietly.

"Everybody knows." She stared at the floor.

"Don't go looking for something you don't need," he said softly. "If you've got questions, ask Gage. He'd be happy to teach you."

"Did he tell you that I passed out the first time we were together?" Frankie blushed with embarrassment.

Quinton put his hand up. "Gage wants you the way you are. He needs you more desperately than you realize."

Frankie looked up at him, her brows knit together. Quinton watched her face move through a myriad of expressions.

"You've fallen in love with your fuck buddy," he spoke softly.

The simple statement was like a slap. A surge of resentment flared up inside her. Frankie stumbled a little. His hand shot out to steady her.

"No," she answered. "I can't. I won't."

"You have."

"It's not supposed to work that way. The reason they call it a fuck buddy is to prevent all the guy-girl relationship bullshit."

"Frankie, stop arguing with me. You're in love. I can see it in your face every time you look at him."

"You can't possibly know what I think when I look at him."

"You were never any good at poker," he replied. "We just let you win on occasion."

She grimaced and fell prone on the bed, smothering her face with a pillow.

"I can't believe this," she moaned.

Quinton reached over and patted her shoulder.

"You look tired. Have you been getting enough sleep?"

"I don't know. Why?"

"Just wondering. Look at me," he ordered.

She moved the pillow to stare up at him.

"Have you been feeling alright lately?" he asked.

"I guess." She contemplated the question a moment longer, added, "I think I came down with the flu in North Carolina."

Quinton started nodding again. "Stomach flu?"

It was Frankie's turn to nod.

"I can't seem to kick it. I'm living on antacids."

Quinton frowned. "Would you do me a favor?"

Her face twisted in suspicion. "Sure, Chief, what?"

"Gage needs to tell you something important and I want you to listen while he talks. Everyone knows he's not very good at divulging his feelings. Don't give up on him. You need to hear what he has to say. I think it will clear up a lot of things for you; make sense out of the nonsense." He quirked an eyebrow and asked, "Do it for me?"

She puckered her lips.

"Please?"

"He's so difficult."

"Do it for me, please."

Frankie took a deep breath.

"I'll try."

"Thank you." He stood abruptly and held out his hand to her. She reached for him and he spread his arms wide. He squeezed her into his chest for a big hug.

"One thing more," he said.

She flashed him a dazzling smile. "What?"

"Don't forget to take your vitamins."

The direct phone line between New Harbor and Harmony Bay rang, sounding loud through the speakers mounted around the station. Frankie pulled away and walked into the living room. Quinton trailed behind her.

"Moriarty here."

"Frankie, this is Andre."

She winced, glanced up to meet Quinton's quizzical look.

"Good morning," she answered.

Andre cleared his throat. "I'm working on several crew evaluations that are due the end of the month and I would appreciate your providing some input into them."

"Certainly," Frankie responded. "Who do you need help with?"

"Garner and Meriweather."

"I've worked with them numerous times. I'll be happy to assist you."

"Excellent. I'll pick you up for lunch tomorrow at noon."

Lunch?

Tomorrow?

Huh?

Before she could respond, Michalet hung up. Frankie's mouth gaped open stupidly.

"Well?" Quinton asked.

"Andre wants to discuss crew evaluations over lunch tomorrow." She scratched her head. "That's a first. He's never sought my input before. He usually does his best to avoid me." She turned her confused gaze on the big flight mechanic. "The man doesn't even like me. I wonder what brought about this sudden change?"

Quinton's mouth pulled up into a sinister grin.

"According to the latest rumor, Andre's divorce was final last week. I think he wants to do some fraternizing."

Frankie's face screwed up in a tight frown.

"Are you talking about me and Andre? Together?"

Quinton smiled again.

"Not in this lifetime," Frankie shuddered.

"Didn't you just mention something about expanding your horizons?"

"That doesn't include sleeping with the enemy."

Quinton waved his hand towards the helipad. Gage sat in the open cockpit, looking defeated.

"Let's not mention this to anyone yet, okay?" Quinton suggested.

She nodded enthusiastically. "Fine by me. I have no problem keeping a secret."

Quinton gave her an amused look.

"I'm going out there to have another talk with Gage," he said. "Try to behave yourself for awhile, okay?"

Frankie snorted and grabbed her fins. "I'm going for a short swim," she said with a laugh, "How much trouble can I possibly get into?"

"You don't really want an answer to that, do you?"

"I'll be on my pager if you need me," she spoke over her shoulder on the way out the door.

"Take Damon with you."

Frankie nodded reluctantly. "Okay."

IT WAS EARLY THAT evening before Gage could work up the nerve to seek her out. Fear of rejection made his senses sharp. He could hear her downstairs; the kitchen chair creaked each time she moved. Her voice was sisterly as she talked to Damon about their swim and the large pod of dolphins they saw. Now and again, the sound of her laughter, pure and joyous, rang through the house.

Gage dug around in his satchel, tried to find the list of things he had written down to discuss with her the night before. *The list they'd never gotten to.* Outside, the weather mirrored his mood—low overcast, drizzle with occasional light rain. He pulled out a neatly quartered paper, took a deep breath and steeled himself.

He promised Quinton no more arguments.

He'd tell her everything. His fears, his doubts, the shame and defeat. All of it. Gage stood up, wiped sweaty palms down his pant legs.

The downstairs radio screeched.

"*BRS-925 Zaitsev* calling American Coast Guard. We request your assistance please."

The voice hailing the New Harbor station had a trace of accent and hint of worry. Russian? Armenian? The second request came quickly on the heels of the first.

"American Coast Guard, come in please."

Armenian.

Gage cocked his ear to the door and listened as an ensign at Station New Harbor intercepted the call.

"Vessel hailing United States Coast Guard, go ahead."

A long pause. The radio squelched.

"American Coast Guard, we have need of your help."

"*Zaitsev*, state the nature of your emergency."

A shorter pause.

"Our engine chief, he is very sick."

All the hairs on the back of Gage's neck stood straight up. He hurried down the stairs. Something about the timbre of the Armenian's voice struck him as odd, strained. Quinton paused in dinner preparations and turned to listen. He gave Gage a frown. They both felt the same weird vibes.

Gage logged onto the computer and quickly accessed the list of registered merchant vessels. Within seconds he had an answer. Merchant Vessel *Zaitsev* was three hundred feet of Russian fish processing boat that normally plied the waters beyond the Bering Straights.

"M/V *Zaitsev*, can you clarify the nature of your medical emergency?"

Gage mentally praised the ensign for keeping the man talking, getting as much information as possible.

Damon peered out of the laundry room, a load of clean towels draped over his forearm. Gage glanced over to meet the kid's troubled look. Frankie edged up close beside him.

"My chief engineer has sharp pains in his chest."

"*Zaitsev*, what is your location?"

A pause. Gage thought he heard yelling in the background.

"We are forty-five degrees, thirty-three point fifteen north and one twenty-six, zero five point forty-eight west."

Quinton arched his blonde eyebrows and coughed. The ship was less than fifty miles offshore, running almost parallel to them.

Their direct phone line rang three seconds later.

Gage snatched it off the recharging cradle.

"We've got the coordinates and are on the way," he answered and hung up.

Frankie and Damon burst into action. Gage turned to Quinton.

"I don't like the sound of this. Be cautious."

"Caution's my middle name, mate."

A FINE MIST CLUNG low to the ocean's surface as *Stella* plied the thick air. It was twilight; the orange globe of the sun dipping lower on the horizon before it disappeared completely. In the water below, Gage watched a small humpback whale sound and dive to the murky depths. The whine of helicopter rotors did little to drown out his unease. He could hear the chatter of Damon and Quinton as they discussed their potential patient.

Damon decided to use the litter. Anyone suffering from a possible heart attack didn't need the unnecessary stress of crawling into a basket. Ahead in the distance, the low clouds parted and the decrepit rigging of a rusted ship came into view.

"I have visual contact," Gage announced.

Frankie had already begun an intercept course.

"Ready at the hoist," Quinton reported.

Gage stared through the reinforced glass window. The closer they approached the target, the more wary he became. The call appeared straightforward enough; language barrier excluded. Over the years they had run hundreds of medical assistance calls, many of which included foreign freighters under strange and suspicious circumstances.

This call didn't feel right.

Years of military training formed the backbone of his suspicious nature. Skepticism wasn't easy to turn off.

Frankie pulled them into a tight hover beside the ship, whipping the water below into a frothy white stew. Gage felt his gut clench. They were sitting ducks in the helicopter.

Defenseless.

Gage turned, craned his neck to see behind them. Two of the *Zaitsev's* crew, clad in rubberized yellow overalls, waved them closer and hunkered down to avoid the rotor wash. He stayed alert, ran through possible scenarios in his head and glanced again at Frankie. She was totally focused on keeping them stable. He frowned and listened intently as Damon got ready to descend.

"Ready for hoist power."

"Affirmative."

Quinton sent Damon and the litter down simultaneously. The kid hung on like a monkey, feet poised on the carabiner that attached litter to cable. The moment he hit the slippery wet deck, his gloved hand disconnected the cable's quick-release. He was on his own now and free to work his medical magic.

Quinton hoisted the cable back up.

"Boom stored. Clear for forward motion."

Gage gave Frankie the thumbs-up signal. With a flick of her wrist, she backed the helicopter off a few hundred yards, affording him a better opportunity to view the ship. Every visible inch of the *Zaitsev* came under Gage's intense scrutiny. His expression hardened into a dark scowl.

He noted the lack of functional lights and lifelines, the two battered lifeboats that wouldn't last five minutes in heavy seas. His eyes roamed over the cracked windows in the pilothouse and a radar system more appropriate for a maritime museum than a working fishing vessel.

Massive piles of old nets cluttered the deck. They had been sewn and repaired countless times. The ship was exactly what one would expect from an aged fleet that lacked the funds for proper upkeep.

Gage blew out a deep breath and glanced over at Frankie. She was deep in concentration, keeping them stable at hover.

"What's taking Damon so long?" Quinton's voice filtered through their headsets.

"Unknown," Gage responded. He grimaced at the glowing numbers on his thick wristwatch.

"What's the frown for?" Frankie's voice pierced through the headset.

"Fifteen minutes, seven seconds. Way off his average," Gage responded.

"Maybe there were complications," Frankie said.

"Damon is one of the fastest working medics in the Guard," Quinton answered.

"Try hailing him," Frankie ordered.

Before he could, the radio crackled and a faint, "clear for pickup" sounded. Gage strained to hear more but there was only a moment of white noise before radio silence.

"Was that a roger for pickup?" Quinton asked. "I don't see any movement on deck."

Gage looked down. Quinton was right.

"I don't like this," Gage spoke.

A metallic glimmer caught his eye. Four men surfaced on deck carrying a litter.

"There they are," Quinton said. "Ready for pickup."

Frankie toggled the controls and maneuvered them back to the ship.

"Ready for hoist."

Gage peered out the window, observing as the litter was lowered and a victim placed inside. As Quinton hoisted it up, Damon clung to the cable, a tentative hold Gage would have ascribed to the less experienced. The litter was spinning wildly.

From the corner of his eye, Gage caught a trace of movement on the ship's deck. He turned and saw a twist of arms and legs, a struggle in the bulkhead doorway. He simultaneously keyed his mike and motioned to Frankie.

"Quinton, drop the litter! It's a trap!"

Too late.

A low warning cry sounded from the back of the helicopter. Gage spun just in time to see their patient fire a taser dart into Quinton's broad chest. Two barbs blasted across the small space and impacted below his left collarbone. Quinton collapsed in a fetal position. The helicopter lurched slightly under Frankie's surprised hands.

"What the hell!" she exclaimed.

An imposter, dressed in Damon's jumpsuit, stepped over Quinton's coiled body. The barrel of a taser gun came up to stare Gage in the face.

"Do exactly as I say and I will spare your life."

"What do you want?" Frankie yelled.

Pseudo-Damon smiled at her, showing a slight space between his crooked front teeth. He kept the taser trained on Gage. "You will land on the ship at once. If you activate the emergency transponder or key the microphone to contact your cutter station, your co-pilot will die."

Frankie darted a quick look at Gage, taking stock of their situation. On the floor, Quinton started to move, slowly regaining control of his stunned muscles. His eyes were glassy but focused. She knew he heard every word. There was an instant of hesitation before she worked the sticks to spin them around.

"Don't do it," Gage ordered. His eyes never left their aggressor.

"I don't have a choice."

"This is a government vessel. You know the rules."

"He'll shoot you," she answered.

"He'll do it anyway. Do NOT submit."

Frankie stared a moment at the hijacker.

"Do *not* submit," Gage repeated and flicked a hand signal to Quinton.

Frankie turned her head and very slowly lowered them down to the steel deck of the ship.

An unarmed man clambered aboard. Gage strained for a better look at the newcomer. He thought there was something oddly familiar about the lanky, dark-haired man with the cadaver-thin face. Like a rocker or druggie, every scrap of clothing he wore was black, contrasting sharply with his pale features. He carried a heavy black case and leather satchel that banged against his hip with each awkward step. The man yelled over the roar of helicopter noise at one of the hijackers.

Gage translated the words in his mind. *"Where is my assistant?"*

The bastard who shot Quinton answered the question.

"He will be here soon."

Gage took a calming breath. His peripheral vision blurred before coming into focus. A name popped clearly into his head.

Dimitri Arhepov.

A memory from the past. Gage had seen his picture many years ago—a Russian computer genius for hire. The man was on every Customs and Immigrations hot list in the world. Apparently he had found new employment in the United States.

"What have you done with my rescue swimmer?" Frankie yelled.

A taser veered to stare her in the eye, wielded by a brute with arguably the worst acne scarring Gage had seen in his life. Gage made a close-fisted hand signal to her. *Keep silent.* Not surprisingly she ignored it.

"Where is my rescue swimmer?" Frankie demanded again.

"He will be safe as long as you comply with our demands."

Gage's mind ran over the possibilities. God help him if Frankie wouldn't shut up. Women! They were going to be the death of him. A rivulet of sweat trickled down his back. He signaled her again to keep quiet. Miraculously, this time she obeyed.

Another hijacker approached them, accompanied by a pinch-faced, frail looking kid in his mid-twenties. Gage stared at the youngster and committed his face to memory.

Two hijackers and two Russian computer hackers.

Gage mulled over their chances. He'd been in worse predicaments. Not bad odds really, especially if Quinton could provide a little help at just the right moment.

He knew he could count on Quinton's assistance if there was any possible way the Aussie had strength to swing a fist. At the moment, however, Quinton was cramped into the space behind Gage's co-pilot seat. His pale head was hung low, his breathing shallow and regular. It wouldn't take long for him to recover. Time was their enemy now. They had to stall.

Their unwelcome guests stowed the empty litter and settled down in the back. Seatbelts snapped into place. The hijacker Gage targeted as their leader shouted above the rotor noise to Frankie.

"You will lift off now."

Her glare pierced the man. "Where?" she yelled back.

"I will give you coordinates momentarily."

"I need to know where to go," she shouted.

"North."

Chapter 21

WALKING THE WALK

ARK SHADOWS SILHOUETTED THE LAND MASS AHEAD. *STELLA* WAS SLUGGISH WITH the added weight in back. Gage glanced over to see the determined set of Frankie's jaw outlined in the dimmed interior of the cockpit. Her jerky movements on the controls, designed to sicken those in the back of the helicopter, almost made him smile. She might be under coercion but she was far from giving up control.

They were instructed to land in a clearing west of the interstate highway. A waxing moon cast the landing zone in an eerie glow. Gage could see activity below. Three darkly clothed figures scrambled from the wind and debris churned up by the helicopter, shielding themselves behind two large vans. He turned his head enough to see Quinton. His breathing was regulated, eyes closed, body preternaturally still and saving strength for the time it would be needed.

Gage knew Quinton's ears missed nothing. Hearing was the last sense to go and first to return. He scanned the forward console. All panel lights were normal. He chanced another glance over his left shoulder. Everyone in back looked airsick.

Frankie's erratic flying had paid off.

Arhepov and his scrawny assistant wouldn't pose a problem. They weren't there to brawl. Whatever computer system he had been hired to hack, mixing it up with the goons in a fistfight wouldn't be part of the program.

So, what *was* the program?

Someone had gone to great expense and danger to hire Arhepov. Talents like his didn't come cheap. Despite his questionable taste in clothing, the man was reported to be worth millions. Gage searched the forested area around them for any sign of exploitable weakness.

As Frankie lowered them to the clearing, Gage emptied his mind of all thoughts and felt a great, cool numbness wash over his skin. There was only one mission now.

Take back *Stella.*

Frankie crunched them down rougher than usual and turned to glare at the man that held a taser on Gage.

"You will shut down the engines," he ordered.

"The engines need two minutes to cool down," she snapped. "I can't shut them down before then."

"You have two minutes. No more," he replied and tapped his watch.

She glared a moment longer and flipped the switches. *Stella's* rotors slowed to a dull thump, thump, thump.

Gage closed his eyes, inhaled a deep breath, taking comfort from the familiar hydraulic smells permeating the cabin. The next few minutes would decide everything. When the opportunity presented itself, he had to be ready to act. He wouldn't fail his team this time. Too much depended on it. Frankie would need him. He couldn't let her down.

Gage licked a thin layer of sweat from his upper lip and scanned the edges of the clearing once more. He refused to blink. Bad things could happen in the blink of an eye. It didn't pay to have your eyes shut when the shit hit the fan. Through the cushion of his seat, Gage could feel the synchronous rap of fingers tapping out a code. Quinton was ready.

A cloud of organic debris flew up to cradle the helicopter. When the blade rotation stopped, three figures descended upon them. Gage shook his head. Five armed opponents against two. Dicey but doable.

Frankie bounded out of the helicopter. She tore off her helmet and started in on their captors. "Where the hell is my rescue swimmer?" Her gray eyes were liquid with violence. "Hey," she pointed a finger in the nearest face. "I'm talking to you!"

A beefy hand motioned Gage out of the cockpit. Staring down the non-wavering barrel of a gun, Gage grimaced, feeling the advantage of timing and patience slip away as Frankie stirred up trouble.

None of the men gave her more than an irritated scowl. Frankie repeated, "What did you do with my rescue swimmer?" She cornered the closest hijacker and jabbed her gloved finger into his burly chest. His disdain made it clear she was not considered a threat.

Gage and Quinton were not treated with the same disregard. A guard was assigned to each of them. Muscle-bound, anabolic steroid types. Both were close enough to throttle but Gage didn't dare make a move yet. Not until he could get Frankie clear of danger. She wasn't helping matters by nipping at their captors like a terrier.

Gage glanced around. Arhepov and his assistant were being ushered into the closest van. The remainder of the hijackers were consolidating their supplies, moving stacks of crates from one vehicle to another. He tried to get Frankie's attention, signal her to shut up. The leader paused in giving instructions to his men and turned to Frankie.

"Captain Moriarty, restrain yourself or you will never see your missing crewman alive again."

Frankie yelled above the noise of their activity. "You went to a lot of trouble to steal my helo. If you want my cooperation, you better tell me what you've done to Damon."

Gage looked over his shoulder at Quinton. The Aussie had been unsteadily moving from the helicopter and was now staring at Frankie. For the first time he realized the danger her furious temper put them in. When Frankie was really mad, there wasn't much that could make her back down.

The stocky leader took an ominous step toward her, brandishing a short coil of nylon rope that made Gage's heart leap. "You are in no position to issue me an ultimatum, Captain. I do not have time for further argument." The man turned to speak directly to Gage. "Lieutenant Adams, you will pilot the helicopter while my men watch over your captain."

Gage wasn't surprised he knew their names. Too much money was involved for them to have skipped their homework. He couldn't afford to wait much longer.

"Who the hell are you?" Gage demanded.

A nefarious smile. "Call me Yuri."

"Where am I going?"

"One kilometer northeast of the hydroelectric plant. I will give you exact coordinates when we are in the air." He motioned to Frankie. "If you make the slightest course deviation, she will be executed."

"You lay one hand on her," Gage spoke icily, "and you'll lose the ability to piss standing up."

Yuri's nostrils flared at the insult. One of the goons tried to give Gage a brutal shove but he sidestepped the blow and stood firm.

"You will comply with my orders."

"Not in this lifetime," Gage sneered.

"Let me remind you of who is in charge." He motioned to the man guarding Quinton.

Frankie sprang into action, getting right up in Yuri's face. "I'm the pilot, not him! He can't fly his way out of a paper bag. I always have to cover for his ineptitude."

The leader mumbled something unintelligible under his breath.

"Adams is a hazard," Frankie raved. "I'm the pilot you need for this job."

"Woman, you are wasting my time."

"I think that the real issue is you're afraid to have a female in the cockpit, even if she is the superior flyer!"

Yuri's nostrils flared. He turned to an underling. "Vladimir, you may entertain Captain Moriarty in our absence," he said. "Perhaps you can teach her some manners on how a real woman should behave."

"Spoken like a true fool," she spat.

Gage groaned out loud. She didn't realize the personality type she was dealing with. If Frankie thought to keep him safe and stranded on the ground, she was going about it the wrong way.

All wrong!

Where the hell was that taser? He'd use it on her himself.

Frankie roared on, "I've been dealing with this all of my life. Stupid men are always afraid of women. Why don't you guys just buck up and deal with it?"

"A truly smart woman would know when to keep silent," Yuri answered in a lethal tone.

"A truly smart man would leave Adams here and let me fly my helicopter!"

Yuri held up his hand for silence.

"Spineless moron," she grumbled.

Yuri's face turned to stone. His jaw clenched. "Are you calling me a coward?"

"If the yellow streak fits—"

Frankie never got the chance to finish the sentence. The rope Yuri held flew up to encircle her neck. Frankie's eyes bulged in surprise. He began to twist.

Baghdad leaped up at Gage as if out of a dream.

He reacted more than acted. A sharp rip rent the air as he slammed a fist into the nearest nose, spun and fractured a trachea with his elbow.

A blur of arms and legs fell in beside him. Quinton joined the fray, blow for blow, matched in speed and intensity. In the space of a breath, the burly guards were sprawled on the ground. There was a brief break in the fight while more hijackers ran to reinforce their downed comrades.

Yuri took a step away, dragging Frankie with him. She struggled, kicked and stomped, her hands searching for a thumb or finger to isolate that would break his hold on the rope.

Gage pulled a gun from the limp hand of an unconscious guard and turned his attention on the bastard choking Frankie. He cocked the trigger.

Fear danced across Yuri's face.

"Put down the weapon, Adams, or I'll snap her neck."

Quinton hissed to Gage, "Be quick about it mate. I'll hold the others off."

Blocking out every other stimulus, Gage took precise aim and pulled the trigger. The force of near point-blank impact propelled Yuri ten feet backwards.

Frankie swayed. Gage rushed to her side and caught her up. "Are you alright?"

She nodded.

"Stay down," he brushed his lips across her forehead. "I'll be right back."

She nodded again. Gage spun, eager to join Quinton.

IT TOOK A FEW moments for Frankie's head to clear. She stood and staggered backwards to the helo as chaos rolled towards her. The fighting had erupted again with incredible violence. Arhepov was trying to escape in one of the vans, his spindly legs pumping with the effort of running.

Her ears were ringing. She thought she heard Gage yelling at her. An order? His voice reached her through the thunder of meaningless noise. Clutching her neck, she felt her way to the helicopter cockpit. She ran her hand blindly over the controls and punched in the transponder code that indicated a kidnapping in progress.

7-5-0-0

The grunting sounds of fighting diminished. Frankie turned to see Gage's boot colliding with Arhepov's jawbone. Twisted bodies were scattered across the trampled grass. Gage looked over at her. She gave him a weak hand signal that help was on its way and sank slowly to the ground.

Chapter 22

SORTING THINGS OUT

QUINTON, GAGE AND FRANKIE SAT ON THE RUNNING BOARD OF *STELLA'S* REAR compartment and watched the procession of government agents lead Dimitri Arhepov and his assistant away in handcuffs. The smell of the clove cigarette Gage had bummed from one of the agents wafted past Frankie's wrinkled nose. At the last moment Arhepov turned and made eye contact with Gage, his hand flew up in mock salute. Gage answered with his raised middle finger.

It was past midnight. The perimeter lights set up for the investigation cast enough luminescence to give the impression of midday. A group of the FBI's finest searched the edges of the clearing for any shred of evidence. Quinton rubbed his aching shoulder and scowled at the paramedic trying to take his blood pressure.

The three of them had been privately questioned, separated from one another, their stories compared for consistency. That two flight jockeys, one of whom was injured, could have overcome six armed mercenaries, was met with a good deal of skepticism. It was not until a female agent named Corley produced old service records on Gage and Quinton that any suspicion of collaboration disappeared. From the abrupt change in Corley's demeanor, the woman had been impressed.

Frankie heaved a deep sigh.

Agent Corley had informed them that Damon was unharmed and in the process of being escorted to the air station clad only in his thermal underwear and a wide grin.

"It figures he would try to screw his way out of a jam," Gage complained.

Quinton rumbled a laugh.

"Do you think it worked?"

"Probably."

201

Frankie paused, a mug of hot coffee half way to her lips. She turned to study Gage's stoic profile. In another hour or so, that dim shadow he sported above his eye would blossom into an impressive shiner. He had fought like a maniac to save her. She caught Quinton eyeing the black eye too.

"I told you to duck, mate," Quinton teased.

"You told me to duck *after* his fist collided with my face. I'm good but I'm not that good."

"Excuses, excuses. I held up my end of the fight," Quinton replied.

"Your end?" Gage responded.

"Abso-bloody-lutely, my end. I did my fair share of ass-kicking after taking two in the chest."

"Two in the chest?" Gage repeated incredulously. "You took two hits in the collarbone and only one of those barbs made it through your flight suit to barely pierce the skin."

"One was plenty enough, mate."

"Plenty enough to make you scream like a girl."

Frankie's voice was scratchy. "Would you two wankers knock it off?"

"Not until you apologize for calling me a sorry-assed pilot," Gage responded.

"I didn't call you that," Frankie smiled.

"She's right, mate. She called you a worthless hazard."

It hurt her throat to laugh but Frankie didn't care. A little pain was small price to pay for being alive. Gage rolled his eyes and took a long draw on his cigarette.

"Where did you learn to speak Russian?" she asked Gage.

"From Greg."

"Your friend from childhood?"

He nodded.

"Greg is short for Gregori. Gregori Buletov. His parents immigrated to the United States when he was five. They moved in next door to us." Gage held out his coffee mug for a refill. The agent assigned to look after them quickly obliged. "The Buletovs were honest, hardworking people," he continued. "At first they were overwhelmed by all the excess in this country. The wasteful, materialistic ways of our culture, Greg's dad was fond of saying. They never got used to it and never took anything for granted. The whole family was into recycling before it was fashionable."

Quinton started to speak then changed his mind.

"My mom taught them English," Gage continued.

"And you learned Russian from them," Frankie deduced.

"Exactly."

Her hands knotted into fists. "How did you know about the computer guy?" She wrapped her chilled fingers tighter around the cup.

"Greg's parents were computer software experts," Gage answered. "Geeks and philosophers were the crowd they socialized with in Russia. I remembered a picture and their stories about a former friend of theirs, some genius gone rogue. Times were really tough back then. Everyone was starving or close to it but good old Arhepov never missed his yearly shopping spree in Paris. He was living the high life at his comrades' expense. A real lie-cheat-steal kind of guy. He made a killing from selling his hacking services to the highest bidder."

"Who do you think hired him for this job?" Frankie asked quietly.

"That's what these fine folks are here to find out." Gage toasted the FBI with his coffee mug and then bummed another clove cigarette from the agent standing a few feet away.

Quinton edged away from him. "Mate, keep lighting those up and you'll need a lung transplant. They can't possibly be good for you."

"Beats the alternative."

Frankie tapped Gage's leg. "Do you know what Arhepov was paid to hack?" she asked.

Gage shook his head. "Beaumont Hydroelectric is almost entirely computerized. My guess is someone paid him to take down the power grid."

Frankie made a growling noise. "That dam supplies electricity for half the west coast. The resulting blackout would cripple us for days and that would just be the beginning."

"Can you spell chaos?" Quinton spoke in seriousness. "Those blokes could've done some serious damage."

Frankie blinked twice while she digested the ramifications of such a deed. "What about the ringleader of the hijackers?"

"Yuri?"

She nodded. "Where was he from? Could you tell anything from his accent?"

"Middle-Eastern, I think. With a touch of Cambridge University."

Quinton clapped his hands twice. "That's a pretty good guess for a worthless, low life fly-jockey."

Gage smiled.

Frankie's head had cleared and she was full of questions. "Who do you think hired Yuri?"

"Somebody who doesn't like the U.S."

Quinton let out a rude snort. "That leaves the playing field wide open. Could you narrow it down some?"

"Do you think the FBI will ever tell us?"

Gage turned to her and winked. "We could ask them real nice," he smiled.

Frankie turned to Quinton. "Isabelle has connections. Can you find out for us?"

"I have a better idea," Quinton answered and pointed to Agent Corley. "Let's get Damon to do it."

They considered in a moment of silence and then Gage started chuckling; softly at first, then growing louder. Quinton and Frankie joined him. Agent Corley paused in her duties and turned to look.

Chapter 23

COMING CLEAN

𝓕RANKIE AWOKE TO THE SOUND OF STEWIE HACKING UP A HAIRBALL IN THE MIDDLE OF her bed.

"Oh my God!"

She flew out of the blanket like a launched rocket and was retching in the toilet before her feet ever touched the floor. A meteor storm of lights wheeled through her pounding head. She reached out for something, anything, to steady herself and ended up in a blizzard of toilet paper.

Hell went on forever.

Each time she thought it was safe to wash her face and step out of the bathroom, her stomach decided it wasn't finished and propelled her back to the bowl.

Pale and shaky, she steadied enough to clean up the mess then crumpled into a swivel chair in front of the fax machine. With trembling hands she checked the weather forecast.

"Clear and sunny for the next thirty-six hours."

She fumbled with the computer and found the incident report begun the night before. She looked it over once and frowned. The report read like the ramblings of some hysterical female, not a decorated officer of the Coast Guard. She hit the delete key and prepared to start over when a knock sounded on her door.

Trouble, disheveled and humble, walked into her room. Frankie took one look at Gage and immediately forgot what she'd intended to do next.

"Good morning," she greeted weakly.

He sat on the edge of the bed, unconsciously rubbing his neck and stared blankly at the wall. A dark shadow of beard stubble set off vivid purple bruising around his injured eye. He cleared his throat and began to speak.

"It was ninety one. A four-man team of para rescue men, were sent to extract a downed *F-15* pilot hiding in a village just south of Baghdad. The pilot had called mayday and ejected. He'd been down less than an hour. His injuries were unknown, assumed grave, and there was pressure from all sides to hurry up." He stopped for a breath. "Risk, rescue and glory. That's what the political gods wanted from us. Rescue the pilot, save the day and make the navy look good, all in one heroic swoop that they could brag about for years. The mission was hashed out quickly. Nobody seemed to think the situation odd at the time. PJ's are trained for exactly that type of quick action. I was trained for it."

The room seemed to swirl around Frankie.

"I was a kid," Gage continued, "younger than Damon, and they put me in command."

A jagged fingernail bit into the palm of her hand. Frankie forced herself to sit still. She wanted to reach out, give him comfort. Hold him tightly. Kiss the pain from his face. Yet she knew if she did, the riddle she'd been waiting four years to solve would remain unsolved.

The enigma needed to talk.

She needed to sit silent and listen to him.

"We parachuted in at night using the coordinates that we assumed were coming from the pilot." Gage paused a moment. "The whole thing was a trap. The pilot was dead. They used his gear and radio to lure us in. My team was taken prisoner in a show of force we weren't expecting." He cleared his throat again. "Iraqis were coming out of nowhere. They completely overwhelmed us."

He squeezed his eyes tightly shut as if trying to block the images.

"At the time, Hussein was offering rewards up to fifty grand for each downed Coalition pilot. I don't know what my going rate was," he muttered. "When the Iraqis realized we didn't have any information they could use, they began to kill us off, one by one. Murdered one at a time, one a day, in front of me. Since I was the team leader, they saved me for last. On the fourth day it was my turn. I was ready to die. I deserved it. Every time I thought about my team, my friends," he shook his head. "I was eager to join them. When night fell, the guards came to get me. I was awaiting my fate when a man in black quietly stepped out of the shadows and disposed of the rear guard. One quick snap and the body slid to the floor."

Frankie's watery eyes grew huge. The raw grief in his voice shook her.

"A SEAL team had arrived to rescue us." He motioned absently to the scar on his neck. "When the shit hit the fan, the other Iraqi guards decided that killing me was more important than running for their lives. They tried to cut my head off with an old piece of razor wire. I was too weak to fight. I woke up a day later in the infirmary on a navy ship, back from the dead and not ready to join the living. I was numb. I couldn't talk for days. The navy docs were worried that I'd had some vocal cord damage. It took days of x-rays and exams before a shrink finally figured it out. He saved me from myself but I could never be a PJ again. I'd lost my edge."

Frankie blinked back tears and swallowed past a lump in her throat the size of a doorstop. "Was Greg one of your team?"

Gage flinched.

"No, a separate incident that happened a few months later. Greg wasn't a PJ. He was a stable part of my other life, the part where people don't die by torture and you get to sleep in your own bed at night."

Frankie rediscovered her legs and eased over to sit down on the bed next to him. She reached out to hold his hand, splayed his fingers between her own. She ran her hands over his blanched knuckles.

A veil of anguish passed across his face. Gage broke contact, jumped to his feet, remained standing as he stared out the window. He couldn't reach out and make direct eye contact. Frankie knew he blamed himself. She waited, silent, for him to continue.

The moment was interrupted by a loud commotion in the other room.

Damon slammed the telephone into the cradle and shouted, "The FBI wants to talk to me again! How many different ways can I say the same thing?" The strain in his voice carried throughout the house.

"Deep breath, mate," Quinton reassured. "There are worse ways to spend the morning than talking to some pretty government agent."

"Yeah? Name one. That woman creeps me out." Damon made a shivering noise.

Frankie glanced over to watch a myriad of looks cross Gage's dark face while the noise of Damon's ranting filtered in from the other room.

Damon mimicked the haughty soprano of Agent Corley, "Seaman McGoldrick, could you explain how we came to find you clad only in your underwear when we boarded the *Zaitsev*?" Pausing before he answered his own question, "Because they stole my mustang suit, lady," he grumbled.

"She's a stickler for detail, that one is," Quinton responded. Frankie didn't need to see the Aussie smirk to know that he did.

"Seaman McGoldrick," Damon's voice became shrill and snotty again. "Could you tell us at what point you realized the intent of the hijackers was to

207

bypass the safeguards of the Beaumont Hydroelectric Plant and take down the power grid covering the western seaboard?"

"After YOU told me about it, lady. I was busy freezing my ass off in the cargo hold."

Quinton's response was ripe with humor. "The girl has to get her facts straight. No use blaming her for doing her job."

Damon sneered. "How about the unflattering way she enunciates *seaman* when addressing me? She's deliberately insulting me. I don't get it. What did I do to piss her off?"

"Don't be so quick to take offense," Quinton answered. "Some women come off as prickly when they're personally interested. Especially the tough ones. She probably wants more detail on where your nickname came from."

Damon made a rude, grunting noise.

"Then why doesn't she ask and I'll show her." He fell quiet, digested the information a moment longer before asking, "Do you really think she's interested in me?"

Frankie watched Gage's busy lower lip curl up in a smile. She reached across the few feet of space that separated them and gently smoothed the skin of his bare forearm.

"Damon reminds you of Greg, doesn't he?"

He spun to look into her face. A flood of grief washed over him. Over her. He moved across the room, hesitated at the door, long enough to break her heart. Without a word, he reached for the handle and slipped away. She watched the empty space where he'd stood, moments before her stomach forced her back to the bathroom.

PAPERWORK.

Endless, tedious and occasionally mindless, it comprised much of what she did for a living. Frankie worked for two hours by sheer will. She forced herself to finish the report while her mind continually drifted elsewhere. Back and forth to Gage. His past. His present. All those terrible memories followed him around year after year, haunted his sleep, weaving his life into a macabre tapestry of sorrow and regret.

She took a deep breath and pushed away from the desk. It was time for some distraction. Stop the pity-party and get a fresh perspective.

She knew where to find it.

Damon was sprawled in the middle of the living room floor, he surfed the web on his laptop computer. He glanced up quizzically. She gave him a wry smile.

"Can I borrow your Audi?"

"Sure, boss," he reached into his backpack a few feet away and tossed her a leather keychain. "Is there something wrong with your car?"

"I just want to go for a drive."

"A fast drive?" His sharp brown eyes flashed with suspicion.

"Something like that."

"You're not going to wrap it around a tree in some kind of estrogen-induced hysteria, are you?"

"That wasn't my plan," she smiled ruefully. "I've got this craving for barbecued chicken wings. Want some?"

Damon made an ugly face. "No thanks. I'm not hungry."

"What? Since when aren't you hungry? Are you sick or something?"

"I'm fine, just busy with a project and I've already eaten," he explained.

"Where's Gage?"

"Running."

"Where's Quinton?"

"In the garage. He's on the phone with Isabelle, trying to convince her he needs a son to carry on the family name."

Frankie lowered her voice conspiratorially.

"Is he having any success?"

"They're negotiating."

Frankie looked over Damon's shoulder at the fuzzy laptop screen. "Doing some research?"

His fingers plied the scroll-down key.

"I'm looking for some information on FBI Agent Margot Corley."

Frankie squinted at the fine print of a news article.

"Any luck?"

"Not so far."

His voice was tight. Frankie knew he was trying hard to conceal how much Agent Corley had him rattled.

"The Admiral called a few minutes ago to congratulate us," she changed subjects. "He says that the mayor is giving a banquet in our honor on Friday."

"We're on duty until Tuesday," Damon pointed out.

"The Admiral has arranged coverage and expects us to attend the function." Frankie gave Damon a little nudge with her foot. "Maybe you should invite Agent Corley along."

"Boss, are you serious?"

Frankie grinned.

"No way," Damon retorted. "That woman is hateful."

"That woman has you stumped," Frankie stated flatly.

Damon rubbed his eyes. "I don't understand why she keeps calling me to clarify stuff. She's so rude all the time. By now she must've figured out that I didn't have anything to do with the hijacking."

Frankie cleared her throat. "Would you like me to talk to her? Tell her to back off before I have to bitch-slap her?"

Damon started to laugh. "I think I better work this problem out myself."

"So, have you asked her what the problem is?"

"She refused to give me a straight answer. Said it wasn't in her job description to be nice to me."

"Hmmmm. Interesting response from a law enforcement professional. Well, keep after it," Frankie encouraged while heading for the door. "I bet you'll turn up something that will give some insight into her behavior. I'll be on my pager if you need me."

Chapter 24

AWARDS BANQUET

THE BALDING, MIDDLE-AGED MAYOR OF NEW HARBOR LOOKED OUT OVER A SEA OF heads in the hotel banquet room, tapped the podium microphone and cleared his throat.

"Ladies and gentlemen. I want to thank you for coming here tonight on such short notice to help me honor some of our Coast Guard's finest."

Frankie's cool gaze drifted over him. No fool to politics, she tuned out most of his speech and waited for the wind-down. The moment came and on cue, every Guardsman present turned and smiled to the assemblage of New Harbor's influential elite.

Admiral White arranged the night off for the crews of Harmony Bay and New Harbor with the caveat they attend the banquet. Like a shotgun wedding, the crews shrugged into their formal, dress white uniforms and arrived punctually at seven.

Gage insisted on picking up Frankie and escorting her to the festivities. Isabelle tagged along with Quinton while Damon brought a beauty of questionable intelligence. Frankie honed her attention in on the women standing beside her. Isabelle had posed an innocuous question to Damon's date, but the woman introduced to them as Amber seemed to have some trouble with it. Her eyes glazed into a vacuous stare. She let out a raw squeak. For a moment they thought she might be having a seizure. Frankie and Isabelle exchanged worried looks.

Amber's breathing increased to short bursts, her attention focused on some mysterious place across the room. The episode lasted only a few seconds. When it was over, she excused herself to the bathroom.

Concerned for her welfare, the two women fell in behind. Frankie searched the crowd for Gage as they made their way to the ladies lounge and found him standing patiently in line at the open bar. Her mouth went dry. He was so damned handsome it was impossible not to gawk. She allowed herself a brief fantasy of running her hands over every inch of that uniform before she ripped it off and threw him to the floor.

"Quinton tells me that you've been sick quite a bit lately," Isabelle said, as they waited for Amber.

Frankie nodded and looked up at Isabelle. The wife and mother of two was simply stunning in dark blue silk that matched her eyes.

"I must have caught the flu while I was in North Carolina. I can't seem to shake it," Frankie replied.

"Have you seen a doctor?"

Frankie shook her head. "I do my best to avoid them."

"Perhaps you should pass on the champagne tonight until you're fully recovered."

"Good idea," Frankie muffled a burp. "My stomach is still a little queasy from dinner."

"Gage looks great," Isabelle commented. "Every woman here's been ogling him. His dark hair and olive complexion are terribly sexy wrapped in a crisp white uniform. The contrast does bizarre things to women."

"It's called female hormonal imbalance." Frankie reached out to brush the leaves of a potted plant she couldn't decide was real or not. "It's the same with any guy in uniform. Even Andre is getting looks."

"Andre too?" Isabelle pondered, her forehead wrinkling with distaste. "I find it interesting that Gage doesn't seem to notice all this female attention," she continued. "I think there is only one person here he truly wants to impress." She gave Frankie a dazzling smile and added, "Gage saw you staring at George Harvey earlier this evening."

"George is a nice kid," Frankie defended.

"Adorable too," Isabelle concurred. "He has a cherubic face and charming personality to match. His manners are impeccable."

"George is sweet," Frankie answered.

"He admires you." Isabelle got a wicked gleam in her eyes.

Frankie turned to stare directly at her.

"It's not much of a secret anymore that Gage and I are sleeping together."

Isabelle fondled one of her dangling gold earrings and watched Frankie carefully. "It isn't widespread knowledge. You've managed to keep a low profile relationship." Isabelle smiled. "Gage was upset to see you talking with George. I thought Quinton would have to douse Gage with his beer to cool him off."

"Are you trying to tell me that he's still jealous of George?"

Isabelle nodded, took a sip of wine. "You do realize that Gage is in love with you?"

Frankie went stone cold. "He's never mentioned those words to me," she replied.

A distressed wail caused them both to jump. They scurried across the polished floor to the bathroom stall Amber had locked herself in.

"What's wrong?"

"I can't get it out," she answered on a sob.

"Just reach over and unlock the door," Frankie encouraged.

"No, I can't get IT out."

"Get what out?" Isabelle asked.

Long moments of silence passed.

Frankie tapped on the stall. "What's wrong? Let us help you."

Amber let out another wail.

"Damon put a remote-controlled vibrating egg inside me. It's stuck. I can't get it out and it won't stop buzzing!"

IT TOOK FRANKIE A FEW angry seconds to hunt down Damon. He stood by a faux-marble support pillar at the edge of the room, manipulating the controls of a small black box. Frankie snaked her way along the periphery of the room and crept up behind him.

"Let me have it," she hissed and held out her open hand.

Damon palmed the box into his vest pocket and dipped his head to speak in a low voice.

"Have what?"

"Don't play innocent with me," she snapped.

"You sound like my mother."

"If I was your mother, I'd be begging the world's forgiveness for the monster I created."

"Are you insulting my mom?"

"Not yet," she replied. "But if you don't hand over that remote right now, I'll start insulting anyone in your family I have to."

Frankie didn't notice Gage and Quinton had wandered up behind her. Damon grinned at them.

"I want the remote," she whispered. "Now."

"What remote?"

"Hand it over, you little pervert."

A few of the partygoers wandered into the area. Damon pulled her to a concealed position behind him.

"Hand *what* over?" Gage asked.

"Is there an echo in this room?" Frankie asked. "He knows exactly what I'm talking about. I want the remote control to his 'toy'."

Gage and Quinton moved fast, using their big bodies to block the general view. If Frankie and Damon were going to play show-and-tell, they didn't want all of New Harbor's finest citizens to see.

"What toy?" Quinton asked him.

"You know the one. I told you about it at dinner the other night."

"I thought you were kidding, mate."

"You said it sounded like fun," Damon said with momentary confusion. "I thought you were going to get one for Isabelle."

Frankie glared up at Quinton and then turned her ugliest look on Damon.

"Boss, why are you staring at me like I'm the Anti-Christ?"

"You little skunk. I can't believe you did that. I know you're obsessed with sex and pleasing women, but you've crossed the line this time."

Damon snickered and looked mildly amused. "What line would that be?"

"Don't get smart with me, buster. Your antics have gone too far." She then asked in all seriousness, "Aren't you worried your toy might accidentally stop somebody's pacemaker or something? There are a lot of older folks here. You could kill somebody."

"I'm a trained medical professional," he answered. "I know CPR." He patted her on the shoulder. "Don't worry so much, boss. The worst it can do is turn on the television in the lounge. Besides, it only has a signal within forty feet."

Gage and Quinton were both chuckling.

"Stop snickering, you two. Don't encourage this brat. You should be setting an example."

"Boss, Gage *was* setting an example. I found that vibrating egg in his catalog."

Frankie blushed, momentarily speechless. She cleared her throat and asked, "Did I hear you correctly?"

"I found it in Gage's catalog. There was an entire section of toys for ladies."

"I think she gets the picture," Quinton whispered.

Frankie looked at Gage. "You need to control your shopping impulses," she stated and puffed an errant strand of hair from her eyes, turned and pointed a finger at Damon. "And you need to be on medication."

Damon stared as if his feelings were hurt. "Medication? What do you mean? I'm still young. I don't have any problem with erectile dysfunction."

Frankie smacked herself on the forehead. "Too much information," she replied. "The real issue here is Amber."

Damon gave her a questioning look.

"She's in the bathroom having a major meltdown right this moment. Your little gizmo is stuck in the 'on' position and she can't get it out."

The atmosphere grew serious.

"I think Amber is done playing," Gage spoke quietly. "Take her home."

"And hurry before the Admiral gets wind of this," Frankie said.

Damon gave them a pleading look. "Amber doesn't need to go home. I can fix the problem. Cover for me while I sneak into the ladies bathroom."

Quinton shook his head. "Take her home. You can extract it there," he ordered.

Frankie punctuated the words by deliberately stepping on Damon's foot with the heel of her black vinyl pumps.

"Ouch! Okay, okay."

"Apologize to her," Gage piped up.

"And make it up to her with some trinket that does not require batteries," Frankie quipped.

GAGE AND FRANKIE WERE left alone as Damon went to rescue Amber and Quinton retrieved Isabelle.

"Your catalog, huh?" Frankie said.

"I think I should plead the fifth."

"I'm not a lawyer," she teased.

"Yeah, but this feels like a court."

"I'll be the judge of that."

Gage smiled at her. "What are the charges, Your Honor?"

"Contributing to the delinquency of a sex addict."

Gage raised his eyebrows. "Guilty as charged. What's my sentence?"

"I thought you were pleading the fifth?"

"I changed my mind." He moved in and bent close to her ear. "I may be guilty of contributing to a sex addict, but she isn't Damon. I was shopping for you and we both know it."

215

Frankie's pulse shot through the roof. She blushed, tried to back away. Gage grabbed her waist.

"What do you have to say to that, Your Honor?"

"I think it's time we left this function while I consider your punishment."

He gave her an evil grin. "Good idea. I've got a long, hard sentence to work off."

Frankie stifled a giggle.

GAGE MADE A RIGHT at the stoplight and crawled out onto the coastal highway. Traffic was slow and thick. His mind racing. He needed to ask her something but he wasn't sure how or where to begin.

"You turned the wrong way," Frankie advised. "I thought pilots were supposed to have a better sense of direction than that."

He glanced across the front seat and smiled. Being close to her made him feel infinitesimally weak and inhumanly strong at the same time. It made him feel *whole.*

"I know exactly where I'm taking you."

"Where would that be?"

"Back to my place."

Frankie stiffened. "The Admiral only gave us this one night off for the banquet. You look tired and we never get much sleep when we're in bed together."

"I'll sleep when I'm dead." He reached over to run his hand along her thigh. "Don't look so worried. I don't bite."

"Oh yes, you do." She tried to sound serious and ended up melting in laughter.

"I nibble. It's different than a bite."

Gage slowed to allow another car to merge into the lane ahead of them.

"I want you with me tonight, Francesca. Sleep beside me in my bed. When you're curled up next to me, I don't have nightmares."

"When we're curled up next to each other you're too busy nibbling to have any bad dreams," she replied.

His answer was a near-whisper. "I need to be inside you."

Frankie blinked against the harsh taillights and cleared her throat. "So is sleeping with me like some cheap form of therapy for you?"

"No," he shook his head. "It's not like that at all."

She relaxed a little, took a shaky breath and inched closer to him. Long minutes passed between them before she softly asked, "What happened to Greg?"

Gage's body tensed but he didn't pull away.

"Two days before I was supposed to get married, Greg and I were skydiving. He was always after me to take him up and show him some new trick. He loved to skydive. He was a math teacher, thought his life was boring and mine was full of excitement. Whenever we got together he wanted some thrill-seeking experience. I guess I gave him the ultimate one."

Gage put on the blinker and turned onto the narrow road that bordered his property. A lone white light flickered by the front door of his cabin.

"Greg had about thirty dives to his credit. All of them with the square parachutes I trained him on." Gage paused for a deep breath. "We planned a stacked formation. It was some simple canopy relative work. We'd done it before without a problem. I jumped first and Greg followed a couple of seconds later. He had an immediate malfunction on deployment. One of his front lines got wrapped around the parachute and pinched it like a bowtie. I was screaming at him to cutaway, open his reserve. He froze up. Shot past me like a rock. I couldn't do a thing but watch him plummet to the ground."

Frankie's vision blurred for a moment. She craned her head to plant a kiss on his dark cheek. "Let me hold you tonight," she whispered against his heated flesh. "Let me love you."

A current moved between them, liquid and hot. He coasted to a stop and turned to meet her lips.

"I can't get enough of touching you," he whispered.

Gage stepped out of the truck and pulled her into his arms. The evening air was brisk. A chorus of crickets sang to them across a cool breeze. They walked slowly over damp grass and onto the smooth, brick porch.

He turned the doorknob and led her inside.

The roaring in Frankie's head remained there. She watched, smoky eyed, as he sat her gently on the couch and began to undress her. When she was down to bare skin, he sat back on his haunches and slowly looked her up and down.

"You humble me with your beauty." He wrapped her in a fleece blanket. "Stay here. I'll be right back."

Frankie watched him stroll to the fireplace and start a crackling blaze. Her flint gaze followed each step he made. He disappeared into the bathroom. She could hear him search the cabinet below the sink, she smelled the acrid sulfur of a lit match, saw the glow of candlelight. Frankie closed her eyes at the sound of a bath being drawn.

The romantic side of Gage Adams revealed itself.

She let the flames from the fireplace absorb her sense of sight, felt the warmth on her flesh. Gage had moved from the bathroom to stand beside his elaborate stereo system. She could almost see him through her closed eyelids. He picked through his collection of music and inserted a disc into the CD player. Frankie counted to herself. One one-thousand, two one-thousand, three one-thousand. A sensual Viennese waltz filtered the air from surround-sound speakers.

"Dance with me," his deep voice urged.

Her breath hitched as warm lips grazed her neck.

"Dance with me," he repeated.

"I thought the purpose of our taking dance lessons together was to learn how to waltz," she balked.

"No," he answered and pulled her to stand before him. "The purpose of taking dance lessons was to get you to spend some off-duty time with me. I already know how to waltz." He pushed the blanket from her shoulders. His hand cupped her breast. He pulled her into his arms.

Frankie smiled. "You big sneak."

Gage replied by dipping her backwards with a flourish. In the back of her mind, Frankie tried to picture what they looked like. Gage—tall and dashing in his white uniform. She—starkly nude and tinged with the erotic flush of arousal.

He danced her to the sofa and eased her down.

"We're perfect together," he whispered and bent his head to nuzzle her thighs. His hands pressed her legs apart and exposed her vagina, dripping wet and begging for attention. His tongue snaked out to lick her juices. Frankie gasped and arched back.

"Mmmmm, you taste so good," he growled and latched his mouth to her wet pussy. "I'm going to get you off and then we're going to bathe together." His tongue flicked across her clit and traced the outline of her labial folds. She moaned, gripping the cushions of the sofa. Gage raised his head and smiled, slid a finger inside. Her entire body jerked at the sensation. He gave her a second finger, moving them in and out as she writhed in delight and met the thrust of his fingers with her hips. His lips captured her engorged clit and gently sucked it into his hot mouth.

Frankie screamed with pleasure.

Gage continued to work his fingers and tongue in synchrony, wrenching the maximum pleasure from her sensitized nerve endings. Her climax was swift and intense. A gush of fluid release squirted into his hand all the way up his wrist.

With a gasp, he drew back and stared at her in awe. A proud grin spread across his face. "I'll be damned." He began to chuckle at the irony of it. "And all those years you thought you couldn't have an orgasm?"

He pulled her off into a tight embrace.

"You're amazing!" He covered her mouth with musky kisses.

"What? Why?"

"You're a squirter! Do you know how rare that is in a woman?"

Frankie opened one glassy gray eye. "Ah, no. Should I be embarrassed or elated?"

Gage burst into laughter. "Elated, sweetheart. You're the best."

Chapter 25

ISABELLE PACKS A LUNCH

"TAKING YOUR DATE TO SEE A RUSSELL CROWE FLICK IS LIKE FOREPLAY," DAMON announced with conviction and folded his cards on the table.

Frankie glanced over the top of her water glass and pondered the revelation. The kid hadn't been paying much attention to the poker game. While everyone else was still dressed except for an occasional shoe, Damon had lost all the way down to his skivvies. He'd been talking nonstop most of the day and getting more and more outrageous with each passing hour. He couldn't sit still. He couldn't focus. Crazy energy shrieked around him. Frankie reasoned that whatever had him acting out the part of a poster-child for Adult Attention Deficit Disorder, couldn't be good for the rest of them.

Ever since Isabelle surprised them that evening with a mouth-watering dinner of steamer clams and grilled halibut, Damon had been wound up tight. When she'd unloaded a box of individual sack lunches, Damon went berserk. The week had been harrowing for all of them, Frankie thought. Maybe he was suffering from post-traumatic stress.

Gage scowled and folded his cards. He steepled his long fingers before his face and stared at their row of flight helmets, absorbed in introspection.

"What's the matter, mate? Is Lady Luck turning her back on you?"

"She can be a real bitch sometimes," Gage scowled and pulled off a sock.

Frankie studied Gage's stark features. She felt her heart jump. Lust rippled across her. She shivered. Thoughts of him bombarded her with images, memories.

Stewie jumped into her lap and demanded attention, kneading her thighs with his paws. Frankie stared at him in shock.

"This cat is getting downright friendly with me lately," she spoke. "What's up with that?"

Quinton interrupted with a statement directed at Damon.

"Hey, mate, I forgot to mention it earlier. The manager of the Seaside Bed and Breakfast called this afternoon. He wanted to thank you for the generous tip you left the maid after trashing the room you were in last week. He also said you left some sort of bizarre leather apparatus there. It's waiting for you at the front desk in a brown paper bag."

Frankie cringed and glanced up in time to catch Gage's smirk.

"I wonder which apparatus it was?" Damon asked.

"You mean you can't remember?"

"Well, it's not as though I don't have a spare. I brought an overnight bag full of toys to use with her."

Frankie shook her head. "You're unbelievable."

"That's exactly what she said," Damon beamed.

Her eyes narrowed in disgust.

"Don't look at me in that tone," he said defensively.

"What tone?"

"That, 'you're such a skanky pervert' tone."

"If the aberrant social behavior fits, wear it," she replied.

Quinton and Gage were both smirking now.

"Damon has never suffered from a lack of depravity," Quinton said and threw two matchsticks into the poker kitty.

"The only thing he suffers from is prolonged adolescence," Frankie sneered.

Damon sat up straight. "Give a bro a break. I am only acting on the normal impulses every male has and I'm doing it without hurting anyone."

"Really? And what about Amber?"

"What about her?" Damon defended. "She had a great time at the banquet. The fun just went on a little longer than she could handle."

"She didn't look like she was having fun to me," Frankie replied.

"There's a fine line between pain and pleasure," he huffed. "I told Amber exactly what to expect and what might go wrong. If you'll pause to remember, I'm always open and honest in my dealings with women." Damon turned to stare directly at Gage. "I can't help it that most guys are wimps when it comes to effectively communicating with the opposite sex."

Frankie sat up straight and splayed her cards face-up on the table for Quinton to peruse. He responded in kind. She glanced over his winning hand and toed off her remaining boot.

"I haven't asked the question yet," Quinton said.

"I don't care. Whatever it is I'm not answering it," Frankie said.

"I'm starving," Damon suddenly exclaimed and bounded out of his chair.

"How can you be hungry again so soon?"

"I'm a growing boy," he replied with a languid shrug.

"You're a growing pain in the ass," Frankie sniped.

He strode to the refrigerator and yanked on the handle and took a deep breath. "There's something really tasty off-gassing in here."

"Good thing you were the only boy your folks had," Quinton observed.

"Feeding another like him would've bankrupted his parents," Gage piped up.

Frankie could see Gage grin at the sidelong glance she sent him. A flash of heat coiled in her belly. She looked down at her clasped hands and willed them to relax. Stewie was purring so she wove a couple of fingers in the fur behind his ears.

"What did my wife leave for you, mate?"

Damon dug through a sack with his name scribbled on it.

"A slab of roast beef and two ham sandwiches." He made a pleased noise. "Hey, boss, can I see what she sent for you? Maybe we can make a trade?"

"Sure," Frankie answered. "But don't eat anything in there until you ask me first." She threaded her fingers through her curly hair and waited for Quinton to deal the next hand. He shuffled the deck again, staring at Damon as he dealt.

A scanner squelched in the background.

A log in the fireplace crackled and popped.

Gage yawned.

Stewie rolled to his back and presented a soft, white belly. Frankie glanced over her shoulder. The house seemed too quiet. "Damon, did you find anything in there to trade for your roast beef sandwich?"

He didn't answer.

She looked over questioningly. He was frozen in place, staring into an open sack.

"Well? Do you want to trade for anything or not?"

"Yes and no." His voice had a peculiar strain to it.

"What do you mean by that?"

"Maybe you should come take a look."

Damon held the bag out-and-away like it contained a poisonous snake. Frankie pushed Stewie from her lap. The cat hissed and sped under the nearest couch.

Plastic rattled when she grabbed the sack from his hand. Behind her, Gage moved stealthily across the floor.

Frankie peered inside and snapped the bag shut.

"Holy shit!"

"What is it?" Gage asked.

She took a breath and opened it again. Inside, a small box with Early Pregnancy Testing Kit printed on the side, stared back at her. All the color drained from her face.

"What's in the sack?" Gage asked impatiently.

"You don't want to know," Damon piped up.

"The hell I don't," he answered and carefully eased the bag from her tensed fingers.

Quinton's voice rumbled across the room. He couldn't disguise the humor in it. "I think it's time for Frankie to go pee on the stick."

"It can't be," she whispered in disbelief. "This can't be happening to me."

"What do you mean it can't be happening to you?" Damon said. "Don't you remember that sperm-egg thing they taught us about in high school?"

Gage reached around her shoulders and gave her a comforting hug. "You haven't sent Quinton to the store after tampons lately," he offered.

"Yeah," Damon quipped. "You've been a real argumentative bitch lately too."

Frankie shot him the finger.

Quinton cleared his throat.

"You've got the same symptoms of pregnancy that Isabelle had."

Frankie looked slowly around. All three men stared back at her.

"Go pee on the stick, boss."

"I'm not sure I can," she mumbled.

Gage gently ushered her towards the nearest bathroom. She felt frail beneath his grip. He wanted to say something to make her feel better but had no idea what.

Fifteen minutes later the three men were still lurking outside the bathroom.

"Haven't you done it yet?" Damon yelled to be heard behind the closed door.

"Shut up," she yelled back.

"What's the hold up?"

"I can't go."

"Turn the faucet on," Quinton advised.

"I already tried that."

"Do you need something to drink?"

"I tried that too."

"How about a beer?" Damon chuckled. "That always works for me."

"No beer," Gage bellowed.

"It doesn't help matters to have you three buzzards hanging around listening to me."

"It's okay, boss, we've heard you pee before."

"Why don't you go play in the street?"

"Okay, okay. We're leaving now."

"That's right," Quinton added. "We'll be out on the helipad if you need us." He nodded when Gage gestured his intent to stay behind.

"Fat chance," she grumbled.

"We're going," Damon echoed through cupped hands. "Here we go. We're leaving now. Later! *Adios!*"

"Goodbye dipshit!"

GAGE GLANCED AT HIS watch. Five minutes had passed. He glanced again. Another five minutes of his life gone. What the hell was she doing in there? He shuffled his weight from foot to foot, stretched his arms. Two more minutes passed.

He couldn't wait any longer. He burst through the bathroom door to find Frankie staring at the test strip. He looked down. The directions were simple. There was no mistaking the result. Two pink lines meant pregnant. He eased his arms around her.

Frankie blinked and looked up at him.

"You deliberately knocked me up, didn't you?"

"It takes two people to make a baby," he said cheerily. "I didn't see you rushing to the drugstore for condoms."

"That's not what I mean. You wanted me to get pregnant, didn't you?"

The harshness of her voice wiped the cheer from his face. "I've always wanted kids."

"Why?"

"Because they're cute and innocent and they smell good."

"That's not what I meant," she replied.

Gage's eyes narrowed. The tone of her voice made him wary. "You're going to keep my baby, aren't you?"

Any remaining color drained from her face. Gage moved closer. "Francesca?"

"I didn't think I could ever get pregnant. I didn't take any precautions because it was never supposed to happen."

"Why?"

"Quinton is the only one who knows about it," she said. "I've never told anyone else. Not even my girlfriends."

"Tell me," he urged. "I have a right to know."

Frankie gulped in a deep breath. "A pretty boy," she answered shakily. "My last boyfriend. He gave me an infection."

She paused.

"I was hospitalized for almost two weeks. Late at night I could hear the nursing staff talking about it, feeling sorry for me. I never saw him again. He didn't even bother to visit."

Gage tensed.

"The doctors told me that I'd be sterile because of all the scar tissue the infection left behind." She waved a hand in the air. "I got this tattoo on my butt the week after I was released from the hospital and have never taken another lover, until you."

Gage had no idea what to say. No slicks words of wisdom popped into his head other than how much he'd like to run into the bastard some dark day. He hugged Frankie tightly.

"I guess the docs were wrong, sweetheart."

Frankie suddenly pushed away.

"It's hot in here," she rasped. "I'm going for a little walk and try to figure out what to do about this," she broke off and rushed from the bathroom.

Gage was silent. He felt his heart break as he watched her leave.

Chapter 26

MAKING PLANS

"SOPHIA, DID YOU ACTUALLY HAVE SEX WITH HIM OR WAS IT ANOTHER OF YOUR pathetic roll and grope sessions?"

Sophia answered Claire with a scalding look.

"Let me put it this way," she announced. "Tonight all the drinks are on me."

A rabid cheer rose up from their table.

"Now that is something to celebrate."

"You never buy all the drinks," Lauren said.

"Frankie needs to save her money."

"Why?"

"Because by this time tomorrow she will be handing her entire paycheck over to the Swordsman."

The Sisterhood collectively gasped.

"You heard me correctly," Sophia turned to wink at Frankie. "I think it's time you told them."

Frankie groaned and hung her head. As if life wasn't complicated enough lately, she thought. Now she was going to have to come clean with her girlfriends.

"Damon won the bet," she whispered.

"What bet?" Claire and Lauren echoed simultaneously.

Frankie rubbed the slight curve of her stomach. "Does anybody have an antacid?" When she didn't respond to the question, Sophia was more than happy to explain.

"Damon and Frankie made a bet for an entire month's paycheck."

Andie moaned under her breath. "Oh no."

"Damon had three months to seduce every unmarried, heterosexual female in the Sisterhood."

226

Sophia tilted her chin up and proudly announced, "I am no longer a virgin."

"Congratulations," Andie patted her on the back.

"Since when is losing your virginity to a man-whore cause for celebration?" Lauren asked.

"Since I said so," Sophia answered smugly.

Kristen and Claire stared at one another, at Sophia and finally at Frankie.

"You sold us out?" Claire accused.

"No wonder you're drinking soda pop tonight," Kristin growled. "Feeling poor these days?"

Frankie looked up sheepishly. Andie jumped to her defense.

"Don't act so righteous. She never forced you to sleep with Damon. In fact, it sounds like she bet against your voracious libido."

"I never dreamed he'd get past Sophia," Frankie whispered.

"It's a shame you couldn't have pulled Lauren and myself in on the bet," Andie addressed Frankie. "We could have given the Swordsman a run for your money."

From across the room, Edgar began to laugh. The noise started low in his ample belly and rolled across the room like a tidal wave. Frankie slid lower in her chair. Another inch and she'd be crawling around on the floor.

"I assume that one of the contingencies of the bet was the wearing of condoms," Lauren spoke in her best, business-like voice.

"It was," Sophia concurred.

"Frankie?" Andie interrupted, "You aren't drinking margaritas tonight. That's as unusual as Sophia paying for them. What's going on?"

Frankie sighed. A long moment passed.

"I guess I might as well make the announcement. You're going to find out soon enough anyway."

She sat up straight and reached deep into the pocket of her vest. For a second it appeared to be empty except for a wad of bills and cherry-flavored lipstick. Then her fingers wrapped around the plastic stick and with a flourish, she tossed it on the table.

All conversation stopped.

Kristin and Claire leaned in close and bumped heads.

"Ouch!"

"Jesus, Mary and Joseph! Is this what I think it is?"

Frankie nodded.

"Oh my God!"

"She's pregnant," Sophia squealed.

Kristin's face twisted. "Frankie, is this a good thing or a bad thing?"

Clearing her throat, Claire said, "Can't you tell by looking at her?"

"Both."

"I don't like the sound of this," Andie stated.

"I'm keeping the baby, of course," Frankie whispered. "I'll raise it myself."

"Are you telling us that Gage won't accept responsibility as the father?" Andie asked. "I can't believe that."

Frankie stared straight ahead. "I never asked him to," she confessed. "Things got busy at work yesterday and we never had the opportunity to discuss it."

"So you assume you're in this alone?"

"I'm the only one who's pregnant," Frankie snapped.

"I think you're making a big mistake," Lauren counseled. "You and Gage should go back to the bargaining table and discuss this. I'd be willing to act as a facilitator if you'd like."

"That's right," Sophia added. "The two of you made that baby. He has a right to have some say in this."

"I never said I wouldn't give him access to his own child. He's one of my best friends. He can have all the access he wants."

"Then what exactly is the problem?" Kristin blurted. "Why so glum?"

Frankie cleared her throat and gazed vacantly across the crowded bar. "I want him to love me the way I love him."

A medley of "oh" flowed from the table.

GAGE PUSHED INTO THE Pioneer Bar. The place was jam-packed. He didn't care. Frankie was avoiding him. "I don't want to talk about it right now" was her response each time he tried to discuss their future. Her last words to him before she sped home from work that morning were, "Relax, you're not under any obligation." It made his chest hurt thinking about it. He had to get through to her, make her understand how much he cherished her. She had to see how much he needed her in his life.

"I love you. Marry me."

He had rehearsed those little words till his jaw ached. It was past time to say them out loud to the person who needed to hear them most.

Gage caught sight of her at the usual Sisterhood table and felt a terrible chill. His heart pounded, his stomach clenched with nerves. Somehow his legs moved him forward. He reached into his pocket and pulled out a black velvet box.

The women at the table fell silent at his approach. He walked to Frankie, dropped to one knee and knelt. He swallowed once, hoping his voice wouldn't crack.

"Francesca Marie Moriarty, would you do me the honor of accepting my hand in marriage?"

Gage offered the tiny box.

Frankie stared dumbfounded, her hands clamped convulsively around the armrests of her chair.

"What did you say?"

"Marry me. I'll take care of you and our baby."

"I don't need your help. I'm capable of taking care of myself and the baby."

"I know that," Gage answered, the words Quinton had told him to say, forgotten. "Marry me anyway."

Frankie sat and stared at him. Sophia's sobbing was punctuated by a firm order from Claire. "Open the jewelry box, you idiot."

Although Gage wasn't sure which one of them Claire was addressing, he replied, "Yes ma'am" and popped the lid open. He shoved a sparkling one-carat diamond engagement ring in front of Frankie.

"Will you marry me?"

Not a soul in the Pioneer Brewpub moved. The entire Sisterhood waited breathlessly. Only the harsh sound of Edgar's nasal breathing could be heard.

A gruff male voice from the corner of the pub drifted towards them.

"Do it, girlie."

Another voice chimed in, "Say yes, red!"

"Come on, lady, marry him."

In moments, the entire pub sided with Gage. Frankie blinked back a tear and thought she might be on the verge of a nervous breakdown. Gage Adams, haggard as though he hadn't slept for a year, on his knees proposing to her in a public place?

Never in a million, billion years!

"I can't agree to something so monumental without giving it time to sink in." She stared at the brilliant ring and shook her head 'no'. Obligation was not what she wanted.

"I'll make a good husband and father. I promise."

Frankie heard the desperate conviction in his voice.

"I'm not leaving until you promise to marry me."

Frankie heard sniffling. Sophia's sobs were joined by others.

"I beg you," Gage pleaded. "Marry me."

Kristin and Claire fidgeted.

Andie was almost hypoxic from holding her breath.

Lauren shook her head and grabbed Gage by the collar.

"Say the words," she growled. "Go on, tell her."

Gage took a deep breath and tried to figure out what the hell Lauren was talking about. His nerves had him strung tight. His proposal was not going well. What was he supposed to do, say next? His eyes darted this way and that.

Edgar came to the rescue.

With a hand held low and close to his chest, the big man slowly spelled the words in sign language. *I love you.*

Gage repeated the words out loud.

"I love you."

When she didn't answer, he blurted loud enough for everyone in the pub to hear.

"I love you!"

Kristin jumped straight out of her chair, clapped her hands.

"It's about time," Andie whispered under her breath.

"I need you, Francesca. I adore you and I always have. There's no room in my heart for any other." His tone grew more desperate. "It's your job to rescue people," he spoke earnestly. "You are duty bound, Captain Moriarty. And you're the only woman who can save me."

"Do it, Frankie!" Claire yelled. "Say yes or I'll say it for you."

Frankie blinked back tears. Staring deep into Gage's eyes, slowly she reached out, tugged the shining ring from the box and slipped it on her finger for a perfect fit.

The pub exploded in celebration.

Epilogue

One Year Later

FRANKIE PUSHED OPEN THE DOOR TO AIR STATION HARMONY BAY WITH HER HIP AND held a squirming, fussy infant at arm's length. "Is anybody here?" she called out.

Stewie jumped down from the refrigerator and strolled over to greet her. She leveled an exasperated look at the cat.

"Is anybody human here?"

Gage appeared in the doorway to the pilot's quarters.

"Hey, honey, what's up?"

"Your son needs you."

He rushed to her side. "What's the problem?"

"He won't stop crying. Nothing I do makes him happy and I'm all out of tricks. He's been screaming for nearly an hour. I can't take it anymore."

From the garage Quinton asked, "Does little Greg have colic?"

"How would I know?" she blasted back at him. "I'm not a medic."

Damon called out from his bedroom on the second floor. "Don't bother asking me to baby sit until you learn how to be a better mom."

"Since when is having colic my fault?"

"You're the mom," Damon replied. "It's always your fault."

Frankie heaved a curse under her breath.

"Hey," Damon nagged, "That's not appropriate language to use in front of the baby!"

Gage scooped his son out of her arms. He and Frankie had arranged their schedules so that each of them worked one week a month as rescue pilots. Today was only the second day of his duty week and there was already trouble on the home front. He cooed and whispered. "You don't have colic. You just want to piss Mommy off."

The infant's wailing ceased.

"Like father, like son," Quinton bellowed.

231

"You're a much better mother than I am," Frankie deadpanned.

"Hey, boss," Damon interrupted. "Can I borrow your luggage when I take Margot to Positano next month?"

"You insult me and *then* ask for a favor?"

"I could do it the other way around if it'd make you feel better," he answered. "Especially if you'd let me borrow your luggage."

It had become common knowledge that Damon was off the sexual market. He had become seriously involved with FBI Agent Margot Corley—the first monogamous relationship of his life. How it happened, nobody seemed to have figured out, least of all Damon himself. Yet the two of them were inseparable and planned an extensive vacation to Italy and Greece. The fact that the kid would make it to Europe before she did irked Frankie more than she cared to admit. Gage reached out and stroked her forearm reassuringly.

"Next fall we'll take the baby and cross the pond together. He'll be old enough to travel by then."

She nodded.

"Put up with Damon's badgering for a little while longer." He flashed her a wicked smile. "I'll make it worth the wait."

"Copy that."

She rose on tiptoes to plant a kiss across his cheek just as Damon's nappy head appeared at the top of the stairs. "Hey, boss," he tried to look serious. "Wanna see my new tattoo?"

In a blur that left Gage grunting in disbelief, she snatched a wet sponge off the kitchen counter and rocketed it across the yards separating them. The dripping sponge struck Damon square between the eyes and rolled down his nose.

The roar of Quinton's laughter filled the house.

"I think that's a negative, mate."

Feelings

by JoDee Strong

Ocean, ocean forever deep
I hear you calling me.
I sense your loneliness
I touch your cold
And I shudder from the fear.

Ocean, ocean dark and stormy
I hear you calling me.
I taste your danger
I feel your pull
And I rise to the challenge.

Ocean, ocean bright and blue
I hear you calling me.
I taste your salt
I feel your breeze
And I know I am alive.

Ocean, ocean sparkling clear
I hear you calling me.
I see your beauty
I feel your magic
And I want to have it all.

Ocean, ocean foamy white
I hear you calling me.
I feel your silkiness
I eye your waves
And I bask in ecstasy.

Ocean, ocean vast and endless
I hear you calling me.
I sense your energy
I watch you ebb and flow
At last I am one with you.

About the Author

Samantha Gail and her husband live in Barrow, Alaska—home to polar bears, Eskimos, snowy owls and arctic foxes, along with amazing northern light shows and plenty of snuggling to keep warm.

Book 1 Forestal series - She was sent from the edge of the galaxy to stop the war ravaging his planet. But for him, she would always be a Cherished Invader.

Forestal series book 2 - He is the last hope his people have... She holds the key to their survival... Time is running out for them all.

Printed in the United States
218266BV00004B/27/P